MIND OVER MIRROR

A romantic beach read for the bifocal set.

by

Jan Allinder Anestis

Wandaleen Cole, Jack Hailey

Bill McDonald & Jo Ann Walther

MIND OVER MIRROR Copyright © 2013, Jan Allinder Anestis, Wandaleen Cole, Jack Hailey, Bill McDonald, and Jo Ann Walther

Cover Design by Daphne Firos

www.studiofiros.com

ISBN: 149277295X
ISBN 13: 9781492772958

ACKNOWLEDGEMENTS

MIND OVER MIRROR, an epistolary novel via emails, was written in real time over a three month period. As coordinator of this group project, I am thankful that Bill, Jack, Jo Ann, and Wanda took on this project; grateful for the blessing of their creativity; and delighted with the nuanced story that resulted.

We five owe an enormous thank you to our better halves – Bob, Julie, Giovanna, Fred, and Em – who were amazingly tolerant of the excessive time we each spent emailing imaginary friends.

TABLE OF CONTENTS

"March is the month of expectation, the things we do not know."

Emily Dickinson

"April hath put a spirit of youth in everything."

William Shakespeare

"Rough winds do shake the darling buds of May."

William Shakespeare

MARCH

"March is the month of expectation, the things we do not know."

–Emily Dickinson

From: Thomas Alexander Scott
To: Olivia Walker MacLearn
Sent: Friday, March 1, 2013 4:43 PM
Subject: Get with it

Hey Walker, Guendaline is pulling this reunion together to celebrate — what — our 46th year since graduating from dear old Morrison College. Weird, I know. She has tracked down this email address for you, used bloodhounds or the FBI or a PI or some such, but no answer from you. So, what gives? Surely you want to see Guen and me and the rest of the grand achievers. We can tell lies about our successes, gossip about people who don't attend, drink as if our livers are still young, and misremember how wonderful life was back in the "golden days." So, whatta ya say? Give me a response, okay? And none of that "out of the office; automatic reply" BS. I told Guendaline that you would surely answer the Great Scott. She said the last thing anyone heard was that you were out traveling, "finding yourself." Well, let me tell you, kiddo, that's highly over-rated. And succeeding at it only brings you back to where you started. So, shelve all that and come have some fun for a change. WRITE BACK!!

Scotty
Thomas Alexander Scott

• • •

From: Olivia Walker MacLearn
To: Mary Alice Schneider
Sent: Sunday, March 03, 2013 5:10 PM
Subject: Déjà vu all over again!

M, did you see the email I forwarded from Scotty? If not, read it now! If so, were you as blown away as I was? He sounds frozen in time. Do you remember how he called everyone by their last name? Apparently he still does. Or that he hit on you the first time you came down to visit me at Morrison, and how forlorn he looked when you told him you were "practically engaged?" I can still hear him declaring in that charming voice of his that a date with him would be the perfect test of whether you should ditch Eddie.

Oddly, Scotty's email triggered a pull to the past I've never felt before. At first I thought it was just the loneliness of life without Ian, but you and I both know I've been without Ian for a long time.

Crap! Here I am again with a Morrison problem and needing your help! Liv

• • •

From: Mary Alice Schneider
To: Olivia MacLearn
Sent: Sunday, March 03, 2013 6:35 PM
Subject: RE: Déjà vu all over again!

Liv,

Scotty. OMG. We were never that young. And yes, he helped me to realize that I should stick with Eddie, who by the way says hi. He agrees with me that you should go to your 46th. You have some planning to do — what to wear, what color hair to have, what truth or lies to tell about yourself.

Don't panic about being our age. Everyone else will be too. Eddie and I walked into our 40th HS reunion at the local yacht club and we thought we were in the wrong place because it was full of old people. Plus there wa█ whole wall of pix of everyone who was already deceased, in█l█ing not just guys who died in Viet Nam but a whole bunch ┫f o█ ers, even our famous drum majorette.

Don't let ANYTHIN█ st█p you from going to this thing. Remember my mom's maxim: you're a long time dead. Whatever you want to ┫o, ┫o it now. More useful pep talks to come. I must see to Eddie's dinner. He would starve if I didn't put food in front of him. He is in his usual scientific fog.

Malice

• • •

From: Olivia Walker MacLearn
To: Mary Alice Schneider
Sent: Monday, March 04, 2013 11:44 AM
Subject: Your sage advice

So basically your sage advice is: Don't let ANYTHING stop me from going? Oh sure. How could it go wrong? Let me count the ways... Liv

• • •

From: Mary Alice Schneider
To: Olivia MacLearn
Sent: Tuesday, March 05, 2013 8:15 PM
Subject: RE Your sage advice

Liv,

Please plan to go to the reunion. Almost nobody will be recognizable, so you can be practically anonymous if you like.

Seriously, at our 40th HS reunion we found only two people looking absolutely the same, one guy because he had a unibrow and a girl with a face not unlike the Yale bulldog. Our perkiest baton twirler, with whom Eddie danced the stroll, had more than doubled in weight. My co-star in "Rebel Without a Cause," every girl's crush in '62, was totally forgettable. People can't notice your varicose veins when they have cataracts. Just go and enjoy.

Malice

• • •

From: Olivia Walker MacLearn
To: Mary Alice Schneider
Sent: Wednesday, March 06, 2013 11:16 AM
Subject: Anonymous

Anonymous? Are you kidding? Oh sure, I carry a few extra pounds. (Stop rolling your eyes – few is a relative term.) I like to think of those pounds as the world's most efficient wrinkle remover. But let's face it, unlike your high school buddies, I went off-radar, dark, unreachable even to my best friends. So, you know I am not going to pull off anonymous.

I better email Scotty and put an end to this now. Shall I send your love? Liv

• • •

From: Olivia Walker MacLearn
To: Thomas Alexander Scott
Sent: Wednesday, March 06, 2013 12:21 PM
Subject: Good to hear from you

Wow, Scotty, your email really took me down memory lane! I forwarded it to Mary Alice. (Hope you don't mind.) You probably remember her as Malice, a nickname she chose in grade school, in defiance of what she called her parents' mundane approach to naming a child. She would answer to nothing else until one of her daughters told her that Malice is a creepy name. She still prefers Malice, but thankfully now she will answer to Mary Alice, or M, as I find Malice the antithesis of all that she is.

I remember that you tried to convince her to go to dinner with you to test her intended engagement. She is, by the way, still happily married to Eddie, so her reason for declining the dinner invitation apparently was solid.

Anyway, the reunion sounds like fun, but I don't think I will be able to come. I've got several major projects this spring and my daughter Holly has a number of trips planned. She counts on me to teen-sit for her brood.

It was good to hear from you. I hope you will give my best to everyone and say I was sorry to miss the festivities. Liv

• • •

From: Mary Alice Schneider
To: Olivia MacLearn
Sent: Thursday, March 07, 2013 10:49 PM
Subject: RE: Anonymous

No love to Scotty. He's probably had too much over his lifetime and needs to cut back anyway.

GO TO THE REUNION. Fie on pounds. Everybody needs more pounds at our age or they will start to look like crypt keepers. I look at some of the women our age who have had "work" done and I wonder what they did with all the spare parts they had removed. Maybe they have a spare person hidden in the cellar somewhere.

One of my local friends who is extremely tall has had so much done that she looks like a female impersonator. You will look great and feel great if you go.

Malice

• • •

From: Olivia Walker MacLearn
To: Mary Alice Schneider
Sent: Friday, March 08, 2013 11:44 AM
Subject: Body image...

M, so it seems I've given you the impression that I am worried about my weight. Well, okay so perhaps I occasionally obsess about what was in comparison to what is, but seriously my weight is not holding me back. I have this amazing ability to focus on my assets — good hair, impressive rack, bedroom eyes. Other than moments of horror when a photo or full-body mirror threatens to destroy my nicely preserved image of how I like to imagine that I look, I am quite confident in social situations.

But this isn't any old 300 person gala or meeting with dignitaries about education for girls in third world countries. This is an event with people from my past, people I slammed the door on when I said my final goodbye to Morrison College in the spring of '67. There will be questions, and I don't know if I will be able to avoid answering.

And, Mary Alice, what if Rich is there? Or even worse, what if he is there with Susan? It's not like I can swoop in on Ian's arm and do my best Katherine Hepburn impression: "Why hello, Richard. So very nice to see you once again, and how lovely that your dear mother could accompany you. What? Oh, I am so sorry, Susan. I did not realize it was you."

Why yes, that would be a tad melodramatic. I'm entitled. Anyway, I already emailed Scotty and told him I was too busy with projects and watching Holly's kids to go to a reunion. So all this chatter is for naught. Liv

• • •

From: Mary Alice Schneider
To: Olivia MacLearn
Sent: Friday, March 08, 2013 6:58 PM
Subject: RE: Body image

Liv, you know you're going to go and I'm sure Scotty senses your wavering. You can't fool us and you know it. You want to go. These people are scary only if you allow them be. Morrison College is as much yours as it is theirs and that is why you must attend. Oh, and to slay a few dragons if the chance presents itself.

If you need advice on parrying questions, let me know. I'm a superb *mendex flagrante* (flagrant liar — thank you Arthur Conan Doyle) and can cook up any answer. We can try one of those sessions the presidential candidates have before they debate each other and come up with all the spin you might need. Just tell me my motivation and I'll be any ghost from the past — even Rich, whose sell-by date has no doubt come and gone.

You'll sail in there with your real bust held high and all your gorgeous hair and bedroom eyes and everyone will admire you. What questions will they ask that you can't answer? I'm starting to like the idea of a spin session. Remember, morality as we long ago knew it has evolved although it might have missed Morrison. All the more reason for us to get together and be creative, not dramatic.

Malice

• • •

From: Thomas Alexander Scott
To: Olivia Walker MacLearn
Sent: Friday, March 08, 2013 10:43 PM
Subject: Welcome back

Hey, hey, hey, Liv lives!! I thought maybe you were in a convent in Cuzco or a cave in Katmandu after taking a vow of silence or chastity or something. Vows are a familiar subject with me. Over the years I have taken a number of them myself, mostly in church aisles or self-help meetings, but I always thought of them more as "immediate intentions" rather than "eternal promises." So anyway, I am happy that you have rescinded your vows, emerged from your shroud of mystery, and reentered the lives of our Morrison menagerie. I have had the occasional contact through the years with Field and Jones and others. (Sorry, still calling folks by their last name. I mean

Guendaline and Gloria of course.) But never with Rich, whose mere name is anathema and whom, I realize already, I should not have brought up in only my second reconnection email to you. Don't go diving back into seclusion and don't thrash your cat or throw your laptop through a window. I'll be more careful. You know me, ol' Scotty. When did I ever make a woman mad at me??

Speaking of women and my misadventures with them — Mary Alice!! Wow, I hadn't thought of her in decades, but now that I do, my mouth begins to water again as if I were still a frat boy on a Friday night. I agree with you, her nickname, Malice, didn't fit at all. I saw her more as delicious than malicious. I haven't a clue why she didn't find me more enchanting than whoever it was she had waiting back on Cape Cod, Eddie or Freddie or whoever. Actually I didn't ask her to dinner; that wasn't my style back then. I'm pretty sure I invited her to accompany me to the movies at the Circle 25 Drive-in. Most likely it was a double feature of "Dr. Terror's House of Horror" and "Dr. Horror's House of Terror." Anything to scare them away from the passenger door and into my lap. You say she is still married to the SAME person since college? So how does that work? I have always managed to avoid major anniversaries with my wives. Cheaper that way – not counting the divorce lawyers.

Too busy to come to a reunion?? Hell, Walker, what project could be more important than getting our crew back together again? The clock is ticking on us, you know. Let your daughter take care of her own children or let your grand-teens take care of themselves (confession here: having a difficult time seeing you as a grandmother).

I always did everything you asked of me in college, but I'm drawing a line here. I'll accept your best wishes for me, but if you want to send them to the others, you'll have to at least write them yourself. Or better yet, bring them to deliver in person at the reunion. Not letting you off that easy.

No concrete list of activities from Guen the Ultimate Organizer yet. I'll let you know. Better yet, WRITE HER YOURSELF! That was said lovingly, even if in loud caps. Write me back and lift the curtain of your life a little bit for me.

Always faithful (in my own peculiar way),

Scotty
The Great Scott

• • •

From: Olivia Walker MacLearn
To: Mary Alice Schneider
Sent: Saturday, March 09, 2013 8:52 AM
Subject: Quick note

M, I just have a minute — it's our first big count down to the gala meeting, and I'm in charge of the whip. But I have to tell you two things. One, I talked to Holly last night, and she said she could not care less whether or not I go to the reunion. Of course while we were talking she was grading papers and yelling things like: "Girls, the dryer is buzzing! Get your laundry out and put it all away! I'm not your personal maid!"

I hate trying to converse with Holly when she's multitasking. Wish I could have just emailed, but as she constantly reminds me, IM and email are passé, and she doesn't have time for long phone calls, so I should just grow up and learn to text. Sadly it takes me ten minutes to write a short text, and I still end up with at least one unintended and misguided autocorrect, so I continue to call and we talk through her distractions. Anyway, minimal attention on her part aside, I did clear it with her — sort of — or at least until she chews on it over the next few days.

Second, I heard from Scotty again. The man is a mystifying combination of Peter Pan and Cardinal O'Connor. I'm stunned by how he seems to have aged without maturing (his memories of you are quite adolescent and very flattering by the way) and yet when he asks me to tell him about my life, I feel like starting with: Forgive me, Father, for I have sinned.

More this evening or tomorrow, depending upon how many divas show up for the meeting. Liv

• • •

From: Mary Alice Schneider
To: Olivia MacLearn
Sent: Saturday, March 09, 2013 10:35 PM
Subject: RE: Quick note

Liv,

My sympathies to you on trying to talk to your daughter. This weekend Eddie and I are at the North Conway house entertaining Amy and her husband and the two little ones. With the entire pack of them in the house it is nearly impossible to talk with our daughter between the competing little divas both trying to suck all the air out of the room and the frazzled parents, and, let's admit it, grandparents too, catering to their every whim. Happily Eddie and I drove up late last night, so we had a night and part of a day alone to decompress before the gang arrived about three. I confess I spent the morning shopping for Josie and then we checked out the ski school where she will have her first lesson tomorrow morning.

After an early dinner Eddie and Dan took Josie, an almost four year old daredevil, for two runs on the mountain coaster at Cranmore while Amy and I bathed Dana. Can you believe she is almost one? If I weren't doing full time day care for Amy, I would probably be a much softer-hearted grand-mother, but Amy and I try to keep order.

Funny you should mention getting permission from our kids to do anything these days. Didn't it used to be the other way around? I know what you mean, though. Amy stands there help-ing me pack for trips with Eddie and vetoes half my clothes. Worst moment last year: I held up a dress I had bought on sale and said "How about this for Bermuda?" and she answered "Not even for an Amish potluck supper." OK, so she hates small prints and Peter Pan collars, even on her little girls. If Holly supports your trip to the reunion, just wait until she rings in on your wardrobe. I promise to come and defend you if necessary.

All this bitching and I never got around to grumbling about Carrie and her four spoiled cats and her sweetie of a partner whom she would probably throw under the next train if he dared to pro-pose. But what do I know? Maybe someday they'll show up mar-ried or maybe marriage is not for them. It wasn't for Carrie the first time around and now she's in love, so why mess with success?

Enough complaining. Just call me when you absolutely decide to go to that gathering and I will rush to you for some spin doctoring and some wardrobe cheer leading. Really.

Malice

P.S. If he took one look at me now, Scotty would soon ditch his foolish memories of our youth.

• • •

From: Olivia Walker MacLearn
To: Mary Alice Schneider
Sent: Sunday, March 10, 2013 1:35 PM
Subject: Welcome to daylight savings — I need a nap!

There was a message on the answering machine from Holly when I got home from church: "Mom, about the reunion. Have you thought this through?"

Annoyed me, so just to annoy her in return, I replied by email instead of text or phone call: "Why no, Holly, I have not yet thought it through. Thanks for asking. However, on the off chance I decide to attend the reunion, be assured that I will prepare a safe dating plan, just like we did for you in high school. I will probably borrow Mary Alice's Amish potluck supper dress. I figure if I wear that dress with a large crucifix and carry a bible with me at all times, that I just might be able to avoid any risky situations. Love, Mom."

If she ever checks her email, that should alleviate her concerns. Liv

• • •

From: Mary Alice Schneider
To: Olivia MacLearn
Sent: Monday, March 11, 2013 1:21 PM
Subject: Safe Dating Plan

Liv,

You are in luck. I stashed the "Amish potluck supper" dress in the third floor closet right next to the two wedding dresses from the girls. It will be too long on you and too tight in the bust, nothing an ace bandage can't correct.

The general appearance of this garment, made in the USA in fact, gives it more clout than a chastity belt, so you should be safe. Pair it with sensible shoes and a straw handbag, circa 1970 (I may have saved one of those too) and of course some horn rimmed glasses (the no prescription kind our son Jamie uses when he wants people to think he's scholarly) and you should be safe with anyone. Eddie suggests you black out a tooth or two, but we don't want to overdo. Your daughter should have no worries about letting you expose yourself to your past.

Eddie is home today with some sort of bug that we think he acquired after Josie gave her mother and me a mild version that morphed into something for which Ed has no antibodies, so he's downstairs watching Winnie the Pooh with typhoid Josie while I scan Dana on her monitor to be sure she is settling down for her nap. She gets fired up every day when we pick up Josie at Montessori and it takes a while to settle her. I was about to say you have it easier with teen grands, but I retract my intended statement. Those years of intercity HS teaching while Eddie pursued his doctorate still give me nightmares on occasion, to say nothing of memories of my three when they were teens. You are a brave woman to take on Holly's kids. I'm hoping to be so over the falls by the time these two are teens that their parents won't trust me with them.

Keep planning that reunion strategy and please refer to the Cape Cod think tank when you need reinforcement.

Malice

• • •

From: Olivia Walker MacLearn
To: Thomas Alexander Scott
Sent: Monday, March 11, 2013 8:43 PM
Subject: You can thank my daughter...

Scotty, my daughter triggered an "I'm the boss of me" moment, and I am thinking about coming to the reunion. Not sure though. You all kept in touch over the years and well, I clearly did not.

So here's to lifting the curtain a bit per your request, although I warn that there is nothing all that exciting to tell.

When I returned from my post-college travels, I lived with Mary Alice on Cape Cod until she married Eddie and moved to Boston while he finished his doctorate. That's where I met my husband Ian — on the Cape, not in Boston. Ian passed away just over two years ago. He was quite a bit older than me and had a serious long term illness that eventually affected his ability to recognize me, so in a sense I've been widowed for more than a decade. Before his illness, Ian was head and creative genius of a non-profit and I have remained involved with several of his and my favorite charities.

And now I'm living in CT, close enough to the Cape for visits with Mary Alice and Eddie, to Manhattan for meetings and theater, and yet suburban enough for deer and fox.

I have one daughter, who, as you already know from my previous email, has teenagers. Holly and family live south of DC, so I have easy train access to them. All in all rather boring as first acts go, wouldn't you agree?

Now tell me about your life post Morrison. Did you ever write your novel? Liv

• • •

From: Olivia Walker MacLearn
To: Mary Alice Schneider
Sent: Wednesday, March 13, 2013 8:43 PM
Subject: From the shadows of my mind...

M, I sent Scotty a short email with a condensed version of my life since college, and have been feeling rather morose ever since. I keep flashing back to visits with Ian, watching him deteriorate and also watching others in his residence fade away as well, people who became part of my world because they were part of his. There was one woman in particular, an ex-stewardess. She arrived about the same time as Ian, and for the first couple years she would greet me with welcome aboard and a big smile. Of course she also would caution me about some perceived danger — be careful, she might say, I don't know where they are hiding — but there was a gentleness to her that responded so sweetly to my reassurance that I would be careful and all was okay. Then sometime in the third year she began to get thinner and thinner, and along with the weight, her spirit seemed to dissolve as well.

Ian never changed much physically — he was handsome to the end. Of course, he wouldn't have known if that were not the case, but I am glad anyway.

Okay, I'm going to pour a glass of merlot and see if there is anything funny on television. If not I will watch another Frasier episode on Netflix. I have an episode of Revenge recorded but will wait until my mood improves to watch it.

How is Eddie feeling? And how about you? You certainly have taken on a lot with full-time grandchild care in your waning years. :) Liv

• • •

From: Mary Alice Schneider
To: Olivia MacLearn
Sent: Wednesday, March 13, 2013 10:21 PM
Subject: RE: From the shadows of my mind...

Liv,

I don't know how you managed with Ian's last years. It had to be terrible. It is one thing when it's your parent, but when it's your husband it must be far, far worse.

We watched Mom drift away while she spent her last years with us, losing the thread of our lives gradually. Because she was as sweet-natured as always, we just humored her, responding as we thought she would want us to. One day I came home from teaching and she asked me if I had picked up the photos she'd taken of Dad's paintings. She had never owned a camera in her life, but I assured her I would keep checking until they arrived.

Of course she forgot that very day. The next night she wanted to know what happened to the apple cobbler she had baked for us (Mom never baked) and Eddie quickly confessed to having lost control and eaten the entire thing. It became a sort of dance with Dad, Eddie, and me, each of us fielding questions or creating believable scenarios to make Mom's life smooth.

Then Dad outlived her by nineteen years, never really losing touch, especially regarding baseball or politics, but still forgetting some short-term issues. One of my favorite little quirks of his was his "anti-answering machine" routine with the girls: "Some boy called!" "Who, Grandpa?" "I don't know who. If it's important, he'll call back." The luckless boy always thought he'd left a message and the offended granddaughter complained to Eddie and me.

We finally removed the phone from his suite when, a week after the sad and unexpected event, he said "Did I tell you Uncle Jimmy died?" After much back and forth and some desperate, apologetic calls to my then still living grandmother and aunt by marriage, we realized that Grandpa needed to let the machine handle incoming calls.

Even the day he died he was pretty much on his game, sending me out for his big recent discovery, box wine. Wine corks had become hard to manage. He'd grown bored with Chardonnay and wanted some Chablis, which he drank every afternoon at five from a tumbler, explaining that it was a lot more stable than those fragile stemmed glasses (and held a lot more, too, Eddie would point out). When I got home to him, he'd lost all his color, the little he had as a blue-eyed Englishman, and had already suffered an aneurysm. It was a quick exit, and right at home.

Away with this topic! I'll share his recipe for his happy holiday drink. I found him one afternoon making his autumn/winter fave, eggnog with rum. As I warned him that eggnog is full of cholesterol and calories, he chirped: "Don't worry, honey. I put in just a little eggnog and fill it up with rum." Can't beat that logic. By the way, Eddie is doing fine again. He's a tough one. Get some sleep!
Malice

• • •

From: Olivia Walker MacLearn
To: Mary Alice Schneider
Sent: Thursday, March 14, 2013 11:36 AM
Subject: FW: I'm still laughing!

M, I had to forward Holly's answer to my email. See below. Gotta love your goddaughter's logic!

Sincerely, your sexless elderly friend

—–Original Message—–

From: Holly MacLearn
To: Olivia Walker MacLearn
Sent: Thursday, March 14, 2013 6:47 AM
Subject: I'm still laughing!

Mom, for some odd reason, I happened to check email this morning, and your safe date plan made me laugh — even at this god-awful hour! Amy TEXTED (hint-hint) me when Aunt Malice bought her Amish supper dress! Sounds awful!

However, I worry that you misunderstood my reason for the message I left on your voice mail. I am not concerned about you being led into temptation by some guy, a'la your OBSESSIVE (Well deserved yelling.) safe date planning during my high school years. I figure you all surely have moved to more mature, less hormone infused relationships, so sexual conquest is unlikely to be a big danger.

No, what worries me is that you don't have a heart safe plan, because I would hate for you to have yours broken once again. Off to work. Talk to you later. Holly

• • •

From: Mary Alice Schneider
To: Olivia MacLearn
Sent: Thursday, March 14, 2013 4:21 PM
Subject: RE: FW: I'm still laughing!

Dear Sexless Elderly Friend,

Where do I start? Should we refer your forty-something daughter to Mark Twain's recently released autobiography in which he airs his views of women's sexuality pointing out that they never lose their physical edge to say nothing of their mental one. No. Let me just remind her that the sexiest organ in the body is the brain and ours are still functioning, not to mention the rest of the equipment.

At the same time I should refer her to my ex-colleague, who now lives in South Carolina in an "over some age or other" compound where she tells me it is high school revisited. Everyone gets it on with everyone else, divorces are rife, and scandal abounds.

Hormones never quit and experience counts. But how can we tell the young? Perhaps one has to be our age to understand it.

Back to my dad as an example: when his friend John had a stroke and sat around drooling, dad, now a widower of some years, stole John's girlfriend, Janice. When we went skiing on weekends, Dad regularly invited Janice to our house during our absence and would request some of his favorite casseroles made in advance. He probably told her he whipped them up himself. After a couple of years they split up because, according to Dad, Janice was too self-focused, i.e. not focused enough on him. It turns out that although she had been married, she had never had kids, so had not acquired the habit of sacrifice.

My book club pals never tire of discussing the divorced men and widowers in our town who will marry any slightly younger woman who knows how to flatter them. I confess that when I'm cooking Eddie's favorite foods or getting all the marks out of his shirts I remind him that no trophy wife would ever do all that for him. Lately it's been blueberries from Dana's breakfast that always get on his fresh shirt. He says he'd never go for a trophy but who knows. Didn't Faulkner say that we know so little of our fellow man? One thing I do know, though, to twist a phrase of the great Dr. Johnson, is that "when a man is tired of (sex), he is tired of life."

Holly will know eventually, but we won't be around to find out. All the more reason for you to go to the reunion and I won't be offended if you pass on the Amish dress.

Malice

• • •

22

From: Olivia Walker MacLearn
To: Mary Alice Schneider
Sent: Friday, March 15, 2013 11:36 AM
Subject: Parts

I hesitate to share this, cause it is uber-silly, but when I read your comment about the rest of our equipment still functioning, for some odd reason the phrase "parts is parts" popped into my head. If you don't remember, it was a line in a funny Wendy's commercial from the 1980's, poking fun at McDonald's chicken nuggets. Absolutely no relevance (hopefully) to what you wrote, but still stuck in my brain these hours later.

More relevant to topic: I guess I was Ian's trophy if you simply count being younger by the fifteen years that separated our ages, but I always considered him the trophy. He certainly was my harbor and my compass during a horridly confusing time. Along with you of course, dear friend.

Ha! Did the wretched lyrics from "You Light Up My Life" just pop into your head? I could hum a few bars. Are they stuck there now? Can you hear Debbie Boone singing: You give me strength to carry on... La, da, da, la, da!

Okay, perhaps I best reset my smaltz-o-meter with a dose of Revenge. Liv

• • •

From: Mary Alice Schneider
To: Olivia MacLearn
Sent: Friday, March 15, 2013 8:15 PM
Subject: RE: Parts

Oooh. Revenge is a sweet topic. I'm still grumbling about the idea of ever being too old for love or sex or whatever anyone wants to call it.

Holly makes me remember Hamlet's criticism of his mother, who admittedly married his uncle, daddy's murderer. When he told his mother, Gertrude "You cannot call it love, for at your age the heyday in the blood is tame. It's humble," he was, as my step grandma would have said, full of shit. He was thirty (still a student and living off the folks) so what did he know anyway?

I'm starting to work up a nasty attitude about all this. That should lead me comfortably into whatever revenge plan you have in mind. Perhaps you could verify the intended recipient, whom I am pretty sure I know. I am guessing that the reunion may be the scene of more than a dragon slaying, but perhaps I am reading too far into your future. First let's dismiss the Amish dress and start dressing you for revenge. Malice (still raging over the "dying of the light")

• • •

From: Olivia Walker MacLearn
To: Mary Alice Schneider
Sent: Friday, March 15, 2013 8:43 PM
Subject: No more caffeine for you!

Yikes, sexy and well-lit M, I was actually referring to an episode I'd recorded of the television series Revenge. I have no dragons scheduled for slaying. And now, with absolutely no medical training, I am going to prescribe two glasses of warm milk and a hot bath, and then of course whatever the glow of night inspires. Liv

• • •

From: Mary Alice Schneider
To: Olivia MacLearn
Sent: Saturday, March 16, 2013 8:18 AM
Subject: Mea culpa

I confess to TV series illiteracy with a couple of exceptions that Eddie and I love (Jeopardy, Modern Family). We always get the TV show questions wrong on Jeopardy by the way. Maybe we will give Revenge a try and cut back on sports and politics. Here's a guilty secret about Eddie the big shot scientist. He loves Wheel of Fortune because he says it is all about pattern recognition and he does tend to get most answers, so maybe he's right. Sadly he can suck the drama and poetry out of anything.

Once when we were young and just married and I was trying to stuff culture into angry urban kids, I read a line from an imagist poem to Eddie, whose nose was in a physics book. "Cats walk thin and sleep fat," I said, thinking how perfect the line was. He replied that it is all a matter of surface area and conservation of heat. What a silver tongued devil he is, but I'm still crazy about him.

Malice

• • •

From: Olivia Walker MacLearn
To: Mary Alice Schneider
Sent: Sunday, March 17, 2013, 10:07 AM
Subject: The joy of purging...

Top O the Morning, M! Are you wearing green and cooking corned beef and cabbage for your crowd? Not me. Skipped church and am wearing sweats and sorting through "treasures." Instead of sweet dreams at 5AM this morning, I awoke to scary visions of Holly and her girls struggling to decide what to do with all my crap when I kick the bucket, as well as having to tackle the boxes in the attic filled with stuff from when I emptied Mom and Dad's Hampton house. (Every time I watch Revenge I think of my growing up years in the Hamptons; not exactly a warm and fuzzy reference.)

Anyway, I remember how impossible it was to figure out what I should keep. There were massive sets of china and crystal from lavish dinner parties, items from trips around the world, heirlooms from the generations before them — how could I dispose of anything without their blessing? Dad could have helped, but his unvarying answer was: whatever you think best, Olivia. So I had everything boxed and shipped to the Cape house, and after we sold it, to the attic here at the Westport house.

After attacking just one of the boxes this morning, I surveyed the butler's pantry in horror. Where was I going to put it all? So began the great purge. It is a bit overwhelming, but frankly so far has not been without some funny memories. First shelf I emptied held the dishes Ian and I registered for when we were married. Basically I chose them simply because my mom hated them, and I was not in a mood to add additional happiness to the ecstasy Ian's social standing afforded her. Same thing goes for the crystal. We used both every time we had my parents over for dinner.

I do like my sterling flatware, but frankly no one seems to use sterling any more. Which reminds me of the plethora of silver service pieces that have turned black from tarnish during decades sitting unused. All of it needs to go. And then I must find the courage to purge what came from my parents' house as well. Back to work. Liv

• • •

From: Mary Alice Schneider
To: Olivia MacLearn
Sent: Monday, March 18, 2013 9:35 AM
Subject: RE: The joy of purging...

Top of the morning after to you, Liv! I skipped the corned beef and cabbage thing. We gave that up after my dad died. With Amy, Dan and the kids at a four year old's birthday party, we opted for a fancy restaurant with Carrie and Mike. Eddie couldn't understand the waiter's accent. He introduced himself as Reynaldo, but his name is probably Bob and I'll bet he grew up somewhere mid-Cape. Can't prove it, however.

Carrie enjoyed watching Eddie deconstruct his frou-frou plate, arranging the beef at six o'clock, the potatoes (to which very elaborate things had been done) at three and the greens off to the left. Who says Amy gets her control freak compulsiveness from me?

You hit a nerve with the heirloom crisis. Here's a terrible confession. We have a house and a barn full of stuff from both sets of parents, but there's no silver or glassware. It's all crap and we don't have the strength of character to ditch it. We have Eddie's father's 1970 car in the barn and the old man's first boat, a piece of junk that no longer floats. They have a whole boat yard to store it and we have to keep that wreck in prime space. I think Eddie's afraid that Jamie would junk it. He would, too. Eddie says if the kids want the big house when we're gone, they'll have to shovel it out.

Our neighbor, Sharyn (love the spelling), sells a lot of the big old beach places to rich New Yorkers and every time she handles an estate sale, she rushes home to eviscerate her closets, vowing not to put her kids through sorting hell - quite the opposite of Eddie's policy. I'm every bit as guilty as Eddie. I save dated clothes that I can't stuff into any more for no reason that I can imagine. If I ever get thinner, will I want to look really out of style? Eddie has 30 pairs of pants up in a third floor closet and won't let me donate them. If he's ever a 34 waist again, he'll have the best plaid pants that the 60's ever saw.

We even store younger people's junk. Back in the early 90's when Carrie sold shoes, she bought all the sale stuff. The front room closet on the third floor looks as if Imelda Marcos gave her extras to a needy Massachusetts teen. Seriously, Carrie has 107 pairs of size 6 narrow shoes, all the latest from the early 90's. I can't imagine where we could donate them. Eddie says maybe to working girls in a third world location where people have small feet. Maybe I should go look in those closets.

Malice

• • •

From: Olivia Walker MacLearn
To: Mary Alice Schneider
Sent: Tuesday, March 19, 2013 2:39 PM
Subject: The joy of full time staff...

M, I just unpacked mom's sterling punch bowl. I remember sipping pilfered cups of brandy punch from that bowl when I was not even twelve. (You would have enjoyed hanging out with me in those days. It is amazing how invisible my friends and I could be, and therefore what we could get away with while our parents partied!) Cannot let that bowl go, but the question is: if I want to keep it out in the light of day, how long before silver tarnishes when left uncovered? This is rather important to know since my full-time staff consists of one person, one day a week.

Oh and my junk mail folder coughed up an interesting email this morning. Seems someone on the committee thought it would be fun to give us all an opportunity to communicate pre-Memorial Day weekend. I now have a list of classmates, complete with email addresses and home state. (Thank goodness no phone numbers!) So my other question is: how tarnished am I for having stayed undercover from my old friends for more than four decades, and do I really want to be out in the light of day now, especially given the fact that Rich's name is on that list? Liv

• • •

From: Mary Alice Schneider
To: Olivia MacLearn
Sent: Tuesday, March 19, 2013 9:02 PM
Subject: RE: The joy of full time staff…

Liv,

First, the punch bowl. That should go at least four months between cleanings and possibly longer depending upon the climate in your house. Here on the beach the air stays wet and nasty unless we seal the place up, so anything silver tarnishes pretty quickly.

When my brother and I were kids the best we could sneak was a bit of cheap rye with ginger ale, the lowest form of highball. It might have eaten through your punch bowl. Maybe that's why I don't drink.

Second, and much more exciting, the email with everyone's information, including Rich's. Now I'm going into English teacher mode. It's all about point of view. We can only speculate about Rich's viewpoint, since he may play a much bigger role in our thoughts of him than in his of you (or us). That topic will need some discussion. However, try to get into the heads of everyone else. What did they think of you? What would they want to know about your life? Try asking what you might want to know about theirs. You can tell them a lot without telling them much if you don't want to. You're a widow with a daughter and grands. You've traveled and had plenty of experiences that they might want to know about. Tell your old classmates what they want to know, but never what you don't want them to know. You could even offer different bits to different people. They're probably eager to share their lives with you, so let them ramble.

Regarding what to do about Rich, perhaps we should get together and work on a strategy. You can come up to us or we can dash to CT, whichever works for you. Eddie is portable and has his mind on physics, so he may or may not have suggestions. He adores you, though, so his old school protectiveness may emerge. Let me know about when to lay our plans.

Malice

• • •

From: Olivia Walker MacLearn
To: Mary Alice Schneider
Sent: Tuesday, March 19, 201, 11:05 PM
Subject: You are so wise!

M, you always know just what to say to calm my excessive what if's!

Punchbowl is outed! I put it in one of the ladder height kitchen cupboards, the ones with glass doors and mood lights. I also ordered some sort of tarnish strips from Amazon to put in the cupboard — they apparently remove sulfa from the air or something like that. Scientific knowledge always goes in one ear and out the other with me. (Well, except for the time Eddie told me that when you plug an extension cord into an outlet it "stores up" the electrical current and will then short out any appliance plugged into it. I spent decades carefully observing the rule of "into the appliance before into the outlet," until someone finally told me that was ridiculous. Certainly amused Eddie when I confronted him.)

Also your point of view lecture was spot on. I imagine Rich is sitting on a pier somewhere, fishing with a dozen rosy-cheeked grand-children, and that seeing me again has never crossed his mind!

Big sigh of relief and off to bed I go! Liv

• • •

From: Mary Alice Schneider
To: Olivia MacLearn
Sent: Wednesday, March 20, 2013 5:02 PM
Subject: RE: You are so wise!

Liv,

Glad to hear that the punch bowl is in view again. Can't stop thinking of "The Brave Little Toaster," Amy's childhood favorite animated movie about household objects and appliances with souls and voices. If that punch bowl could speak, what a lot of memories it would share. We anthropomorphize plenty of our household objects, imagining that they remember events. I used the same linen pastry cloth (a monkey riding in an open sports car—purchased in Bermuda in '69) for thirty years and it seemed like an old friend, almost unfolding itself the day before Thanksgiving when Amy and I would make pies all afternoon. I felt like a murderer when I had to toss it.

And cars! They do have souls. When I totaled the '84 Chrysler GTS turbo right before Carrie left for college in '92, I was bereft and could barely face it at the wrecking yard. It seemed to be a wake. After that I could never love another shift car and switched to automatic. That model, to be fair, had the worst clutch in automobile history.

If anyone read what I write to you, they'll have me committed. Maybe a panel of wives would pardon me if they met Eddie. He can tell some fantastic tales with a straight face. Just last year he pointed out a homeless guy he sees around town and said he was looking better. I gazed with pity in the man's direction and discovered it was our neighbor, an investment guru with more money than God. "Almost had you there," Eddie said. Every time I go to that man's house for book club with his wife and the other neighbor ladies, I shudder to think what they would make of my husband. Perhaps they write Eddie off as a mad scientist. You owe him a major practical joke of your choice for what he told you about appliance cords.

Who cares, by the way, if Rich has any number of grandchildren? Sorry, but not very, for being harsh on him, but I still harbor some hostility about how he treated you. Tell me to shut up if I'm trespassing here and I will. If you give me permission to continue, I'll have trouble stopping. Love from Eddie, who is sorry about his lies to you.

Malice

• • •

From: Olivia Walker MacLearn
To: Mary Alice Schneider
Sent: Wednesday, March 20, 2013 11:45 PM
Subject: Rich and the Aliens

M, I would never tell you to shut up about anything, let alone about Rich! Considering my state of mind in the year post Morrison graduation, and all you did to keep me safe and sane, you are entitled to harbor a bit or even a lot of hostility.

Still, I've moved on. Rich would not have entered my mind if not for this reunion stuff, and I think I prefer to go back to not thinking about him, as I am sure he is not thinking about me.

Now, about aliens… This evening I watched several recordings on my DVR, and just finished with the latest episode of *The Neighbors*. It's a silly show; not something I ever would have said you must watch, except that the teenage daughter is you! Holly texted me this evening to confirm that she agrees. To quote her: "OMG, mom, u r so right! A Weaver is Aunt Malice reincarnated!"

In my humble grumpy-old-person opinion, texting reduces everyone to the verbal equivalent of a twelve year old! I'm off to bed. Liv

• • •

From: Mary Alice Schneider
To: Olivia MacLearn
Sent: Thursday, March 21, 2013 8:15 AM
Subject: RE: Rich and the Aliens

Liv, in spite of Eddie's devotion to sports, politics and game shows on TV, I promise to check out *The Neighbors* and see if I can feel seventeen again.

Regarding reignited hostility to Rich, I must admit that I had not been thinking much about him either until this Morrison reunion thing came up. Lots of water under a lot of bridges. I should let it go.

Malice

• • •

From: Thomas Alexander Scott
To: Olivia Walker MacLearn
Sent: Thursday, March 21, 2013 11:31 AM
Subject: RE: You can thank my daughter...

Hey Walker,

Thanks for lifting your curtain for me; I enjoyed the peek. That doesn't make me a Peeping Thomas, does it? Should I even be joking like that with a grandmother? Hold on, let me set this in my mind again: you have a child (strange as that sounds to me) who has children (picture my brain frying). How can all this be? Aren't we still 18 or 21 or at most 22? I think I am having so much trouble swallowing this reality because I've seen most of the other inner circle types a time or three over the years, but I haven't seen you since graduation! So your face has no wrinkles (except those two worry lines carved into your brow by I'm-not-going-to-mention-his-name). You still carry the blush of youth and the passion of the unscarred-by-society. At least that's you in my mind's eye. It's a good picture; I almost wish you wouldn't come to the reunion so I can keep that image intact. Of course, you may be a really hot grandma, so there's that! Sometimes, as I pass a mirror, the face that glances back startles me. Who is that guy and how did he get into my apartment? But when I look into my mind, I see the same old familiar Thomas Alexander Scott that I have always known. So which is truer, Liv, the mirror or the mind? As you can tell from my emails, I have pretty much refused to grow up. Like they say, you can't always be young, but you can always be immature. Suits me. Anyway, according to your last email, the first act of our life-play has just concluded. Means we are going to live pretty damn long – unless it's a one-act play!

So...Ian, huh? Must have been a great guy if you liked him enough to take the matrimonial plunge. You were always so serious about relationships. Sorry that it ended like it did. All of my spouses are still alive; it was just the marriages that died.

My life post-Morrison? Ah, anything but boring, Walker, I can promise you that. Not always fun, not always fulfilling, not always sane, but never boring. You knew that I was heading to Memphis State University (excuse me, now it's the University of Memphis – much more profound, no?) for a Master's in English. Got that, graduated, and as the Dean waved my diploma, Uncle Sam waved my draft notice. Enlistee sounded much safer than draftee so I joined the Air Force. That's where I got my first big break in writing. My great novel? No. Patriotic speeches for the big brass? No. Short stories about soldiers, combat, and other human tragedies? Nope. I wrote training manuals at an air base in west Texas. Go ahead, laugh, I can hear you sputtering from here. I did try to slip in some double entendres and a few malapropisms just to liven up the drab rigidity of military life. I also published a little weekly sheet entitled "The Reveille Rag." That was fun – till some stars and bars actually read it. And it suddenly changed to "Taps." But I was allowed to remain in the Public Affairs Office, just under a shorter leash. Fortunately, or perhaps unfortunately, the leash was long enough to allow me access to an off-base watering hole where I met Wife #1. If Texas weren't as hot as hell already, her very presence would have made it so. She was a lotta woman. I still get a fever when she crosses my mind. But like Delbert McClinton sings, "Yeah, we had our good times, but I think I'm better off with the blues." Anyway I got discharged and divorced in the same month. Literally didn't know whether to laugh or cry. And as the curtain comes down on that marriage, I think I'll drop it on this email as well. Or else this will become that "great novel." Let me know if you want to hear more.

So drop the maybe from your reunion plans. And say hello for me to Mary Alice, the sweet Mary Alice, the one that not only got away but never even bit! And say hello to your daughter Holly for me. Does she know YOU, I mean the you that I know? And, how do I say this tactfully, I want to know more about you than just the you I know. Care to do more than just lift the curtain? Care to remove some of the face paint? To paraphrase an oft-used line from college days, you tell me yours and I'll tell you mine.

Sorry. Brevity was never my forte.

Then and now,

Scotty
Thomas A. Scott

• • •

From: Guendaline Field
To: Olivia Walker MacLearn
Sent: Thursday, March 21, 2013 1:32 PM
Subject: FW: Hello!

Liv,

I just talked to Scotty, and he said you might come to the reunion. That would be wonderful!

However, I thought you should know that I also heard from Rich a couple days ago. See his email below. Let me know if you want me to send him a bogus "change of date for the reunion" email. I'd be glad to.

Guen

—-Original Message—-

From: Rich Stapley
To: Guendaline Field [Guendaline Field]
Sent: Monday, March 18, 2013, 10:58 AM
Subject: Hello!

Hello Guen,

The fairest college sent me some sort of notice of an off-year reunion — with you as the contact person. Thanks for doing this. I'll try to make it, although I have projects to finish that I'm behind on (not a good excuse, I know).

I've stayed in touch with some close friends, but few travel to the West Coast, so it's time to make an effort to see people while I'm still reasonably upright. Put me on the list of absolute maybes.

Rich Stapley

• • •

From: Olivia MacLearn
To: Guendaline Field
Sent: Thursday, March 21, 2012 10:23 PM
Subject: Our 46th

Guen, Hard to believe it's been 46 years since we left Lexington with our Morrison diplomas tightly clutched in our hands. I am thinking about coming to the reunion — am not sure yet. And although your offer re Rich made me smile, it is not needed. As my friend Mary Alice said, lots of water has passed under that bridge!

This must be an enormous amount of work to organize. What made you take it on? Liv

• • •

From: Olivia Walker MacLearn
To: Mary Alice Schneider
Sent: Thursday, March 21, 2013 10:41 PM
Subject: My cup runneth over!

M, stop smirking and swallow whatever comment you were going to lead with. I am referring to my overflowing inbox not the new midnight blue lace bra I just ordered from the Wacoal site. All the usual garbage is there, your ever-welcome emails not included in the garbage comment of course, plus while I was out picking up the overlays (which I love by the way) for tomorrow night's gala and helping set up the ballroom, emails arrived from Scotty and Guen.

Scotty continues to amaze me. What is it with that man? He writes like he's still a college junior. You know how we were in that wonderful year when we were just beginning to think we would be big man on campus and not yet feeling the cold air of reality from the big bad world outside of college. Yet despite his persistent Peter Pan persona, the urge to confess all persists. I wonder if he forgot to mention a detour to a monastery in Tibet!

And while I expected that the email from Guen might be a "how come you answered Scotty but haven't so much as sent me a hello" guilt-fest, it was not. She seemed to simply want to tell me that Rich might be at the reunion. No sarcastic remarks or thinly veiled digs. She even offered to send Rich a bogus change of date email! She was such a good friend, yet I don't feel the urge to confess all to her. Wonder why. If I had a shrink, a real one, not you, M, that would definitely be a question for my next session.

I did send Guen a quick reply and now it is bedtime for me. Doubt that you will hear from me again until Saturday afternoon. I leave for the florist at the crack of dawn tomorrow and won't be home until well after midnight, and then will have to detox from the diva sweetness I've inhaled. Liv

• • •

From: Mary Alice Schneider
To: Olivia MacLearn
Sent: Thursday, March 21, 2013 11:15 PM
Subject: RE: My cup runneth over!

Liv, I think there's a simple explanation for why Guen is so improved. Women mature well. Men just seem to age. Really, there's an eleven year old boy trying to get out of every 65+ guy I know. Scotty probably found the age he loves best back in junior year and he's wearing it well. Don't know about you, but I would not go back. I think of Emily in "Our Town" going back after she is dead to her favorite birthday and realizing it's time to return to the cemetery on the hill. Brr. Time for a subject change.

On a happier note Eddie and I just got home from babysitting the girls while Amy and Dan went to a cocktail fund raiser for Josie's pre-school, the same one Amy and Carrie attended. Even though Amy is still a size 4, she wore a sort of Spanx thing under her dress because she thinks she needs body work after the second child. It's hard to feel sorry for a size 4, but I confess I enabled her by going out and buying the undergarment this afternoon after she freaked out while trying on her favorite dresses. That's the closest I've ever been to a size 4, just watching her. The kids take after Eddie's mom.

Good luck with your gala. Just maintain your usual balance of Mary Poppins and Auntie Mame and the thing should work out. Try some encouraging beverages too.

Malice

• • •

From: Guendaline Field
To: Olivia Walker MacLearn
Sent: Friday, March 22, 2013 10:15 AM
Subject: Thanks for asking!

AAAARRRGGG or however one can express complete frustration. Who made up the fiction that retirement is the "golden years?" When you are in a routine you can brush off minor and major frustrations by concentrating on your work. AND, people know that you have obligations and they leave you alone. If I go to one more meeting where there is a request for a volunteer and someone else volunteers me because "Guen is retired," I think I may... Oh who am I kidding; I always agree to do whatever thankless task is put on my plate.

Before I got covered up with an avalanche of "volunteer" work and family obligations I talked with the Alumni Office to make sure we could be accommodated in our off year reunion. They were actually very pleased that we may be able to pull it off. They even offered to help us plan a special event. There was some joking about a class that couldn't get things pulled together for a whole year. I have to admit that I have had some reservations about making all the contacts since as a townie I was a bit removed from campus. But, things seem to be going very well and I am starting to really get excited.

Well once I get started I do ramble. Hope things are going well with you and your family.

Guen

• • •

From: Olivia Walker MacLearn
To: Mary Alice Schneider
Sent: Saturday, March 23, 2013 10:47 AM
Subject: So much for sleeping 'til noon...

Oh, M, my mom would have been so proud of Amy's approach to body armor. Mom believed every woman should be girdled and lifted, and that one's hair and makeup should also proclaim perkiness. I wore a size 5 in college and yet I was fitted with girdles to keep my tummy from protruding and bras intended to pull up and point outward two breasts needing help with neither. She was a stickler on weight too. In high school I once gained 10 pounds, which would have had me tipping the scales at a whopping 115 pounds. When I foolishly mentioned it, mom put me on a diet "before it's too late!" She refused to answer my question "Too late for what?" because she also bought into the idea that information was bad for the virginal soul. Strange times those 50's and 60's.

The gala was incredible. We raised more money than we hoped and frankly my fear of diva sweetness was unnecessary. Apparently the offspring of my parents' wealthy friends have all moved to Palm Beach and LA, and the room was filled with real people.

On the reunion front, which seems to be a daily topic now, Guen answered my email and she sounds extremely hassled. Seems she did not really want to undertake organizing for this reunion; and I have to wonder if it is more than that. I would ask but then what goes around comes around and the last thing I need is a true confessions fest. (Since I seem to be leaping from subject to subject: did you ever read any of the original *True Confessions* magazines? My maternal grandmother had boxes of them. Great bedtime reading and helpful in researching the whole "too late for what" issue.)

Time for some brunch, maybe a nap, and definitely an evening in front of the television. Tomorrow I've got a well-earned massage followed by dinner with big brother. At least dragon lady is not coming with him. Liv

• • •

From: Mary Alice Schneider
To: Olivia MacLearn
Sent: Saturday, March 23, 2013 4:15 PM
Subject: RE: So much for sleeping 'til noon…

Thank goodness your gala is over at last. Your mother and my mom and her sisters must have come from the same mold. They opposed any sort of bounce and crammed my ninth grade body into panty girdles. One of my aunts would try to pinch my behind to be sure I was wearing a proper foundation.

Apparently girls who jiggle attract undesirable men. And yet our busts were presented as if on platters. It was the "look but touch me not" era for certain.

Amy and Dan came through Thursday evening's fund raiser/ cocktail party unscathed and without a single prize from the silent auction. It appears that the other parents at Josie's school, all older and more in funds, bid shocking sums for the treasures. At first Amy felt a bit too young (just turned 30 among a lot of fortyish women) and out of place at the event, but after two of the host's signature cocktails, things went smoothly for her. She admitted that a couple of the dads, also into the cocktails, hit on her, but she was always good at deflecting that sort of thing. Carrie's even better at that, but being a redhead has trained her in parrying unsuitable attention.

You must have been chasing them away in your girlhood. I remember the first time I set eyes on you at Yale. I said to my brother "Your roommate has his work cut out for him with that cute sister." He replied "No such problem for me." Of course I punched him.

I took a shot at knitting again. Don't tell my physical therapist. Repetitive motion is bad for the arthritis, but every once in a while I try again with the knitting needles. This time I picked a complicated hat which is the knitting equivalent of one of Eddie's double black diamond genius level Sudokus. (As Eddie was kind enough to point out, at least I might have a hat to show for it some day.) This frigging hat pattern must have been created by some monster just to see how long a crazed knitter will keep at it. It's impossible to do anything else, even listen to music, while working on the pattern.

If I knew Guen better, maybe I could hazard a guess at what her true confession might be, but you're a better judge of that. Does she have some hidden agenda? Tell me more as you find out. Everybody deserves a guilty secret. Yet, if it never gets revealed, what's the point?

Malice

• • •

From: Olivia Walker MacLearn
To: Thomas Alexander Scott
Sent: Sunday, March 24, 2013 10:25 PM
Subject: Mirrors and Minds...

Scotty, I have to say you aptly summed up the battle of the inner twenty-something vs. the elder ghost who haunts us via mirrors and photographs. Which is truer, you ask, the mirror or the mind? That is a bit like how different your voice sounds when you hear it from a recording than when you hear yourself speak. Which is the "true" sound? A related thought is: if a person never looked in a mirror or saw a photograph, would he or she run freer in the forest? My guess is yes.

Sorry to disappoint, but I don't think I qualify as a hot gramma. The only time recently that someone seemed surprised to learn I have grandchildren was at a Manhattan nail salon. Holly had just texted me a photo of her daughter Mary in her dress for the junior prom. I showed it to the manicurist and identified the girl in the photograph as my grandchild. She looked shocked and asked how old I was. When I told her, she protested loudly that she would have guessed no older than fifty. I sure wish she'd said that after I'd tipped her, so I could have luxuriated in the compliment just a bit more. Still did though.

As to your comment about Ian, he indeed was a great guy, at least for the first thirty-some years of our marriage. I sometimes struggle to hold on to the memory of just how wonderful Ian was before the disease took hold. What makes focusing on the good times harder, I think, are the years before I knew there was a physical reason for his irrational demands and especially for the bouts of unfounded jealousy. Wow, I don't quite believe I wrote that. Other than Mary Alice and Ian's shrink, I've never talked about those pre-diagnosis years with anyone. So tell me, Scotty, did you perhaps spend some years in a Tibetan Monastery, because I seem to be removing more face paint than I am prone to do.

More on Holly and your other questions at another time. I am down for the count after a tiring but (mostly) fulfilling weekend. Friday evening was a gala I co-chaired, a fundraiser for a group that supports women who start small businesses in third world countries. It was stressful but quite fun once all the things that could go wrong did not. (I always nervously anticipate such issues as "It appears the chef prepared ground beef patties in lieu of salmon fillets." Or "Does anyone know where the band is?")

Then this evening I had my once-a-month dinner with my brother. We avoid discussing taxes, gun control, The Marriage Act, the Tea Party, and a rather long list of other subjects as well. His lovely (gag) wife bowed out, so that saved the evening a bit. (See what I mean — it's like I'm in the confessional or on some sort of truth serum! Were you ever in the CIA?)

I can definitely imagine your antics as an Air Force enlistee, and I patiently await the tale of wife two. Liv

• • •

From: Rich Stapley
To: Olivia Walker MacLearn
Sent: Tuesday, March 26, 2013 12:58 PM
Subject: Greetings

Hello Liv,

Greetings across the miles and decades—and apologies for this wave of nostalgia. I saw your email address in the list of alums for the off-year reunion. Are you thinking of going? Anyone else you know of? I'm considering it — years in California mean I rarely see anyone from Morrison and thought maybe I should go to this one.

Hope all is well with you — and is this MacLearn a true Scot — pole throwing and visits to ancestral villages and conservative politics?

Rich

• • •

From: Olivia Walker MacLearn
To: Mary Alice Schneider
Sent: Tuesday, March 26, 2013 7:31 PM
Subject: I just forwarded an email from Rich to you!

Holy cow! Rich's email reminds me of the first time (actually the only time) I got on a toboggan. The hill was not all that steep, but while we were chugging hot chocolate, it began to sleet and a thin coat of ice formed on the top of the snow. The ride was exhilarating until the toboggan flipped over about halfway down the hill. I returned to school that Monday looking like I'd had an encounter with an angry cat.

Rich back in my life, even in a small way, could be ever so much more dangerous. Liv

• • •

From: Mary Alice Schneider
To: Olivia MacLearn
Sent: Monday, March 25, 2013 8:45 PM
Subject: RE: FW: Greetings

Liv, are you going to write back to Rich or just assume that he will be at the reunion? Interesting to note that he has questions about the man you married (as if he were a platonic friend concerned about the fate of an old pal).

Conservative politics!! Hurling the caber?!! Stereotypes are such a time saver. He does not say much about himself.

Malice

• • •

From: Olivia Walker MacLearn
To: Mary Alice Schneider
Sent: Tuesday, March 26, 2013 9:31 PM
Subject: Braveheart…

I don't know what I will do, M. You would think I could give a simple and resounding no to the idea of replying to Rich, rather than a wimpy I don't know. Ask me tomorrow, or perhaps the next day, or perhaps in a week or two or three. Maybe my backbone will have regenerated by then, and I can take a stand.

Stereotypes are strange things, aren't they? I am not sure what Rich envisioned when he mentioned an ancestral village. Thirteenth century Scotland a'la the movie *Braveheart?* Probably should not tell him that there was nothing resembling that in Ian's impressive ancestral digs. Remember how much fun we all had roaming the grounds and exploring the various buildings when you and Eddie joined us there that glorious spring before everything got complicated?

And politically conservative would be way off. I remember time after time when we championed various liberal causes, although Ian did inject a tinge of conservative thought on certain matters. As it should be, I think.

Maybe he was thinking of Colton. Dinner with my dear brother last night was the usual ping pong match of views on most issues. He brought up Bloomberg and grumbled about Obama destroying the Second Amendment. I offered to buy him a musket just in case all his weapons were confiscated, and it deteriorated from there. Finally we agreed on one thing, we both have our fingers crossed that Mary applies to Yale next year. What a joy it would be to have her there. Liv

• • •

From: Mary Alice Schneider
To: Olivia Walker
Sent: Tuesday, March 26, 2013 10:30 PM
Subject: RE: BRAVEHEART

Liv, you are a martyr to dine with your brother. I'd love to send a pack of my left-wing pals to bedevil him. They're a bit off the edge, but to see them with Colton would be like watching scorpions in a jar. He should own a musket just in case the starving hordes ever try to take over and steal any of his stuff.

If you do decide to write to Rich, what will you say? Will you simply give him the party line or will you be frank? I would love to know.

Remember 'way back when online dating started? Cassie was in college then and filled in a couple of profiles, as did her pal Lena. They were swamped with replies from men. Eddie pointed out to her that there were four people in any exchange: who she said she was and who she really was and the same deal for each guy. She took some offense, but when a man who claimed to be a professor in NC wanted to fly her down to see him, she decided her dad might be right.

It reminds me of that great New Yorker cartoon of a nondescript mutt and his smaller pal sitting before a computer. The larger one is saying, "On the internet nobody knows you're a dog." What if Rich is a major dog now in whatever sense you want to imagine?

OK, maybe you could write him, but don't meet him before the reunion. I know it is none of my business but I just love butting in to your life.

Malice

• • •

From: Olivia Walker MacLearn
To: Mary Alice Schneider
Sent: Wednesday, March 27, 2013 9:31 AM
Subject: Lessons learned at the pool…

M, do you remember how you all would laugh at me from the water as I sat on the edge of the pool, legs dangling, refusing to come in because the water was too cold? Finally after some annoying taunts and bribes, I would, with agonizingly slow movements, walk down the steps into the water. And how every darn time you would point out that once in I was fine?

Well, after tossing and turning all night, ruminating about when and how I would respond to Rich, I decided to just jump in and get it over with. It may take a couple, okay a few rewrites, but I am determined to be done with it before my body next makes contact with my mattress. I'll blind copy you on the email. Liv

• • •

From: Mary Alice Schneider
To: Olivia Walker
Sent: Wednesday, March 27, 2013 10:30 PM
Subject: RE: Lessons learned at the pool...

OK, I can deal with this, but please remember that I am a vengeful person and if he hurts you again, I am coming after him. Silly me. A 67 year old grandma should not speak this way. Instead I will travel over to Providence or up to Revere and hire somebody else to do the job. I mean it. And don't attribute my vendetta plan simply to my Italian ancestry. I did some research and found that the Welsh are famously vengeful (think old Comitatus maxim: "It is better to avenge a friend than to mourn him long"). Don't even get me started on the English and Irish ancestors. Truly, the only good thing about Dad's decline is that in his final decade he forgot whom to hate. He even mellowed on the New York Yankees. Outrageous.

Seriously, I am right here behind you and I have a plan if Rich so much as upsets you.

Malice

• • •

From: Olivia Walker MacLearn
To: Richard Stapley
BCC: Mary Alice Schneider
Sent: Wednesday, March 27, 2013 11:04 PM
Subject: RE: Greetings

Hi Rich,

The reunion list was certainly a walk down memory lane. I am amazed at how many names I was able to connect with faces after all these years.

So you moved to California. There are a few states with such distinct personalities that it's almost as if they are separate countries: Arizona, New Hampshire, New Jersey, Oregon, Texas, and of course California. It must be interesting to live there. Connecticut is pretty close to where I grew up, so not a big change for me.

As to reunion weekend, I didn't do a good job of keeping in touch with classmates through the years, and haven't attended any reunions, but I've been catching up with a few close friends, and I'm excited at the chance to see them. However, I am involved with several charities from a large non-profit that Ian ran in the 80's and 90's, and I have not checked schedules yet for conflicts.

Unfortunately I have no info about attendees other than Guen and Scotty, but I imagine someone from the reunion committee could answer that.

Good to hear from you.

Sincerely,

Olivia

• • •

From: Olivia Walker MacLearn
To: Mary Alice Schneider
Sent: Wednesday, March 27, 2013 11:06 PM
Subject: Written, edited, and sent!

I blind copied you on my email to Rich. Am off to bed now —
to sleep, perchance all through the night. Liv

• • •

From: Mary Alice Schneider
To: Olivia Walker
Sent: Thursday, March 28, 2013 10:02 AM
Subject: RE: Greetings

What a diplomat you are! You are wasting yourself on those
charitable organizations Ian founded. You should be at the
UN. About what was I worrying? (Note that I did not end the
sentence with a preposition even in my agitation). And the
phrase "didn't do a good job of keeping in touch with classmates through the years..." Let's see. What might you have
failed to mention to the creep who broke your heart? I love
"connect names with faces..." I'll bet there's more you can
connect with than his face.

I still have Providence and Revere in my sights, so don't think
Rich is off the hook. Let's see how he responds. Since I have
known him only in the negative sense for over forty years, I
can't help thinking that he may have evolved into any number of nasty forms, perhaps starting forest fires for fun or
throwing litter out his car windows, not flossing, or worst of
all, doing a little fortune hunting among wealthy, sexy widows
(I'll name no names).

Just don't forget to keep me informed. Let me be your Jiminy Cricket on this trip to Pleasure Island. As soon as his Donkey ears start to show beneath his hat or within his thinning hair, I will alert you.

Malice

• • •

From: Olivia MacLearn
To: Guendaline Field
Sent: Thursday, March 28, 2013, 8:30 PM
Subject: Thinking about you…

Guen, I keep thinking that you sounded so stressed in your email. I'm sorry you were thrown into organizing this off-year reunion, although given that only — what did your initial email say? Maybe five people? — showed up for our 45th reunion, and you already have at least a maybe from thirty of us, you seem to be the perfect person for the task!

How is your mom's friend, the one you lived with? I know you hated being a townie, but we all sure loved going home with you to a real house, to hang out in a bedroom that did not have two twin beds, a chunky double desk, and concrete block walls.

Anyway, I just wanted to say that I hope all is well with you, and that your committee does its fair share so you can de-stress a bit. Liv

• • •

From: Olivia Walker MacLearn
To: Mary Alice Schneider
Sent: Thursday, March 28, 2013 8:45 PM
Subject: The perfect antidote to clothes shopping!

M, your email made me laugh. No mean feat given an afternoon of clothes shopping. If I were in charge of the world, mirrors in dressing rooms would be redesigned to provide multiple functionality: Press A for above the neck reflection, B for waist to head, and C for full body reflection. And the image that sneaks up on a person from the tri-mirror version, well, talk about something that ought to be outlawed as a threat to life, liberty and the pursuit of happiness!

So I now own a few new items to wear in DC over Easter weekend. Sunday looks promising at a high of 61, although rain could spoil that. What's the forecast for the Cape? Liv

• • •

From: Guendaline Field
To: Olivia Walker MacLearn
Sent: Friday, March 29, 2013 9:46 AM
Subject: The Bat clarifies

Liv:

You misunderstood me. I actually initiated the 46th reunion project. I suddenly really wanted to see people again. Retirement makes you look back and get nostalgic. When I called the alumni office they said none of our class showed up for the 45th reunion. That made it seem even more important that we get as many to come as possible.

All the "involuntary volunteering" I made reference to was at places like church and civic committees. Now when someone else volunteers me I can say, "Sorry I have no extra time, I am working on a project with some college friends."

Believe it or not the response to date is forty-five attendees. I believe that is at least a third of the class. I'll have to check that.

Unfortunately, Mrs. Banks died about three years ago. One of the last things I said to her was that she had been a real sport about all my college friends dropping by. She said she thought she enjoyed it more than we did. She really was a sweet lady, we had our moments of course, but you tend to forget the little bumps in the road and just enjoy the ride. Do you remember how the whole house smelled of Youth Dew cologne? She must have bought it by the gallon. I never encounter that smell without immediately thinking of her. My Mom was devastated by her death. They had been such great long-term friends.

I just reread my last email. I can certainly see why you thought someone had volunteered me to put together the ad hoc reunion. I did dig into my frustrations about retirement with a vengeance. Someone had probably suggested that I clean Fellowship Hall again! I am actually doing well.

I was glad to see that you are comfortable with ALL the possible attendees.

Guen

• • •

From: Olivia MacLearn
To: Guendaline Field
Sent: Friday, March 29, 2013 10:22 AM
Subject: Vive le technologie!

Guen, I'm on the Acela Express heading to my daughter's for Easter weekend and a welcome dose of spring weather! I just read your email on my iPad, and I'm replying as the train crisscrosses New Jersey on its way to DC. So cool! I feel quite technologically hip.

I'm glad I misunderstood about your frustration with being volunteered for everything! I sure hope heading the reunion committee will help with your "let's ask Guen to do it" problem. I remember facing the same issue as a stay at home mom when Holly was young. Hard to say no if everybody thinks you are eating bonbons and watching soap operas all day.

I noticed from the list of alums that you are back in your home town. Funny how so many of us gravitated to our places of origin. I grew up on Long Island, lived most of my life on Cape Cod, and am now firmly rooted in CT. Almost like going home in the scheme of things. Liv

• • •

From: Mary Alice Schneider
To: Olivia Walker
Sent: Friday, March 29, 2013 8:30 PM
Subject: RE: The perfect antidote to clothes shopping!

L, I like your ideas about clothes shopping. For years I've longed for a cubicle (a large one) with candle light and small hand mirrors artfully placed. I must have been in my mid fifties, longer ago than I would like to admit, when I first began to believe that the vile young designers had replaced the try-on mirrors with fun house mirrors, the ones that widen everything.

DC over Easter! Sigh… I just checked my weather app and it shows a blob, maybe the sun, covered in what looks like cotton balls, so it looks as if we'll have another damp, cloudy, chilly Cape Cod Easter. Josie will be annoyed that people won't notice that she and little Dana are wearing matching dresses. They have distinctly different coats.

Remember when we went all out in our Easter garb, complete with hats and gloves? I used to worry about not wearing the same hat for Palm Sunday that I planned to wear for Easter. Now it's all I can do to change out of jeans before the horde arrives for dinner. And forget about heels. My mother-in-law used to wear heeled bedroom slippers. Her feet would have worked on a Barbie doll. Eddie said it was because she was only 5 ft. tall, but she was from a glamorous age, long gone I fear. Also, let's admit it that New England women tend to "have" their clothes, their hair color (no worries about roots) and often their original husbands. We are very behind the times.

Don't forget that I have my eye on you, so dish up everything that happens with this reunion planning. That includes any letters from Rich. Long years ago, during our student teaching, my roommate used me to help her dump a boy. She let me red-pencil his love letters. I gave him a C minus and told him "misty mountain tops" seemed a bit trite.

Waiting to hear more,

Malice

• • •

From: Olivia Walker MacLearn
To: Mary Alice Schneider
Sent: Saturday, March 30, 2013 3:52 PM
Subject: Ah Spring!

Hi, M! I spent the first half of today staring in wonder at trees with leaves of green and at crocuses and daffodils. Everywhere I look spring is evident. This is not Connecticut!

Holly and the girls send their love. Tim is off at a Kiwanis meeting—big pancake breakfast fundraiser next weekend.

Tomorrow the girls will humor Holly and Tim by searching for their Easter baskets, and then we will leave for brunch at their club. I'm not sure when church slipped off of their list of "Things to do on Easter," but it seems it has. I would be more upset if they were not a family who walks the walk so to speak.

I heard back from Guen. Seems she was not upset about organizing the non-reunion-reunion, and in fact volunteered for the task! It appears the "Guen will do it" issue applies instead to her life in general. When I think back about Guen's college life as a townie, it was that way then too. She was allowed to go to college away from home only if she would agree to live with a good friend of her mom. I know Guen often missed doing things with us because Mrs. Banks needed help with this or that, and Guen would acquiesce. I swear some people are born with an "I cannot say no" birthmark on their forehead.

Oh and Guen closed with the comment that she is glad I am comfortable with ALL the possible attendees. I am quite sure she means Rich. I did not correct that in the reply I sent (techie that I am) from my nifty iPad while aboard the train. But am I really comfortable seeing him again? I suspect not. Curious? Oh just a tad.

What am I? Thirteen? Fourteen? I feel as if I should close with: OMG, M, what if he and I are MFEO? Liv

• • •

From: Mary Alice Schneider
To: Olivia Walker
Sent: Sunday, March 31, 2013 1:07 PM
Subject: RE: Ah Spring!

Ah, yes! Easter. A happy one to you. Our two grands went to their first ever neighborhood egg hunt yesterday and they're still wild with delight. Being four and one they find everything delightful. I'm such a heathen than I don't ever go to a church unless someone dies, get married or gets christened. We have a christening in a few weeks.

Yesterday our doorbell rang and I found two evangelical ladies on my front porch. What makes them think that at 67 I've been waiting all my life for, as Oliver Goldsmith called it, "a slice of their scurvy religion?" Wouldn't I have one in place by now if I wanted one? I used to have one and I abandoned it. I explained to them that I am not in the market for religious information and wished them well, but honestly, I think they could spend their time better. I must abandon this topic or I'll start ranting about draft dodging presidential candidates trying to convert the French in the 60's. Please!

Guen sounds like a sweet type right from central casting and not the Annie who "cain't say NO" to men in "Oklahoma!" She's trying to make everybody happy except for herself, but everyone is grateful I'm sure. That indentured servitude she had to endure in order to go away to college sounds pretty grim.

Eddie and I still don't discuss the time he signed me up to be a brownie leader when he was enrolling Cassie. I was feeling ill that night (turns out I was newly pregnant with Amy) and found out about my volunteering when he got home. Blecch! Had to manage a brownie troop with my neighbor for a whole year, allowing two weeks off for delivery. Then the little monsters all wanted to get their baby care badge – can't remember the actual name - while using Amy as their guinea pig. Give me all the acne-covered parolees from an urban high school or all the drab part timers at a Cape community college, but rescue me from elementary school girls.

Oops, I'm ranting again. Have a great Easter weekend and don't forget your white gloves (channeling my mother).

Malice

• • •

From: Olivia Walker MacLearn
To: Mary Alice Schneider
Sent: Sunday, March 31, 2013 7:52 PM
Subject: Look what the bunny brought!

Another email from Rich! (Pasted below.) M, he addressed me as Olivia. Yes, I know that is how I signed my email to him. But he never called me Olivia, so it feels so strange.

And he has children. Are they old children or does he have a trophy wife now? Or did Susan never age? Third child at 58?

Fourteen is too mature. Thirteen too. I believe I just turned twelve. Liv

Pasted below is his email:

*   *   *   *

Olivia,

Thanks for the note. I think my sense is the opposite: I see the names and wonder who ARE these people? Did I know them? Might as well be random names from the Montpellier phone book. I did go to one reunion, started conversations with each person I saw, and after about 15 minutes realized that I only wanted to spend time with friends — not a great insight, but it was a moment. So this Memorial Day thing probably depends for me on who's going to go. If you have a way to figure out who's going (still haven't heard from Guen), let me know.

It's Easter weekend — glad to see that Peeps are still around. My parental solution for all the sugar of Easter and Halloween was to re-hide the candy countless times until it was so groty that even my kids didn't want to touch it. I suppose hard-boiled eggs are a different thing — real food that shouldn't be wasted. (Child of Depression-tempered parents talking.)

Anyway, take care. And what's the large non-profit? What do they have you doing?

Cheers,

Rich

• • •

From: Mary Alice Schneider
To: Olivia Walker
Sent: Sunday, March 31, 2013 8:50 PM
Subject: RE: FW: Greetings!

Liv, or should I say Olivia!

Wow. So Rich is a father. How nice. The kids could be any age.
My old childhood buddy Salvatore, surprisingly a contractor
in CT now, started fathering kids at age 52 with his third wife
and now he's on his own with them. He did not mention what
happened to his wife, but she's out of the picture.

Why does Rich not mention his wife? Is this a man over 60
issue? Does he count you as a friend? One would think so
(note steam coming out my ears)! Who re-hides candy until it
gets grotty (note correct spelling)?

We need more information.

Malice

p.s. Twelve is an excellent age. It is never too late to have a
venomous childhood.

APRIL

"April hath put a spirit of youth in everything."

–William Shakespeare

From: Olivia Walker MacLearn
To: Mary Alice Schneider
Sent: Monday, April 1, 2013 6:48 AM
Subject: You may stick with calling me Liv

Reserving a Monday morning train back to CT seemed like such a good idea at the time. It does make for a crack of dawn beginning to the day though. If I can keep from nodding off, I'll write from the train! Till then, Liv

• • •

From: Olivia Walker MacLearn
To: Mary Alice Schneider
Sent: Monday, April 1, 2013 10:39 AM
Subject: chug-chug-chugging along...

Literally and figuratively, M. Thankfully I was able to stuff my inner teen back inside and I am now functioning as a reasonably intact adult. Not sure why I reacted as I did to Rich's email. I suppose there might be a few unresolved issues. Slight understatement, I know.

So here is my plan, which didn't work last time but ever the eternal optimist: rather than waste time ruminating what-if's, I am going to whip off a quick answer with a few facts about my work with the charities. I'll ask Rich what took him to California and if it is a good place to raise children. That should help clarify, don't you think?

The weekend was wonderful. Tell me exactly why we are still living in a part of the US with such a tardy springtime. Liv

• • •

From: Olivia Walker MacLearn
To: Richard Stapley
Sent: Monday, April 01, 2013 7:58 PM
Subject: RE: Greetings

Hi, Rich. Just got home from a wonderful Easter weekend with Holly and her family, an easy trip on one of the express trains. The blue skies and sunshine were such a treat. Spring is definitely making itself known south of here, but CT is struggling to leave winter's grasp.

You asked what I do with the charities. Mostly I plan fund raising events — kind of like my parents' Hampton parties only with socially redeeming value. One recent event I co-chaired was for a charity that helps women in third world countries by providing start up money for small businesses. The gala was very successful and quite fun once all the major things that can go wrong did not.

So what took you to California? Do you enjoy living there? Is it a good place to work, raise kids, etc.?

I have no specifics about who will be at the reunion, but Guen did say that almost a third of the class is planning to attend, so you should have friends to hang with if you decide to go. I'm still a maybe. Liv

• • •

From: Mary Alice Schneider
To: Olivia Walker
Sent: Monday, April 1, 2013 11:13 PM
Subject: RE: chug-chug-chugging along…

Tardy springtime!? The Cape is two weeks behind Boston. Seriously. My Arlington cousin's lilacs bloom way ahead of ours in May and it's always cold and damp around here through June. Eddie's aunt from Florida stayed with us one June and we couldn't keep the old girl warm. Hmm. Now that I think of it, she was about the age we are now. Funny how our point of view changes. Remember when we didn't trust anyone over 30?

Speaking of people we shouldn't trust, don't get me started on unresolved issues between you and Rich. Sure, ask him about raising kids in California and maybe he'll open up about who "mothered" them. I trust he knows. OK, I'm being spiteful — my specialty.

Parenting and relationships are a challenge. Did I mention that this year we have not one but two feral barn cats? Our younger spoiled house cat growls injuriously at them from the dining room window but would have a heart attack if she ever set paw outside. We've been feeding the feral male, Tybalt, prince of cats, named for Juliet's cousin, for a year and a half, ever since our previous big male feral, Fluffy, disappeared. Now Tybalt has brought home a girlfriend whom we have named Maggie after the role Elizabeth Taylor played in Cat on a Hot Tin Roof. Maggie looks remarkably like the late Fluffy and we suspect she is his daughter.

The point of this apparently pointless tale is that we are pretty sure Maggie is pregnant. She remains in and around the barn, eating lavishly and basking in whatever sunny patches she finds. Tybalt considers himself unattached and roams away for days, probably courting other women. I knew a pigeon like that near my urban classroom many years ago. The kids observed that while his mate sat on their eggs right outside our huge windows, he was getting it on with other girl pigeons nearby, in full view of the nest, on our flat roof. Baby pigeons, by the way, are not a bit cute. I'll leave you with that thought.

Got your back,

Malice

• • •

From: Olivia MacLearn
To: Guendaline Field
Sent: Tuesday, April 02, 2013 10:38 PM
Subject: Question…

Guen, I've been wondering about your email address since you first wrote! So unique and creative, unlike mine! Does it have any special meaning?

It's an early bedtime for me tonight — Holly's girls joke that I get jet-lagged every time I take the train between CT and VA. They may be right. Liv

• • •

From: Guendaline Field
To: Olivia Walker MacLearn
Sent: Wednesday, April 03, 2013 10:10 AM
Subject: The Bat

Liv, My thinking process in selecting my email address shows just how warped I am becoming. I arrived at the descriptive email address as follows: When I was young I could remember a tremendous amount of information. For instance I never forgot why I had gone into a room. When I did start forgetting why I had traveled from the second floor to the first floor I questioned how my brain was working. I envisioned a file room in the center of my brain. When I was young there was a junior file clerk who knew before I asked what I wanted and had it waiting for me. As I aged so did my file clerk and he finally got to the point that he couldn't remember which file cabinet the information was in and finally where the file cabinets were. I decided in my frustration that my clerk morphed into one of those bats you see in horror shows that have big yellow eyes and clearly don't know where he or she is or which way to fly. Therefore I have a confused bat in my belfry.

So I say to all those folks in college who thought I was a little odd: "You should see me now." And I hope to display this personality openly at Memorial Day Weekend. Yesterday was the first time my daughter Elaine knew that I was working on a college reunion. She immediately asked me what I was obsessed about. She wanted to know if I am trying to lose ten pounds in two months or shopping continuously to find just the right dress. That's when I realized that I wasn't doing anything like that. I admit for most of my life I was prone to going off the deep end about things that probably didn't matter much. This time around I just want to see a lot of people I haven't seen for years and be comfortable with them just the way I am. Guen

• • •

From: Olivia MacLearn
To: Guendaline Field
Sent: Wednesday, April 03, 2013 10:23 AM
Subject: RE: The Bat

Guen, I don't remember anyone thinking you odd in college. But then I don't remember thinking that Gloria was "just a farm girl" and sometime in our senior year she confessed she thought that was my impression of her since I was from "The East!" I wonder how many false assumptions we all made in our college years; indeed how many we still harbor or make anew in our golden years.

I think your bat in the belfry imagery quite descriptive! You always had a talent for business. Who knew you were creative as well. Liv

• • •

From: Rich Stapley
To: Olivia Walker MacLearn
Sent: Wednesday, April 3, 2013 9:45 PM
Subject: RE: Greetings

Liv and MacLearn,

Easter is an English major's favorite holiday — from George Herbert to T.S. Eliot. Even do secular agnostics and woolly atheists pause and reflect. (Thank God for Spell Check — "woolly" and "atheists" needed attending.) A train trip under blue skies seems like the way out of winter's tunnel.

The fund-raisers sound important - a hard kernel of purpose beneath the gaiety and Champagne. A friend from around the time of my divorce got her kids through college and then parlayed her experience as a social worker with a caseload of Cambodians into a US-AID grant to establish a program in a Cambodian coastal town. Instead of being for women, it was for amputees (all those land mines) to learn a micro-micro enterprise — small engine repair, raising chickens. She said their one planning error was buying a foot locker to put by each bed (the participants come into town from far-flung villages for two weeks and stay in a dorm — no one had clothes besides what was on their backs. She's still there, 20 years later. So, nice work, Liv. Hard to think of anything more important.

I should know, but who's Holly? I don't remember her from Morrison.

California — studies brought me here and suddenly there was a job and friends and roots and families not so close that they could drop in unannounced. Then, blink, 20, 30, or 40 years have passed. I have plenty of friends who left for Oregon-Arizona-Nevada-lower-taxes as soon as they retired, but I can't imagine being back in Arizona, and what would I do in Oregon? My bridge game has me ranked dead last in the world (I was briefly ahead of a girl from Pakistan then her family made her drop out) and last time I went fishing was 1963. Plus, as a tax-and-spend liberal, I should stick it out here paying my fair share (which, truth to tell, isn't much).

Should I apologize now for the breezy tone? It's a pleasure to ramble on with you — in slightly more depth maybe than a cocktail party and more shallow than dinner and a movie. (As for movies, if you haven't seen it, treat yourself to "Millions" — the last two minutes will show you how important those fund-raising events are.)

Best,

Rich

• • •

From: Olivia Walker MacLearn
To: Mary Alice Schneider
Sent: Wednesday, April 3, 2013 10:24 PM
Subject: Oh my…

M, I just heard from Rich again. Will forward to you as soon
as I send this. No red lining, please. Best not to make me want
to come to his defense. I'm feeling just a bit too nostalgic for
my own good. Liv

• • •

From: Mary Alice Schneider
To: Olivia Walker
Sent: Thursday, April 4, 2013 8:15 AM
Subject: RE: Oh my…

Liv,

I'm simmering as I read Rich's missive, especially the "Who's
Holly?" bit. Of course he doesn't remember her from Morrison.
He gets points from me, though, for being a non-runaway tax
and spend liberal. He seems to be less than affluent. What
a shocker for an English major. I can slam them, being one
myself.

Back in my city teaching days, one of my homeroom partners,
another English teacher, kept providing cartoons to keep
up our morale. My favorite was of a bookish looking young
woman with an armload of platters in a smoke filled truck

73

stop asking "To WHOM goes the chili special?" We could slap each other five and say "This beats waitressing!"

So we still don't know what Rich did to keep chili on the table or why he devoted the lion's share of his letter to his Coastal Cambodian volunteer friend. Maybe it's his way of keeping it breezy and rambling — wouldn't want to get too personal, would we, such as over a dinner and a movie? Hey, Rich, remember when you and Liv couldn't sit through a whole movie? Bet you could sit through a double feature now with no future need for matching claw footed bath tubs on a misty hillside!

Wow! He plays bridge. You two have lots in common. Just being nasty. One way to stay at the top of our class at Pickering was NOT to play bridge. Seriously, that place was a dumping ground for all the chicks who couldn't make the seven sisters. The favorite phrase out of their superglued teeth was "Anyone for bridge?" The school took scholarship kids like me so that somebody would be awake in class and keep the Profs busy.

So back to being a male English major. What would I know about that, having been at a women's college? One night our dorm neighbor, a girl my roommates called Giant Sequoia legs, asked me to take her Princeton fiancé to a program at our chapel, an evening with some dude pretending to be Robert Frost. GS legs, a chem major, had no interest in poetry, so I took her man with me and was surprised at his alertness and perception. OK, I admit that I knew only MIT nerds and my Yale brother, soon to be lost in actuarial tables (very original choice in CT), so at first I thought the guy was a freak, some sort of trained monkey. Then I learned to drop the prejudice and accept that he really loved lit. He seemed dismayed that his woman lacked the humanities gene, so I cheered him up with Eddie's interpretation of my favorite imagist line: "Cats walk thin and sleep fat." He completely understood. It turned out to be a fun night and GS was grateful. Ah, precious memories, how they linger.

Take the advice of this secular humanist. Don't let Rich's references or his silver tongue woo you again. English majors are a manipulative lot. "Words are all (we) have" and all that. Eddie, all his awards and Ph.D. notwithstanding, tells me he is an unarmed man in our war of words and that men in general don't have a clue or a chance. Just remember that when and if you take on this guy again.

Still got your back!

Malice

• • •

From: Olivia Walker MacLearn
To: Richard Stapley
BCC: Mary Alice Schneider

Sent: Thursday, April 04, 2013 8:45 AM
Subject: Oops…

Rich, Sorry for the confusing reference to a name you have no reason to remember. I'm getting reacquainted with several Morrison friends, and in an email to Scotty I mentioned the possibility that I might be watching my daughter Holly's girls over Memorial Day weekend. Probably figured I'd mentioned it to you as well. I need to be more attentive to what I've written to each person.

I'm sad to hear of your divorce. That must have been difficult since you mentioned children, or are they from a second marriage? Colton — you remember my brother I'm sure — is on marriage number three, and has children from each go-around.

I'm not much for heading out to movies but will look for "Millions" on Netflix. Liv

• • •

From: Olivia Walker MacLearn
To: Mary Alice Schneider
Sent: Thursday, April 04, 2013 8:50 AM
Subject: Blind copied you on my email to Rich...

I probably should stop that. It seems rather impolite. Liv

• • •

From: Mary Alice Schneider
To: Olivia MacLearn
Sent: Thursday, April 04, 2013 9:05 AM
Subject: RE: Blind copied you on my email to Rich...

Liv, maybe my brain is not up and running yet, but what should you stop? Did I miss something?

Malice

• • •

From: Olivia Walker MacLearn
To: Mary Alice Schneider
Sent: Tuesday, April 04, 2013 9:30 AM
Subject: RE: RE: Blind copied you on my email to Rich…

No problem with your brain, M. I just meant I should stop blind copying you on my emails to Rich. (The thought of someone doing that to me makes me cringe — do unto others and all that.)

Thankfully, I have refrained from forwarding your emails to him. "Matching claw footed bath tubs on a misty hillside," huh? Made me laugh! Liv

• • •

From: Thomas Alexander Scott
To: Olivia Walker MacLearn
Sent: Thursday, April 4, 2013 8:20 PM
Subject: RE: Mirrors and Minds…

Ah, Liv, so sorry for the lapse. I have always had great intentions, haven't I? I had intended a quick reply to your revealing email, but life intervened…or interfered, more like it. Okay, to be frank, that sumbitch Mr. Mortality has been peeking in the windows of my life which sometimes shuts me down emotionally. A close Air Force buddy in Texas didn't make it through a risky cancer surgery. My reality-based mind told me he might not, but my ever-optimistic heart had convinced me he would. Left me pretty shaken. I guess we all live with that conflicting duality of realism and hope. Or do we? Maybe I only like to think that everyone has the same struggles I have. Anyway, couple his death with the death of an old man, the father of yet another deceased close friend, and me being expected to "say a few words" at the crusty old geezer's funeral and it has been a rough ride recently. Actually, I kind of enjoyed telling a few borderline racy stories about the old man and watching the good folks at the First Fundamentalist Church go pale. Shock and awe, baby, shock and awe. I still love the chance to wreak a little havoc. But these deaths open the carefully-crafted shutters of my world for Mr. Mortality to ominously appear, reminding me that it's a short ride at best.

You know, Walker, life goes a lot faster in the living of it than it does in the reading about it. Those Western Civilization classes in the old auditorium at Morrison seemed to drag on forever but the truth is that those ancients were alive just yesterday. Think about it: my grandfather was born in 1889. Sounds dusty and historical, right? But ask any freshman entering college next fall about *our* birth year. Most of our circle were born in 1945; those frosh were born in 1995. That is the same time span as us as freshmen talking about 1895! How's that for perspective?? So when that damned limit-dangling Mortality hovers, I typically recede into the shadows for a few days, flip the channels between late night movies that no one ever liked, and pour myself into a bottle of fine old Scotch which reminds me that age is sometimes beneficial. Now I have emerged finally, a little unsteady perhaps, but that describes a lot of my life anyway. Loved your comment about "running freer in the forest!" I once jumped naked from a high boulder into a frigid fast-flowing creek ten feet below in the Gorge. Ah, wilderness! Ah, youth! Now it has to be mild before I sit out on my balcony and tepid before I will step into my shower.

No, I'm no guru or priest magically pulling secrets from you. I'm just pretty much one open book inviting another book to flip a few pages and feel the freedom it brings. When you hold everything in, the space inside you gets filled up. And, as more stuff happens to you, there is no room for it without internal compression, leading to emotional pressure, leading to splits and cracks in your psyche, leading to all kinds of inappropriate spewing. It's not a pretty sight to see; it's not a healthy thing to be. Maybe another reason you can let your hair down a bit with me (do you still wear it long?) is that I haven't got a judgmental bone in my body. We are what we are — and what's wrong with that? Under all the years I am still Scotty and you are still Liv, sitting lengthwise on the bench under the big tree in front of the library, using each other as a backrest, sharing the ups and downs of the life opening up all around us. Just because we forgot that for 46 years doesn't mean it isn't still there.

Honestly, I had forgotten all about your brother. Now I recall how different he was from you. Hands down, I think you got the best genes. Your compassionate heart still shows in the charity work you seem to be doing. What was the word you wrote — fulfilling? Has life been fulfilling for you, Liv? Mine has been full, but I'm not quite sure about filling.

After my discharge from the Air Force and my first divorce (God, that sounds terrible — even to me!), I had nothing planned, so I naturally gravitated back to school. I used some veterans' benefits to get another Master's degree, this one from a state university near Austin. And what field would complement my English degrees? Why, Cultural Anthropology, of course! Don't ask me why. Maybe just my attempt to figure out society and why we do what we do, a sort of post-Vietnam War reflective stage.

When I finished the degree, it was spring and the mountains called to me. At Rocky Mountain National Park in Colorado, I found a message board advertising a park ranger position. Someone would pay me to hike, explore, and talk?? It was my image of heaven. Little did I know that my heaven would also, a few years later, bring me a living angel, and then a lot of hell. But I think I'll save that for my next email, which I promise will shortly follow your next reply. I have had enough melancholy from Mr. Mortality for a while. Besides I am out of Scotch.

I'm hoping now that, having tasted the freedom of self-revelation, you might tell me more about your life. About Ian. Or the joys and pains of life since Morrison. Or even perhaps why you disappeared so completely after college. Not pushing, not prying, just listening.

Scotty
The Great Scott

• • •

From: Olivia Walker MacLearn
To: Thomas Alexander Scott
Sent: Saturday, April 6, 2013 9:30 AM
Subject: RE: RE: Mirrors and Minds...

Dear Scotty, I am so sorry about your friend and the inevitable pain caused by your close encounter with Mr. Mortality. He was my roommate for a while too, and I was ever so glad to see him go. I think of him as the Shingles virus, hiding out 'til you forget about him, then reappearing to wreak havoc. (I've never actually had Shingles. I just watch the stupid commercial for the vaccine every time it's on, even though I've already had the vaccine, and even though I know watching will leave me with a case of nasty free-floating anxiety. Why not stop if I know that about myself? Train wreck syndrome, I suppose.)

Oh and I must thank you for the reality check on how damn old we are. Pass the scotch!

Now on to answering one of your easier questions: Yes, my hair is still long, although I think about cutting it frequently, because of something my mother said at some point in my mid-fifties, right after subjecting me to one of her famously slow head to toe visual evaluations. She sighed and then said: "Last weekend I saw a woman standing across the room at a party. She had the sexiest long hair. Beautiful! But then she turned around and I swear everyone in the room gasped in disgust at how old she was. Later we all said she should have had it cut decades before."

"So you think I'm too old for long hair?" I barked in my best insulted teenager voice.

"Oh, Olivia," she simpered, "You do take everything I say so personally."

More open book moments to follow. Second wife? Liv

• • •

From: Guendaline Field
To: Olivia Walker MacLearn
Sent: Saturday, April 6, 2013 1:17 PM
Subject: RE: RE: The Bat

Liv, your last email caused me to wonder whether or not I actually knew myself before college. I think my Morrison years taught me who I was. Even if I just look at the yearbook pictures I can see a different person each year. I am absolutely sure that I left there with more sense of self and something else that I can't define. Maybe that is what college is for everyone — or should be.

Thank you for the nice observations about my business and creative sense. Actually I have very little creative sense and I had to work hard at the business side. But my start-up business did do well, and I have passed the reins to my very competent daughter. It is so satisfying that she wanted to continue my work, and I am very flattered when she asks me for advice.

In my previous email I said pretty negative things about retirement, but in truth, I love retirement. It is the first time in my life that I can do what I want when I want. As you know I worked the night shift while I was in college and continued to work even in Grad School. Then I threw myself wholeheartedly into the start-up. As an adult I never had time to just stop and look around me. Now, I keep my iPad on my night stand and slowly wake up in the morning checking my emails and Facebook communications. I should also be embarrassed to say that I also check out what the Queen is up to on the Unofficial Royalty News site. Then, at my own pace, I decide what I want to do on this new day and whom, if anyone, I want to be in contact with. There are some minor demands, but now if I become weary of something I can just withdraw gracefully. This excludes family demands of course — but that is another corner of my life.

I can also take time to be nice. If I have a full cart at the grocery in the checkout line and someone comes up behind me with two or three items, especially if it is a woman wearing navy blue, black, or brown, I let them go first. Oh, how many times did I, in my business dress trying to get somewhere quickly, wish that someone had shown me that little courtesy. Guen

• • •

From: Thomas Alexander Scott
To: Olivia Walker MacLearn
Sent: Sunday, April 7, 2013 10:11 PM
Subject: RE: RE: Mirrors and Minds

Oh, yeah, your mother. Liv, my girl, how did you turn out so normal with her as your materfamilias? I remember the first time you introduced us. She lifted her nose and looked down at me even though I was a foot and half taller than she was! Maybe it was my southern drawl or the blue jeans I was probably wearing. Her whole demeanor just dripped of disapproval. Freud must have been wrong because certainly your early childhood influences did not form your personality. At least not THAT influence.

Ahem, please note for the record that my response to your email is quite prompt enough to be considered "quickly, shortly, forthwith, straightaway, PDQ," and perhaps even "in the flash of a very slow eye." The Great Scott always keeps his promises! Well, this one at least.

Okay, okay, Wife #2. In my years as a park ranger at Rocky Mountain National Park I met some interesting, odd, and intriguing people. But one particular summer I walked into something quite different. At the first meeting which included our summertime ranger staff the well-ordered rows of Smokey the Bear stiff Stetson felt hats always brought an inner chuckle to me, looking as if they were brown pizza trays with a glob of dough in the middle waiting to be kneaded and spun. (Okay, truthfully, I loved my hat.) The uniform brought a uniformity (duh) and anonymity to our group, as it was intended to do, I'm sure. But there was no hiding the brilliance of the smile emanating from under one of the pizza trays. I just happened all summer to get myself assigned to wherever she was. Since she was a college biology professor back in Louisiana, that usually meant that we were out on a trail leading nature discovery hikes. I fell in lust with her the first time I saw her lounging on the front porch of her cabin, wearing her official white t-shirt and a pair of boxers. But watching her keen eye spot an almost invisible hummingbird nest wedged onto a branch in the crevice of a rock or listening to her expand our universes by pointing out a common weed and describing its medicinal value to ancient cultures, I felt something deeper happening — a respect, a valuing, a treasuring. I fell in love with her mind. Her last night of the summer we camped together in a high meadow, laid back on our sleeping bags and watched the Perseid meteor shower light up the night sky like the Fourth of July on the Potomac. That night she asked if I had any plans for my future. Obviously she had mistaken me for a normal person. At my "not really" she suggested I pack up my gear and come home with her to Louisiana.

The next thing I knew, I was in a church aisle (my first wedding had been at the county courthouse) and was looking for a job in a small city stuck in the middle of piney woods split by the Red River. Since her beloved town had only a tiny four-year college and a two-year branch of the state university, I should have known that my chances of landing a teaching position were slim to none. When the waiting got tiresome, on a lark

I took the written test for a position on the fire department. You know I always tested above my real ability. So I became a firefighter, working 24 hours on followed by three days off. Being an adrenaline junkie, the 24-on hours were great, though they meant being away from her. But, ironically, it was the three days off that did us in. Too much beer, too much inertia, too few ambitions, too toxic a mix of her success and my failure, too many edgy exchanges, too few shared experiences, and over the years the relationship slowly melted in the humid heat of Cajun country. Oh, I wrote a twice-a-week local color column for the Daily Talk, a little humor, an occasional insight, but not enough to fill the coffers or the void. I have never believed that being busy was the point of life, but the word *fulfillment* does imply fullness in your days, doesn't it? So the local teaching job never came but the marriage went under the weight of low expectations and odd hours. You know what's funny, Liv? The day our divorce was finalized, I received an offer to teach at a small college back in Kentucky. Life sure has a warped sense of humor.

Jeez, in just a few days I have pounded you with my existential despair and now dumped the sad saga of my marital un-bliss in your lap. Bet you will think twice before including "write soon" in your emails to me! But, listen, I'm not some woebegone whiner. I go at life like a puppy — all unrepressed zeal. And I have learned a lot from my adventures and misadventures. From Wife #2 I got to see close-up what passion for your work looks like. She was living out her core values, bringing to bloom the seeds that Mother Nature or God or The Cosmic Gene Pool had planted in her. I still admire her. I just haven't managed yet to find in my life what she has in hers. I wonder, if we asked everyone at this upcoming reunion whether they had become what they were destined to be, what would they say?

So, have you ever gotten back in touch with Guendaline? Have you written REUNION in red ink on your calendar? Does Mary Alice need a poet-in-residence at her place on Cape Cod? Could she use a publicist? Or a firefighter? Or an anthropologist??

If you are you interested in hearing about the next ex-Mrs. Scott, there is just one more to go. So far.

Holding you to your promise of more open book moments to come.

Scotty
Thomas Alexander Scott
The Man with Three First Names

• • •

From: Rich Stapley
To: Olivia Walker MacLearn
Sent: Monday, April 08, 2013 12:14 AM
Subject: RE: Oops...

Liv, I understand there are few joys to compare with being a grandparent. Are you grandma Liv, grams, or maybe granny or abuelita? I'm amused by friends who extol their grandchildren, who are like the children of Lake Woebegone — but the grand-paternal/maternal feelings must be real. Are you finding it wonderful and unexpected?

The children are mine and what's-her-name's. At least she told me so. Two of them, older daughter, now a semi-scientist running an animal lab at a college in the Pacific Northwest, and younger son, who started an art gallery with a friend not long before the recession hit, which they survived some-how. They have no children, and it's likely to stay that way. I shouldn't be disrespectful of Susan — it was good while it lasted and great for a lot of it — but now it seems like a long time ago. Can't say we were completely solicitous and courteous to each other during the divorce, but no linger-ing resentment, more a fading set of memories with no sen-timental need to reconnect. I did come out of it with one Letterman-worthy line: "Like many employed guys in their 40s who divorce, I bought a sports car." "Oh? What kind?" "I don't know, my attorney drives it."

Are you still married or did you visit the Great American Divorce Theme Park? Shooting range, hand-to-hand com-bat training, bankruptcy court, fantasyland, the on-line dating ride, used-car lot, and the complex of tiny apart-ments with too much furniture you negotiated to keep and a too-friendly neighbor. You don't need a ticket, you just get on board.

Enough. Enough. Are you getting the urge to go to the reunion, or are these notes convincing you to sched-ule root-canal work that weekend as a more pleasant alternative?

Cheers,

Rich

• • •

From: Olivia Walker MacLearn
To: Mary Alice Schneider
Sent: Monday, April 08, 2013 8:02 AM
Subject: Baby pigeons...

M, I know you won't get this until you return from your cousin's birthday/wedding/baby shower? (Sorry, can't remember which) tomorrow, but I could not wait to report! I woke up to another email from Rich. Quick summary: Divorced from Susan. They have two grown kids. No grands. He is curious about my marital status.

I was going (with some editing) to quote daytime TV: Like sands through the hour glass, so go the (emails) of our (inboxes). But in deference to your English major, I will offer up Shakespeare instead: "Lord, what fools these mortals be!" Liv

• • •

From: Guendaline Field
To: Olivia Walker MacLearn
Sent: Monday, April 08, 2013 7:20 PM
Subject: You might be a member of the Class of '67 if...

Liv, I thought I would share that I am putting together a list of hopefully funny indications that "you might be a member of the Class of '67." My concept is copied from the comedian who jokes about folks who might be a red neck. One of my indicators was, "If you had a crush on Dobie or Annette you might be..." Almost as soon as I had written that I had a pop-up news report that Annette Funicello had died. Suddenly it just didn't seem funny anymore. I don't know about you but for me the Mickey Mouse Club was a constant after school entertainment. I don't remember being "into" the beach movies, but I certainly knew about them. Within recent years I have looked back to consider whether I had met my formal and informal life goals. The only one that I clearly missed out on was being the same size as Annette. I was so disillusioned as a teenager to read that she was only 5'3" tall. I was 5'5 1/2". Today it dawned on me — I'm shrinking. I may reach that goal yet. Guen

• • •

From: Olivia Walker MacLearn
To: Richard Stapley
Sent: Monday, April 08, 2013 8:15 PM
Subject: The Rapture…

Rich, I just received an email from Guen that Annette Funicello died.

Like so many of The Mouseketeers, Annette was there in the beginning of my years of swaying to music, of fast dancing, of slow dancing. Maybe this is the beginning of that slippery slope everyone talks about. Instead of our elders dying, it is members of our own generation. One big Sarah Palin Rapture and we're all gone. Whoosh.

I hope The Daily Show is on target tonight, because I sure could use a serving of laughter with my Merlot.

On a cheerier note, you asked what my granddaughters call me. At Holly's request we chose the traditional Scottish names for grandparents: Seanair—pronounced 'Shen-ar'—for Ian.

Seanmhair—pronounced 'Shen-a-var'—for me. As is often the case when grandparents try for specific names, the babies had other ideas. Ian was NarNar and I became LeLa. Later the girls adopted the official names for us, mostly to please Holly, who takes great pleasure in all things Scottish. I would have been quite happy to remain LeLa.

Well, I best dash off a reply to Guen. I owe Scotty an email too, but that one will have to wait until tomorrow. The night is not young, and it seems neither am I.

Well, that was morose. Perhaps I should sing a few verses of "the sun will come out tomorrow." Liv

• • •

From: Olivia MacLearn
To: Guendaline Field
Sent: Monday, April 08, 2013 9:03 PM
Subject: RE: You might be a member of the Class of '67 if...

It was just the opposite for me, Guen. I don't remember watching the Mickey Mouse Club, but I loved the beach movies. And at 5'2" I considered Annette tall. :)

Great idea on your Class of '67 email! Liv

• • •

From: Rich Stapley
To: Olivia Walker MacLearn
Sent: Tuesday, April 09, 2013 11:03 AM
Subject: RE: The Rapture

Thanks, Liv, for the note. I doubt that my sister, my brothers, and I missed an episode of the Mickey Mouse Club, with Annette as my favorite. What a great fantasy life she provided.

I saw a photo yesterday of her, in a wheel chair in the mid 90's, with Frankie Avalon and Fabian. I'm sure there are books, articles, and dissertations out there about the contribution of Italian-Americans to early rock and roll and the birth of youth culture. Annette, Fabian, Frankie, and the other Philadelphia singers. I hope Dick Clark sent a check to the Pope every year in appreciation for the boost they gave his career.

I did a little YouTube memory-lane searching after hearing about Annette's death. I watched the Ronettes sing "Be My Baby" — another New Jersey group, I think — and two of the three of them had rough lives. (Anyone married to Phil Specter couldn't have been all that happy.)

As for funerals, yes, they'll be an increasing part of our social lives. For a while, I'd attend the occasional funeral of a male friend; now they're more frequent and some are for women.

So, LeLa and NarNar. Great names. How far does this love of all things Scottish go? Haggis for Christmas? Insert here some sort of Robert Burns inspired greeting to both of you, and not the one about the best laid plans of mice and men. I hope the Daily Show cheered you up.

Rich

• • •

From: Olivia Walker MacLearn
To: Richard Stapley
Sent: Tuesday, April 09, 2013 3:12 PM
Subject: Ah, yes, dear old Robert Burns...

In 1785, he fathered the first of his fourteen children. His biographer, DeLancey Ferguson, had said, "...it was not so much that he was conspicuously sinful as that he sinned conspicuously."

Thanks for the thought though. Liv

• • •

From: Mary Alice Schneider
To: Olivia MacLearn
Sent: Tuesday, April 09, 2013 7:45 PM
Subject: RE: Baby pigeons...

We're back! Thanks for the update on Rich. So he has two kids. Are they his former wife's by a previous relationship or are they Rich's biological children? Just asking. Inquiring minds and all that. He has grown kids but no grands. What may we deduce from that? Maybe nothing, but possibly a lot. I look to my book club for examples. The sweetest lady in the group (and you know how it gags me to say anyone is sweet, but Belinda absolutely is) has six adult children fourteen grands. Another lady in the group, quite unbearable (now I sound like myself), has only one grand even though she had eight children and raised them in our idyllic beach town (hah!) with a committed spouse. Then I keep thinking back to Faulkner's premise that we know so little of our "fellows" and maybe even of ourselves.

You may recall that when our Cassie got divorced from Carl, she told us we had given her false expectations of marriage. Well, excuse us! Eddie and I should have made more of an attempt to wage war on one another or perhaps cheat. Fat chance of that. Eddie's favorite MIT joke is that the physicist tells his wife he has a mistress and his mistress he has a wife so that he can spend all of his time at the lab. I believe that physicists have the least time or inclination of any academics toward cheating. Watch for it. We'll probably find out tomorrow that Eddie has another wife and kids somewhere. We had our first date 52 years ago Sunday, but I don't like to sound overconfident. Sentimental fool that he is, Eddie pointed out that we spent our first date making out behind Rosie Jenson's basement water heater. That was back in the day of the semi-finished basement rumpus room.

Ply me with chocolate and I'll share my favorite English teacher joke. Oh, all right. A guy gets into a cab at Boston's Logan Airport and says "This is my first time in Boston. Where can I get scrod?" The cabbie replies "I've heard that question asked a thousand times, but never before in the pluperfect subjunctive." This knocks 'em dead at English department meetings. But oddly enough, I did not get reappointed chairman of the hospitality committee. If you're really desperate for a yuk, I'll share my brother's best insurance joke next time. They gobble those up in CT.

I crave more details about your newfound connection with Rich. Keep them coming. I'm not from Morrison, so who cares if I want to spy on the whole project.

Malice

• • •

From: Olivia Walker MacLearn
To: Mary Alice Schneider
Sent: Wednesday, April 10, 2013 10:13 AM
Subject: RE: RE: Baby pigeons

Oh, M, you are so funny!

I agree that you can relax about Eddie cheating, and I seriously doubt that you will discover one day that he has had another family tucked away somewhere. However should we both be wrong, I imagine clueless wife-two as an unattractively pale woman, who is so clueless that she would buy Eddie's story that they cannot have sex or get married until his Great-Aunt Alma Matter passes because Eddie will only inherit her millions if he is a bachelor and a virgin. So poor horny wife-two would spend her nights browsing Sears catalogues in anticipation of the house they will furnish when they finally tie the knot.

Now, on to Rich: Susan is four years younger than Rich and I, and she and Rich knew each other (I assume biblically based upon their behavior at various frat parties) by the end of her freshman year of college, so I think the kids most likely are his. I have no comment on your theory that the maternal grandmother's personality is linked to the production of grandchildren. (I actually try not to think about either your or my grandchildren in terms of what effect having us as grandmothers might mean!)

I want to satisfy your need for details, but my newfound connection with Rich is hard to describe. I find myself checking my email more often, and I definitely reply sooner than the author of *He's Just Not That Into You* would recommend. Our emails have been fairly innocuous, so nothing to report there. The biggest problem I am having is that I have been ignoring any comments/questions that should have been answered with the fact that Ian no longer strides the earth in his ancestral kilt. And now it seems impossible to weave the whole widowed thing into an email without it sounding like an invitation.

More later. I have an urge to browse the Sears catalogue. Liv

• • •

From: Olivia Walker MacLearn
To: Thomas Alexander Scott
Sent: Wednesday, April 10, 2013 11:22 AM
Subject: Chapter One... Ian

Okay, Scotty, as requested, here's chapter one of "Liv the Open Book."

When I met Ian I was lost. I know that sounds melodramatic, but it really does describe my memory of that time in my life. Rich was gone from my life, and then my parents and Colt pretty much wrote me off — not financially thank heavens, but emotional support was at zero percent. Granted, emotional support had always been on the downward curve of average, but that time our views clashed more than usual, and when I would not capitulate, they shut the doors to their hearts and I was on my own.

So Mary Alice became my family until I practically shoved her out of the nest so she could marry Eddie and move to Boston, where he was in grad school. (Plans she had put on hold to be there for me.) And then one beautiful fall day as I was biking to a small family run café not far from the house, I almost ran into a wonderful man with the most beautiful Scottish accent. We talked for hours under the watchful eyes of the café owners, and before summer was official we married. My parents were ecstatic as I had finally accomplished something they appreciated — Ian was both wealthy and well-bred. Just for spite, I briefly considered dumping Ian for a Hell's Angel biker who worked summers at the local gas station, but thankfully love won out over annoying mom and dad.

We both enjoyed the Cape so we bought a wonderful old house with a view of the water and more yard than one hopes for in that area. It was a perfect place to raise a family, and despite his travel schedule — none of the meetings for the non-profit Ian ran were where we were — life was good. After Ian retired we stayed on the Cape until a few years after Holly finished grad school and moved with her new husband to DC, at which point we bought the Westport house so we could have the best of both worlds — the beaches of Cape Cod and reasonable proximity to Manhattan for theater and other city pleasures.

Sadly it was not too long after we bought the Westport house that Ian began to change. (As I look back the end of wonderful began in imperceptible ways in my forty-ninth year of life.) We would come home from the theater or a wonderful dinner out, and I'd hear noises coming from his study. In the beginning he would just be slamming drawers or stomping around, and it would stop and all would be fine. But within a few years it got worse. The slamming of drawers would be just the beginning to an evening of anger. Sometimes it would end when he gathered up his things and retreated to a guest room for the night because, as he would tell me, he was not about to stay in a marriage with someone who was cheating on him. When I would push for an explanation, begging him to tell me what I'd done to make him think that I was cheating, he would consistently say: you know what's going on! Then in the fall of 2000 he retreated to his side of our large king size bed, never to return to mine.

Years later his shrink explained that what Ian was thinking felt completely real to him, but he couldn't explain it because he didn't understand it either. He was misreading normal social behavior, struggling with interpersonal interactions that felt wrong, but not in a way he could verbalize. It was the beginning of, as Nancy Reagan called it, our long goodbye.

That is pretty much the worst of my life story, so don't stop emailing me. I promise cheerier chapters to follow. Liv

PS Yes, I am writing to Guen. Oh, and did I mention that I am writing to Rich as well?

• • •

From: Mary Alice Schneider
To: Olivia MacLearn
Sent: Wednesday, April 10, 2013 10:15 PM
Subject: Advice

Liv, you should disregard any of my advice about relationships because my personal experience is very limited. As you well know I've been with Eddie since I was fifteen and have known him since first grade. Our kids try to keep this dark secret from everyone because it is too corny for words.

Our daughters are both big experts on relationships. I can scarcely count the number of boys they dated, each beginning at a very early age. One crazy summer night Eddie and I got the giggles trying to decide who was the worst of the bad boys our girls collected, and decided to call it a tie among a murderer, a drunk neo-Nazi, and somebody else's husband. Yet the girls are with great guys now, so maybe Chaucer was correct, or more correctly, his Wife of Bath had it right. She was a firm believer in sampling before buying and she was way before our time.

When I was in a John Donne seminar senior year (only four students and the dept. head teaching) I recall being unable to deal with "I wonder, by my troth, what thou and I did till we loved." The other three students and even the elderly fearsome single female dept. head shared stories about feeling just this way. I couldn't remember a time before I loved Eddie. Perhaps you could rephrase Donne's line to "I wonder, by my troth, what you and I have done since we loved." It might make a nice ice breaker. Or not. Maybe a jaunty Nantucket limerick would be better. Cape Cod humor. Sorry. We have to do something while we wait for the first daffodils and the summer people to arrive.

By the way, lots of people our age are divorcees and widows, neither of which makes anyone in your face available. Single is single, no matter how one arrives at the category. Rich knows that already. Notice how I can't stop dishing up advice in spite of my earlier caveat.

I must dash off to iron blouses for our upcoming "vacation" at Disney as part of the whole gang of eight. Nothing beats a crowd of sun starved New Englanders standing in line together.

Luckily our next door neighbor has promised to care for our indoor cats, the feral cats, Mr. & Mrs. Zeke (the possums), the raccoon family and our two new additions, a pair of wild turkeys who showed up today and really enjoyed the left over pasta that baby Dana and I tossed to them. Amy was explaining to Josie that we'll have a savannah view at Animal Kingdom and I found myself wondering how that is different from home. Josie thinks that crocodiles will be just outside the window.

Be strong. Go ahead and answer any emails that take your fancy. With plenty of bad or at least clueless advice, I've got your back.

Malice

• • •

From: Olivia Walker MacLearn
To: Mary Alice Schneider
Sent: Wednesday, April 10, 2013 11:02 PM
Subject: RE: Advice

Disney World! Have a wonderful time! As you well know that is one of my favorite places on earth! When I was little I wanted to be Peter Pan's Wendy. I also wanted to be Annie Oakley, so there was hope for me until mid-life crisis time, when I switched my inner fantasy self to Tinker Belle. (And we laugh at men and their motorcycles and leather fringe pants.)

Give Mickey a hug for me and tell me all about the new fantasy land. Will you eat dinner in the castle? Will you go to the

Hoop-Dee-Doo Musical Review? Will your granddaughters dress as princesses?

I will email instantly if I do anything foolish or admirable. Otherwise, I will try not to interfere with your "vacation." (Just echoing your quotation marks.)

Sudden memory: years ago, on a frigid December day, I was on a bus from the Contemporary Hotel to Animal Kingdom. The route included a scheduled stop at Blizzard Beach and a group of Wisconsinites, all dressed in skimpy swimwear, were on the bus on their way to swim in what must have passed for warmth to them. I believe the shirtless males, hairy arms raised high as they held on to the safety straps while standing for the trip, would absolutely trump the sight of a crowd of sun-starved New Englanders standing in line together. Liv

• • •

From: Rich Stapley
To: Olivia Walker MacLearn
Sent: Thursday, April 11, 2013 10:27 AM
Subject: RE: Ah, yes, dear old Robert Burns...

Liv, 14 wee bairn. No wonder every Scot is a direct descendant of Bobby Burns. And no wonder he spoke of the best laid plans of mice and men going awry. Reminds me of one of those lists of SAT essay errors: "Johann Sebastian Bach had 14 children and practiced on a spinster in the attic." Or the flip side, in a Welsh accent, "Posh are we? Having a wedding and not even pregnant."

I looked at one branch of my family tree, descendants of an English line that arrived here in 1630's, and there is at least one grandmother of mine (well, great-great-etc. grandmother) who was 13 when she gave birth. Awful. Nobody's pure.

Have you gone on a walking tour of Scotland? Or at least the occasional trip to Edinburgh and Glasgow?

Tìoraidh (or so says my English-Scottish translator),

Rich

• • •

From: Olivia Walker MacLearn
To: Richard Stapley
Sent: Thursday, April 11, 2013 9:27 PM
Subject: RE: Ah, yes, dear old Robert Burns...

So imagine this, Rich: you receive a gift for which a thank you is appropriate. You see the gift-giver at work and could simply say thanks, but you say nothing because you plan to send a note or flowers or maybe wine instead.

You head home, get a business call from a colleague, have a beer and watch something recorded on your DVR, and then it is bedtime and besides you want to stop at Papyrus to buy a thank you card to go with the gift. Only life continues to get in the way and you send nothing the next day either. Eventually so much time passes that you realize there is no good way to say what would have been a simple statement early on. AWKWARD!

I find myself in a somewhat similar situation, other than it has nothing to do with gifts or thank you notes, rather just with the awkward part.

When you first emailed me, I was surprised to hear from you (understatement) and writing back felt odd (ditto on understatement) because you were neither stranger nor someone I knew anymore.

I shared bits and pieces of my life, but for some odd reason, even though there were numerous opportunities to do so, I kept not writing something that became more awkward to address the more we emailed. So, addressing it will have to be awkward, because I don't see a "glad you asked, have been meaning to tell you" moment on the horizon.

You asked me about divorce and I ignored your question. Had I replied the answer would have been no, I have never been to that theme park. Just the opposite. Ian and I were magic together. He was an incredible husband and father, but older than I by some 15 years, and about twenty years ago an insidious disease began to slowly steal his personality, some ten years later his memory, and eventually two years ago, his life.

N'uff said. Time for a glass of Merlot and HGTV. Liv

• • •

From: Mary Alice Schneider
To: Olivia MacLearn
Sent: Thursday, April 11, 2013 11:45 PM
Subject: RE: Advice…

We're complete suckers for Disney World. Eddie and I just got back from Dan and Amy's house where she explained what we will be doing minute by minute during our four and a half days. Dana will see the place for her first time at just a week over her first birthday. Amy herself visited Disneyland at six weeks, so I think Dana can file charges against her parents if she wishes.

What is it about Peter Pan that grabs us all? In just over a month, Josie's fourth birthday will feature a Peter Pan theme and the birthday girl, who intends to visit Disney as Rapunzel, complete with the princess tea at the Grand Floridian with her dad, wants to go to her own party as Captain Hook. She has her girly and non girly moments. Maybe it is because the event is at one of those indoor play arenas with a pirate ship and any number of other places where the kids can break bones or destroy their friends.

My most degrading Halloween costume, in 1954, still humiliates me. That year big brother and I went as Peter Pan and Tinker Belle. Of course he stole the show as Peter with his red hair and cherubic face. I skulked behind him, my dark hair showing under the cheap mask and my chubby body crammed into Tink's costume. Parents at doors shouted "OH, LOOK! It's Peter Pan! And who are you supposed to be, little girl?" I recall thinking that the candy had better be worth the humiliation.

Funny you should ask about the castle dinner. We will be eating both in the castle and at Be Our Guest, the first place to serve alcohol in the Magic Kingdom. Eddie will celebrate his 68th birthday at the Beast's castle. This was Amy's idea and we all think it should be great fun, except maybe for Eddie who would be happy having a steak in the family room while watching the Red Sox in high def and swearing at the umps and players. Luckily he did not have a vote in the restaurant selection.

I love your Wisconsinites story. Eddie was down near Cocoa Beach one winter for some physics thing and decided to go swimming, reasoning that if you can't stand on the water, you should swim in it. Floridians walking along the beach in parkas watched him and shook their heads.

And here at home one December 26th, just after he first started wind surfing, Eddie put on all the new cold weather equipment that Santa had delivered and went out on his board. A police officer was waiting for him when he came back to the beach. Somebody had reported a madman out on Buzzard's Bay. Luckily the cop had gone to high school with us and recognized a case of Eddie being Eddie.

So you should just be Liv and do whatever you want regarding Rich. You have good instincts and will know what is right. If it sounds wrong, I'll be sure to mention it. Just don't leave out any details. I don't really know the players in this unfolding drama and I need your input.

Malice

• • •

From: Olivia Walker MacLearn
To: Mary Alice Schneider
Sent: Friday, April 12, 2013 10:43 AM
Subject: Full Disclosure

M, I watched HGTV from bed last night. I did not have my iPad with me, so I missed your late evening email. If I'd known you were up so late, I might have called you.

I decided to tell Rich that Ian had passed away, so I sent him an email last night. (I will forward it to you as soon as I send this.) I guess after living forty-five years in my own version of witness protection, I am tired of treating life as a three act play. Liv

• • •

From: Mary Alice Schneider
To: Olivia MacLearn
Sent: Friday, April 12, 2013 6:02 PM
Subject: RE: RE: Full Disclosure

Let's start thinking of a five act play. Maybe we are just reaching the fulcrum and have plenty of denouement still ahead, to say nothing of a resolution. But Liv, full disclosure???!! Are you serious? This almost allegorical style might just confuse the man. It has been a long time after all and you are so ladylike that you frighten me.

Malice

• • •

From: Mary Alice Schneider
To: Olivia MacLearn
Sent: Friday, April 12, 2013 6:16 PM
Subject: RE: FW: Ah, yes, dear old Robert Burns..

I wrote my previous note after reading your last two letters. Now that I take a closer look at this most recent missive, I admit that I am seriously impressed by your mannered approach to the subject. It has the pace of a tea ceremony. I'm more the throw some dishes and use a few Anglo-Saxon words type, but chacun à son goût as the French say. If your dignified style ever fails, I'll show you some of the colorful hand gestures Mafalda (AKA dirty Mafalda because of the sanitation level in her beachfront store. Mafalda's sausage sandwiches were legendary, but you didn't want to see them being cooked.) used to use on the bread man when he was late with his delivery. It's amazing how body language makes universal statements.

So you are going ahead with this "disclosure" to Rich? You have courage and circumlocution on your side. Let me know how it goes.

Malice

• • •

From: Olivia Walker MacLearn
To: Mary Alice Schneider
Sent: Friday, April 12, 2013 7:30 PM
Subject: To the north of glass half empty...

M, you keep me sane! The pace of a tea ceremony is so much nicer than "can you please get to the frigging point?" which is not an unusual comment when I use my mannered approach to subjects. (You were actually yelling that under your breathe right now, weren't you?)

But to assuage your disclosure concerns, perhaps not quite full disclosure, but at least to the north of glass half empty.

Have a wonderful time in Orlando! And try not to worry about me. Seriously, what can go wrong? :) Liv

• • •

From: Mary Alice Schneider
To: Olivia MacLearn
Sent: Friday, April 12, 2013 10:14 PM
Subject: RE: To the north of glass half empty...

I really wasn't yelling at you to get to the point because I have great respect for your diplomatic approach, of which I am entirely incapable. It must be your ladylike upbringing.

I'll bet you didn't even mind wearing the white gloves on Sunday. Ever the contrarian, I used to listen to Father Tom's too frequent sermon about how thinking a thing is as bad as doing it and concluded that I might as well do it then. Wrong interpretation, I know, but it worked for me (and Eddie too if truth be told).

Do your thing. It suits you.

Malice

• • •

From: Rich Stapley
To: Olivia Walker MacLearn
Sent: Saturday, April 13, 2013 8:36 PM
Subject: Does poetry sooth grief?

Oh, Liv, I'm so sorry — for your loss and his, and for Holly and her children. Two years ago is yesterday.

Rich

• • •

From: Olivia Walker MacLearn
To: Mary Alice Schneider
Sent: Saturday, April 13, 2013 10:13 PM
Subject: Rich's answer...

I hope you are having a wonderful first day in Orlando, M. I forwarded Rich's answer to my email to you. I assume you've read it.

Suddenly the thought of going to Lexington is terrifying, because that message came from the Rich I once thought I knew, right up until the day I realized I did not.

Armor back on? Check! Glass half empty? Check! Liv

• • •

From: Mary Alice Schneider
To: Olivia MacLearn
Sent: Saturday, April 13, 2013 10:25 PM
Subject: RE: Rich's answer...

Maybe the glass is half full. Maybe Rich grew up instead of just aging as many men seem to do. Perhaps you don't need full armor — just a bullet proof vest to protect your heart.

Malice

p.s. I see why you love Animal Kingdom. We've got a great view of the wildlife from our balcony. Tonight after Josie and Dana had their baths and collapsed into sleep, we grownups sat on the balcony and watched the animals get their evening meal. A giraffe foursome walked right by us. We're hooked.

• • •

From: Olivia Walker MacLearn
To: Richard Stapley
Sent: Sunday, April 14, 2013 9:56 AM
Subject: In the echoes of my mind...

Thank you for your kind words, Rich. We do miss Ian, and he certainly lost his "golden years" to his disease. In some ways his death was less difficult emotionally for us, because we all had missed him for so many years before his body died.

You said two years ago is yesterday. I think in many ways all our "years ago" are yesterdays. I am feeling especially philosophical about time this morning. (I suppose it could be the effect of a long night of celebrating with friends.) I joined Colt and the newest version of Mrs. Colt at Mory's in New Haven to watch the Yale hockey team compete in the finals of the NCAA hockey tournament. After the first period, we moved from the bar there (too crowded and noisy) to the home of old friends for more drinks and an easier view of the television. What an exciting evening! Both teams in the championship game were from right here in CT. And when Yale won, we celebrated as if we were young enough to do so — well, I suppose the newest Mrs. Colt actually is young enough, but that is another story.

Anyway, when thinking about your comment that a year ago is yesterday, I found myself reflecting on those poor souls who believe they have been abducted by aliens (the outer space kind, not the enemies of the GOP version) and returned to earth in an altered state. Before you call the psychiatric hotline, perhaps I best clarify a bit. I don't believe I was ever abducted by either kind of alien, I just feel as if the real me is a teenager, or at tops, a twenty-something, trapped in a body that belongs to a cast member from *The Golden Girls*. And it appears that no one but me is aware of my real age. People don't say, "Nice try," when I order a senior ticket at the movie, or choose the senior rate at a hotel, and they rush to open the damn door open for me! What's that all about? Do they think I failed door opening 101?

Many of my friends say they would not return to a younger age if they could. They appear serene, content, at peace with their age and place in the universe. Not I. I would take a go-back in an instant, not because any specific time was better than now, nor to fix any decisions, nor to change my life journey in any way. No, I just want the rush of time to stop, and I want the image in my mind to match the image in the mirror.

Actually, I am having second thoughts about attending the reunion. Scotty said it in one of his first emails to me. He wrote that in his mind I was still the innocent young woman he last saw at graduation, unlike most of his aging college friends, whom he has seen at a reunion or two over the years. If I stay away we can all still be young — at least in the echoes of my mind. Liv

• • •

110

From: Olivia Walker MacLearn
To: Mary Alice Schneider
Sent: Sunday, April 14, 2013 9:04 PM
Subject: Just marking time…

…until your next email, when I can experience all things
Disney through your descriptions!

Did you get to see the Yale-Quinnipiac hockey game? I
remember that the television stations are somewhat limited
at the Disney hotels — on purpose I am sure. After all, the
last thing Disney wants is for everyone to curl up before the
television. They want you out and about, and don't forget
your wallets!

Anyway it was such an exciting game! Well, the third period
was. First Yale goal happened literally seconds before the
second period ended and then three more in the third
period for a 4-0 win and a national championship! I was at
Mory's with Colt and the third version of Mrs. Colt. I believe
she has already produced a second egg for his never-end-
ing sperm, as her stick-thin figure has a noticeable bump.
So unless she swallowed a large grapefruit, she is already
preggo with baby two.

So tell me all about Disney Day Two. Oh and I wrote back to
Rich, but with my body armor on. Liv

• • •

From: Mary Alice Schneider
To: Olivia MacLearn
Sent: Monday, April 15, 2013 8:10 AM
Subject: RE: Just marking time…

Liv,

Disney is going well, but is very exhausting because of the energy level of our daughters and granddaughters. We seem always to be running for a bus or dashing for fast pass tickets. Maybe Eddie and I are just too old for the pace of pre-schoolers and thirty-somethings. Everything is as magical and happy as ever, though, except for some of the freaky looking humans we see around the park. If one is seriously overweight, doesn't it seem wise not to wear revealing clothing and cover all the exposed flesh with tattoos? Just wondering.

Amazingly we did receive the hockey game here, but Eddie, a rabid hockey fan, did not discover the fact until I had hogged the TV for two **PBS** favorites, *Call the Midwife* and *Mr. Selfridge*. He wasn't too disappointed, though — just glad that a school we both love won the whole thing.

So Mrs. Colt is going for seconds. I thought trophy wives were required to produce only one trophy offspring. How OLD is Colt? Does he really long for the chaos of little ones at his age? It must be some sort of right wing status symbol.

One last piece of advice, borrowed from Miss Pross in *A Tale of Two Cities*, when she passed on the advice of her brother, a criminal called Solomon: "Hold your head high and fight low". Maybe this will come in handy for you in the weeks to come. BE CAREFUL. Malice

• • •

From: Guendaline Field
To: Olivia Walker MacLearn
Sent: Monday, April 15, 2013 9:43 AM
Subject: 1, 2, 3, For a woman your age...

Liv, I have so much enjoyed "just talking" with you the last few weeks. How on earth did we lose each other for so many decades?

I just had another old woman episode which has turned me on. So, lucky you get to hear me rattle. :) Perhaps I just didn't notice exactly what was being said to me in years past. But I certainly do now. I had reason to dress up today for a luncheon and a long term friend came rushing up to compliment me on my appearance. "What a lovely outfit. It looks so good on you. Is it new?" I said no it was really quite old and then came the phrase. "Well you just look wonderful — for a woman your age."

Recently I spent practically a whole day cleaning Fellowship Hall at church. Our pastor was walking through and stopped and looked around. "What an incredible amount of work you have done Guen you must be exhausted. The hall hasn't been cleaned this completely for years. You certainly are a good worker — for a woman your age."

The only people I now know who deviate from this pattern are my doctors. Each of them always starts out with the phrase for a woman your age. Example: "For a woman your age your blood work results were actually quite good." Now one could interpret this to mean I'm going to die within the next two hours.

Don't people realize that the use of that phrase, especially after a compliment, almost diminishes the compliment to a criticism? Okay, maybe not a criticism, but certainly no compliment either.

Hope you are having a good day. Guen

• • •

From: Olivia MacLearn
To: Guendaline Field
Sent: Monday, April 15, 2013 10:45 AM
Subject: For my age...

Guen, I too regret the loss of our friendship over the past four plus decades. But thanks to your remarkable efforts, we are now in touch again. (I have also had some great conversations with Scotty and, how strange is this, with Rich.)

Your reaction to backhanded compliments and quantifications of good test results resonated with me. I find myself railing against the night, which as I think about it, is probably different than your reaction. I imagine you might just want people to treat what you accomplish or how you look or what your cholesterol measures without regard to your age. I seem all of a sudden not to want to be my age.

Maybe it is a Walker curse, this resistance to aging. My mom, thanks to incredibly talented plastic surgeons, numerous trainers, beauticians, personal fashion consultants, etc., looked thirty until she was lowered into her casket, and actually she looked pretty damn close to that age then too. Dad at ninety-five still stands tall and has his full head of hair. From what I hear, he apparently is considered a hunk at his assisted living residence on Long Island. (If you have to move to assisted living that is definitely the place to go!)

And my brother Colt has found his own way to keep young. He is on his third wife and third set of offspring. And each new wife has been younger than the pervious one was at time of acquisition. If the pattern continues wife number four will be too young to have a drink at their wedding reception...

Other than monthly hair color appointments, I have forgone the various methods of age alteration (so far) but I find myself more and more wistful about youth. This is not good. If I had a shrink, I would have booked some double appointments! Since I do not, you were the lucky recipient of today's angst. Liv

• • •

From: Thomas Alexander Scott
To: Olivia Walker MacLearn
Sent: Monday, April 15, 2013 1:07 PM
Subject: Re: Chapter One... Ian

You're what?? You can't be emailing Rich! That's a betrayal of Liv! Wait a minute ... you *are* Liv. So, wait ... you're what?!? My mind is doing the Mt. St. Helen mushroom cloud ... can you tell? After all my years of faithfully hating him for you, after dutifully shunning him (though I doubt he noticed), after all the evils I wished upon him, you now tell me (and awfully damned nonchalantly, I might add) that you are writing him. Hell, Walker, I would have bet at any odds that I would never hear that sentence from you.

So, how is he? Did he marry that little freshman twit? Actually, I know he did; I have kept tabs on him a bit from a distance. He may have been an asshole, but I did care about him. He was my friend. Of course, looking back, most of our conversations were about beer and sex, but that was, and is, true about most guys in college. It's hormone-induced. I don't know if he ever knew the real me, nor I him. But then, a person doesn't get many of those to-the-core relationships in life. Some people never have any. Those like you and Mary Alice need to treasure the closeness. I'm not sure I have ever had anything in my life like you two have in each other.

Well, so, is Rich's wife still his wife? If not, will there be a little reunion going on at the big reunion? Tell me, Walker, what changed to make it possible for you to talk with him after all these years of dry despair? Did you change? Did he? Or has the world we knew just fallen away and taken our walls with it? Seriously, what changed?

Humph, think I'll punish you a little by dragging out my Wife #3 story. After "leaving Louisiana in the broad daylight" (thank you, Oak Ridge Boys, for another lush, alliterative line I wish I had written), I came back to Kentucky to do what I had intended to do since we were in college: I became an associate professor at a small school much like Morrison. I was afraid that my lack of teaching experience would eliminate my name immediately. I also feared that they would do a background check and find mine too checkered for their tastes. But to my surprise, they saw me as a "Renaissance Man" who had tasted "real life" as opposed to so many whose worldview had never peeked outside a classroom. So they gave me lots of space to create my own courses and try out inventive techniques in the classroom. Plus I was allowed to teach cross-curriculum classes. In one which combined literature, philosophy, and sociology I was teaching Bonhoeffer's *Letters and Papers from Prison*. So I took my dozen unsuspecting scholars to visit the tiny county jail, really just a concrete block holding-pen. They scampered inside the one cell, eyes agog, all jokes and pokes. Then I had the jailer close and lock the door. That clanging of steel got their attention. I assigned them to write a treatise on the goodness of humanity and told them I would return in the morning. They screeched and screamed and cursed at me as the jailer and I shut the outside door and headed off in search of a beer. Of course I went back for them later that afternoon. And for the next two weeks we had fabulous discussions about cheap grace, about inhumanity, about poetry arising from the moldy filth around a toilet, about the justice of our penal system, about the fickle nature of fate, about the condition of our prisons, and the abandonment that all prisoners feel.

I don't think I ever felt more alive, Liv, than those first years of teaching. Nor less enthused about the last several. Small schools often make for small-minded politics among faculty and administration. I was expected to be limitless in my teaching but happily fettered as an obedient faculty member. I could teach free; I just wasn't to live free. Besides, how many times can you lock students behind bars and still enjoy it? Actually, the answer to that is "unlimited!" But after six years or so, I was bored with the students, bored with the school, even bored with myself. So, I resigned to go find my destiny elsewhere, ready to spread my pedagogical wings and fly to greater heights. The Dean in a show of mean-spiritedness tried to maim my future fame by claiming that I was fired — for lack of classroom preparation, for failure to publish in a peer-reviewed journal, and for breaking the student-faculty restrictions as defined in the college handbook.

Well, to be perfectly honest, he was correct about the last one. One of my students, a starry-eyed coed of comely nature, had indeed found my apartment more to her liking than the dorm. But in our defense, though there was a considerable age gap, we were deeply in love with each other. Plus we shared a love of the works of Nikos Kazantzakis, Kurt Vonnegut, and the wizardly poetry of the Eagles, who sang, "You can spend all your love making time." We should have listened more closely to them. Oh, our love was deep; it just didn't have much length. But, of course, we married anyway ... for a while, a record short while in the list of my mangled marriages. Once she and I stepped out of our neo-hippy, pseudo-intellectual roles, we found that neither of us had much interest in the other.

So there it is, Walker, the unabridged List of Wives, shamefully presented by Great Scott III (not quite as infamous as King Henry VIII). Do you still think kindly of me? Hell, Liv, I'm 67 years old and still waiting for the right girl to come waltzing into my life. Since I seem to live through the verses of songs, I leave you for now with a thought from the BoDeans: "She's lookin' for me somewhere."

Can you relate?

Scott
Thomas Alexander Scott

• • •

From: Olivia Walker MacLearn
To: Olivia Walker MacLearn
Bcc: Guendaline Field, Mary Alice Schneider, Bill Smith, Thomas Alexander Scott, Richard Stapley, Lois Franke, Holly MacLearn, Colton Walker, Mary Myers, Lilith MacLearn
Sent: Tuesday, April 16, 2013 1:13 PM
Subject: I am weary this day after the bombing...

Everyone,

Please excuse me for using a blind-copied group email to communicate my feelings this day after the Boston Marathon bombing. This is such a stressful time. Every time there is a breaking news alert I feel my stress rising. So far the breaking news reports have added nothing new, but there is a sense of "another shoe might drop" that has not been with us since the 9/11 attack. That said I could not imagine writing separate emails to each of you — a few old friends, some I've known for decades and some just recently back in my life, and to my daughter Holly, brother Colt, and sister-in-law Lilith, and yet I feel a need to share what I am feeling with each of you.

I feel as if I were personally touched by the violence of what has happened in Boston. The Mandarin Oriental is just a block from where one of the bombs was planted. I've stayed at the Mandarin many times when visiting friends in Boston or attending meetings for various charitable funds. I've sat sipping wine in the bar that fronts on Boylston, a bar which, according to one news article, had its furniture fly from the blast, and its air fill with smoke after the explosion.

I've had breakfast in the adjoining restaurant, enjoying both the delicious food and the flow of people and cars and Duck

Tour buses that is Boylston Street. Yesterday as the horrific scenes were displayed over and over on various stations, I felt as if I were watching my own neighborhood. This store, that restaurant, this sign, that landmark...

The last time I felt such a personal invasion was days before your second birthday, Holly. It was an especially raw winter day. We'd returned home from a dinner out and Ian drove the car into the garage. While he retrieved our bag of leftovers, you and I walked over to the door that opens from the garage into the mudroom. It was locked.

Your dad and I laughed as we both immediately figured you had turned the little button in the doorknob to the lock position before we left the house. (Playing with those door knob locks was your greatest enjoyment at that time of your life. We thought nothing could be more annoying. Had we known about your eventual fascination/obsession with horses, we would have been less anxious for that phase to end.) Anyway, we did not carry a key to that door so I waited there in the garage with you, and Ian went around to the front door to let us in. What he quickly realized when he opened the front door was that a burglary had been in progress.

One of the thieves must have heard us drive into the garage and had the sense to slow our entry by locking the door to the garage. Footprints in the snow indicated they'd used the time they bought to exit through the still open family room sliders, leaving behind the pile of loot they'd been accumulating. We lost little in valuables, but we lost so much emotionally. I believe that was when we began to use the security system in a home we had thought safe simply because, well, because it was our home.

120

Life altering as that was, I can at least understand stealing. I accept that it comes with the territory — that such behavior is inevitable. Sometimes from people who have less, and sometimes from those who have just as much or even more, but are deficient in character and so they take what they want. It doesn't feel right, but it just feels like a sad defect in otherwise human beings.

But I cannot understand those who commit acts of terrorism, not from foreign shores, and especially not from domestic groups or individuals. I do not understand the paranoid fear of government in those domestic groups, but far more than that, I do not understand how they move to a willingness to sacrifice innocents. For me, yesterday's evil acts and those that preceded are beyond my comprehension, and I imagine God must be weary with it all as well. Liv

• • •

From: Mary Alice Schneider
To: Olivia MacLearn
Sent: Tuesday, April 16, 2013 8:35 PM
Subject: RE: Weary this day after the Boston Marathon bombing...

Hi Liv,

We are all stuck to the TV here at Disney, especially because the place is packed with New Englanders. Given our youthful roots in the Boston area during all Eddie's academic years, this act of terrorism feels all the more personal. I know what you mean about seeing familiar places. Boston remains our "go to" city for getaways, especially because Eddie often returns to MIT and I still enjoy prowling the city.

One of Amy's college roommates called her to say that her father was standing right across from the second bomb blast waiting for his wife to finish the race. They were unhurt but emotionally traumatized. Amy and Dan's summer back fence neighbor is an emergency physician at Mass General, so we assume he is doing long shifts. I love that the Boston Police and Fire unions have chipped in and put up a $50,000 reward for information leading to the capture of the perp. It's the kind of blue collar generosity I often saw growing up. You have to love Boston.

Malice

• • •

From: Mary Alice Schneider
To: Olivia MacLearn
Sent: Wednesday, April 17, 2013 9:38 AM
Subject: Heading home

Hi Liv,

We are packing up the gang of eight here at Animal Kingdom Lodge and preparing to fly to Logan late today. Our sweet neighbor, Karen, whose son drove us to the airport on Saturday, was planning to meet us in our Suburban, but Cassie checked and found that there is amplified security at the airport now and we don't want Karen impounded or harassed in any way, so we'll take a car service instead. The little girls should sleep on the plane and then we hope they'll continue sleeping in the car for the hour plus ride back to the Cape. Whoever coined the advertising phrase "Getting there is half the fun" did not have kids or grands.

• • •

From: Olivia Walker MacLearn
To: Mary Alice Schneider
Sent: Wednesday, April 17, 2013 5:13 PM
Subject: RE: Heading home

Safe travels!

A memory just flashed! One week after 9/11 I was flying to Dayton, Ohio for a conference and I stopped at Saks to buy a new raincoat. (Mine had a hard to miss stain.) The sales clerk and I talked about how 9/11 had changed so much, especially travel. After she rang up my purchase, she handed me the bag, reached out to give me a big hug, and said the same words I just wrote above, her voice catching, as if we were dear friends, not total strangers.

With apologies to Dickens: The worst of times often begets the best of times.

Please let me know when you are home safe and sound. Liv

• • •

From: Rich Stapley
To: Olivia Walker MacLearn
Sent: Wednesday, April 17, 2013 11:12 PM
Subject: The mirror, the puck

Liv, I finally got round to logging in to reply to your note from three days ago about aging, attending the reunion, and the joy of being with friends while watching Yale's hockey win — and there were your reflections on the Boston tragedy. The psychic wounds as well as the scars on the body politic last a long time. (NPR ran a story that after terror attacks, people become more set in their partisan ways; we're less cohesive as a society.)

I'll leave it at that for now, having little to add to your thoughts, which took me close to the scene in ways that photographs and eye-witness accounts didn't.

But to your note about time, and about time and the mirror, that the real you is a teenager trapped in Bea Arthur's body (or is it Rue McClanahan?). I have two reflections, and I like at least one of them.

Maurice, the retired astronaut in *Northern Exposure*, hated it when teenage clerks at the movie theater gave him a senior discount without his asking. And he found other ways to complain about being classified as a senior — and thus an object. In the last scene of the episode, he's standing on top of a cliff above a lake. We see him from behind at a distance. He's naked, lets out a shout, and dives into the water.

My other thought comes right from your email. You had an exciting evening when you watched the hockey game. No, the rush of time won't stop, but there's no mirror around when you're having a good time with friends. So, the challenge is to have as many of those moments as possible. Okay, I'm not discovering relativity, but, as the Owen Wilson character says in *Midnight in Paris*, "I'm having a moment here." I think you should assess whether to come to the reunion based on if you think the lot of us can create two or three of those Yale Beats Quinnipiac (I had to look it up) moments during the weekend.

Scotty may be overdoing the existential angst that accompanies reunions. Or, as Ezra Pound might tell him, "Pull down thy vanity, I say pull down." Or, as Dylan would have it, "Do not go gentle into that good night ... rage, rage against the dying of the light." I think one way to do that is to ask, "Is this where Yale is playing hockey?" If yes, go.

I've meandered long enough. Thanks again for the emails, Liv. A tip of the Zin glass in your direction. Rich

• • •

From: Olivia Walker MacLearn
To: Richard Stapley
Sent: Thursday, April 18, 2013 1:01 PM
Subject: RE: The mirror, the puck

I kept trying to understand your Zen reference (is the glass half-full, half-empty, or am I to experience the contents in the moment) when suddenly I realized that you were simply referring to a glass of Zinfandel! Understandable communication difficulty: As a loyal Merlot gal, I don't speak Zin.

Also, I know I was the one who referenced being trapped in the body of one of The Golden Girls, but seriously, Rich, Bea Arthur? I may look older than when we last spoke in person, but I think one would have had to look at least a little like a young Bea Arthur to end up as an old Bea Arthur!

Anyway, I have a busy weekend and week ahead, so I thought I should get these important observations to you, in case replying to emails gets bumped from my red-flag list. :) Liv

• • •

From: Mary Alice Schneider
To: Olivia MacLearn
Sent: Thursday, April 18, 2013 9:19 PM
Subject: Back

We are back and beginning to settle in to our routines. It's all about shopping to fill the empty fridge and doing the laundry again to say nothing of atonement with the cats that missed us. Today the contractors decided to begin insulating Amy's house, so she and the girls came here to take a group nap. Normally it would be only Dana napping in her crib, but Amy and Josie were exhausted from the late flight home from Disney, so they plopped on the big bed that Amy and Dan will share when they move in for the renovation. The baby slept three hours and mom and sister two. It gave me the chance to make a big pot of minestrone. Everyone will be full of zip when Dan drags himself home tonight.

Eddie and I have to go to Barnes and Noble tonight to get another Nook reader. I don't know what he did to his, but it is simply fried. Something happened while he was out in the hot sun reading a good police procedural by Tana French so he nabbed my reader and I switched to reading on my I-phone. Given that Eddie has read about four books on his reader and I've read scores on mine, it's an odd twist that his should expire first. He doesn't keep it in a holder, so perhaps it takes more hits.

Eddie lost his sun glasses and watch too, but I found the watch. Let's not even discuss the horrible sunburn he picked up because he didn't remember his sunscreen. The man needs me for sure.

The girls make fun of me for being his personal servant, but I think it's a generational thing. Of course I create three meals a day for him and do his laundry. I would hate to think of his wearing mismatched socks or eating whatever he might scrounge up for any meal. Ergo I am older than dirt, a real fossil.

Negativity be gone! You seem to be a girl in her first bloom again. It must be the reconnection with your old flame. My mom's favorite joke was "The light of my life has gone out, but I found another match." She had a strange sense of humor and this joke hardly applies. However, you may be rekindling a very early light.

I'm too tired to make sense. Maybe I need a nap. Malice

• • •

From: Olivia Walker MacLearn
To: Mary Alice Schneider
Sent: Friday, April 19, 2013 10:33 PM
Subject: Even matches have a "Best By" date…

Yes, sadly I Googled it. As one person replied to that very question: Matches are cheap. Why bother worrying if your old ones will perform. Toss them and get yourself new matches. Just saying…

Tonight I drove over to Finalmente Trattoria for dinner. Andre asked about you both, and I promised we would be sure to go next time you and Eddie come to Westport. I could happily dine there nightly. For me it has all the advantages of owning a restaurant with none of the downside. Andre treats me like family, but I don't have to bus tables or help in the kitchen. And just about every item on the menu is superb, especially because they will tweak any recipe to fit my special requests, like my inevitable request for "without the mushrooms." (If ever there was a chance that I would revise my opinion of mushrooms, it was squashed last fall when I took a Chinese cooking class and the teacher referred to adding the mushrooms as adding the fungi.)

Well, I'm babbling and obviously have nothing of merit to say so I will sign off for now. Liv

• • •

From: Mary Alice Schneider
To: Olivia MacLearn
Sent: Saturday, April 20, 2013 1:03 PM
Subject: The joy of Finalmente

Hi Liv,

I drool at the thought of another evening at Finalmente. Eddie and I love mushrooms, whatever people want to call them, even the ones that Cassie gathers with her mycological crazies. OK. She belongs to a mycological society whose mother ship is at Harvard and she is decades younger than the average mushroom hunter. On one occasion (fearing marauding perverts - I tend to scare them off) she asked me to accompany her to a state park to gather Hen of the Woods mushrooms and I began to wonder if dogs use them as a blog site. I see them sniffing everything and have no doubt that they are reading the opinions and personal data on dogs who have recently visited. Think of this. When we smell a thing, it is the size of a postage stamp, metaphorically speaking. When a dog sniffs it, it is the size of a big silk scarf. For bloodhounds, the scarf is the size of a pashmina. Bloodhounds also love to leave their scent everywhere, which is why they don't house train so well (this from my vet neighbor). Seriously, have you ever seen one as a house pet?

On the local animal front, the raccoon from our barn appears to be a nursing mother, so I'm putting out lots of healthful stuff for her to eat, and no doubt share, or compete for, with the pregnant fluffy cat. This morning I cooked a good sized pile of chopped chicken liver and put it in the barn vestibule, so I await the first smart mother to find it.

It appears that babbling is one of my strong points too, so I'll go downstairs and see if Eddie wants some lunch. He really wouldn't eat unless I put food in front of him.

One last detail. Today Dan and Josie stopped by to borrow some painting supplies on their way back from the town recycling center (dump) with Josie, dump notwithstanding, in full Rapunzel attire. She is still protesting having to come back to Massachusetts from Disney. More as it happens, Malice

• • •

From: Olivia Walker MacLearn
To: Thomas Alexander Scott
Sent: Saturday, April 20, 2013 11:34 PM
Subject: You just might want to grab a scotch first...

Scotty, something you wrote (and not about wife #3 — that deserves its own separate response) has stuck in my mind the past couple days, pushed aside most of the time by the Boston horror, but popping back at unexpected moments. You wrote: "Tell me, Walker, what changed to make it possible for you to talk with (Rich) after all these years of dry despair? Did you change? Did he? Or has the world we knew just fallen away and taken our walls with it? Seriously, what changed?"

Did I change? I'll answer that in a moment. Did Rich? No way to know. Our emails have been a dish of courteous topped with formality and a sprinkle of remembrance. His caring response when I told him about Ian was spot on the Rich I knew pre-Susan. In fact for a few moments after I read it, all things Susan (they are divorced btw) were erased. But then I remembered that by the time Rich told me about her, they were firmly in love.

Now I suppose it is possible, in a Disney princess animated movie kind of way, that they met the very morning before he told me about her, that when they locked eyes the earth parted and the heavens sang, and that little blue birds danced in the air and wove them together with ribbons. Yeah, I know. So ditching that fantasy, I have to accept that they were together for some period of time before he told me. Days? Weeks? Months? No matter. A second would be too long. Whatever the measure, it was time during which I was clueless that my world was atilt, that gravity was not working, that nothing was as it seemed. So which was reality — the man I thought I knew or the man I think I did not? Since I have no answer, I have no way of assessing change.

But I will say that I have changed since those college years, perhaps not so much in action as in reflection. You and I were innocent but uninhibited in our conversations. In fact we had discussions that almost make me blush to remember. Do you recall how we dissected each others love lives — never failing to offer, no wait, offer is too mild a word, to proclaim our opinions about what the other one of us should or should not do? And how we shared our conquests and our defeats? I do, and I remember that when Rich fell for Susan, you listened as I endlessly repeated the same what-if's and should-I-have's and what-will-I-do's. Most people would have hit me over the head and left me by the roadside, but you never so much as sighed loudly.

So I should be able to speak freely about anything. Still, it has been decades since we spoke without filter, so this is difficult, but I will try.

I would say I have changed because I have known love in all its forms and I miss it in all its forms. I miss pet names and quick little hugs and a knowing wink across the room. I miss making up after an argument and giving in just because. I miss Valentine cards and long walks on the beach. I miss coffee on the deck in the morning and plays in the city on date nights, and what else … oh yes, I really miss multiple mind-blowing orgasms.

Do you remember the song *All By Myself*? It was originally recorded by Eric Caemen, but it was the Celine Dion version that was playing in the car today. And as I listened to it, I thought that it sums up my willingness to walk too close to the fire again. Too hot seems less scary than too cold.

131

Of course I eventually come back to the eternal struggle about what is appropriate for people of "a certain age." When I see two elderly people hold hands, I think it is cute. A gentle hug? Sweet. A quick kiss on the forehead? Adorable. But the image of them doing the deed with vigor and enjoyment is: Eww! Yuck! OMG, I'm outta here!

So why do I remember each heavenly touch from those college years and wonder how it would be to know that again, when he and I would be the elderly couple of my nightmares, so perhaps it would be best for me to think: Eww! Yuck! OMG, I'm outta here!

You say you are "67 years old and still waiting for the right girl to come waltzing into (your) life." And you ask if I can relate. Indeed I can, Scotty. Too well I fear. Liv

• • •

From: Rich Stapley
To: Olivia Walker MacLearn
Sent: Sunday, April 21, 2013 11:33 AM
Subject: Zen

Liv, Sorry about comparing you to Bea Arthur — she was the savvy one, though. Can't remember if she thought she was a teenager trapped in an alien body. I guess that would be Betty and Rue.

Anyway, hope the weekend and the week ahead are memorable. It's a planting weekend for me (well, maybe an hour): tomatoes and herbs. We'll see if the basil takes. If it does, it will be a first for me.

I even have a few grape vines reviving from last year. No wine, but I did try for grappa with some wild grapes. It turned out to be rocket fuel, undrinkable, but it looks nice on the marble counter. "Yes, that's some grappa I made. It's a bit raw, so I'd suggest pairing the flourless torte with the Frivolo." See, I talk West Coast.

Cheers,

Rich

• • •

From: Guendaline Field
To: Olivia Walker MacLearn
Sent: Sunday, April 21, 2013 2:16 PM
Subject: Aging

Liv, your email caused me to stop and assess how I feel about being older. I am still just me. The same person I have always been, only with more experience. I don't mind being experienced. Age seems to be a different thing. My body has indeed started to react differently. I have my ailments. I just adapt to those. There are several sagging areas that I just try to ignore. And yes, I have actually placed my fingers on each side of my face at the eye line and pulled up.

I went blond fairly early. I felt it was necessary to maintain my appearance for business reasons. I started with highlights and nature finished the progression. Once you start that kind of process it takes over. Several times I have considered letting my grey "grow out." It doesn't take many days for me to change my mind.

At this point in my life my age does not stop me from doing anything that I want to do. It is only when I am physically out of sorts that I feel negatively about aging. I am with my parents almost daily and the restrictions that their ages, 90 and 91, have placed on them are very depressing. They were so active and alive. After retirement they threw themselves into volunteer work. Now, they just sit in their chairs with hearing and eyesight problems that result in almost total isolation. I will truly hate being old if I reach that point.

So how do I feel about aging? Would I want to be young and do it all over again? Damn good question Liv. Damn good questions. One thing I do know is that it is good to be in contact again. Even with all the years of silence between us, when I write to you I can feel you understand what I am saying. Guen

PS I have contained myself long enough. HOW DID YOUR FIRST CONVERSATION WITH RICH GO?

• • •

From: Olivia MacLearn
To: Guendaline Field
Sent: Saturday, April 20, 2013 5:15 PM
Subject: Rich

Funny you should ask. Our first conversation was followed by a number of others. In fact, I just heard from him again this morning.

I would say that talking to him again is surreal. I feel like I know him. I feel like I don't know him. I feel as if I could sit and talk with him over a glass of wine. I feel as if I would rather duck behind a column to avoid seeing him if we happened upon each other. We've talked some about what has gone on in our lives since college, but neither of us has mentioned that we were "together" or that we came apart.

I would say it is a little bit like on-line dating. You tell a little truth, you float a white lie or two, and then you just wait see what develops. My guess is little or nothing. Liv

• • •

From: Thomas Alexander Scott
To: Olivia Walker MacLearn
Sent: Sunday, April 21, 2013 10:20 PM
Subject: RE: You just might want to grab a scotch first…

Ah, there's my Liv. I knew you were in there somewhere behind all the polite and proper. Been waiting for your bare-naked honesty to reemerge. And there you are. Nice to see you again, my lovely, lovely friend.

First of all, the "multiple mind-blowing orgasms." Guys are generally satisfied with just one, administered at fairly frequent intervals. But I think Wife #1 knew what you're talking about. First she would screw the bar owner in the stock room at the end of her shift. Then she would meet some barfly cowboy at the Rendezvous Motel for a little roll in the hay. Then she would come home and jump my bones. I think that counts as multiple orgasms. I would guess that she had many lovers before and after our marriage, but I am certain that she did during. She was one hellaciously hot honey, pure raw woman. I don't hold it against her. I wasn't so monogamous myself during those unsettled 1970's when we grabbed for whatever felt good at the moment. But, damn, I miss the fire now.

Other than the crying phrase, "Don't wanna be all by myself anymore," I couldn't remember the lyrics to that song you mentioned, so I Googled them. Damn if you didn't nail it, Walker. The perfect expression of what plagues us both – that a vague and unreachable love is the only cure for what ails us.

So, are we doomed to only view love from a distance now? Your "Eww! Yuck! OMG!" reaction to elderly PDAs (Public Displays of Affection) recalled a similar moment for me. I had always seen Paul Newman as the quintessential babe magnet with those crystal eyes and that cool, detached demeanor, not to mention his pearly whites. Then, late in his career, came the movie, "Nobody's Fool." Newman at age 69 flirts with sexy, curvaceous, 37-year-old Melanie Griffith the whole movie. Finally the moment comes near the end of the movie when they embrace and the camera pans in on a torrid, tongue-laced kiss between them. I recoiled in disgust. I honor the man but I couldn't get past the wrinkles and the idea. Now as I tiptoe toward that age myself, I have to put aside what it would look like in order to crave what it would feel like. I've come to understand that I may be 67 years old, but it is still me inside here. Is passion past tense for us now, Liv? Are we to encounter it only in our memories? Hell no! So, if there is a window of opportunity to revisit the passion of the past with Rich, I say jump through it, girl! Let the morning light bring whatever frustration, regret, or bitterness it may. But seize the moment. *Carpe diem,* Walker, because *tempus fugit.*

Okay, just a few words of confession here. I am currently living with a woman. After leaving my teaching post in Kentucky, I was accepted for a Ph.D. program back in Texas. I completed most of the class work and actually started on my thesis, working title, "Angst, Rage, and Sex: the Lyrical Truths of Rock and Roll." I whiled away four or so years on that, picking up work where I could, tutoring some, writing freelance stuff. Then, out of patience and money, I took a teaching job at a community college in Ft. Worth where I have been ever since, going on a dozen years now. I teach a variety of courses including one for social work students called "Transgender 101." Don't ask. Except for high school, I have never kept at anything this long. I think maybe I have settled. I don't mean settled down; I mean settled for less than I wanted. But most people my age are retired or getting ready for it. The only thing in my safe deposit box is a dead spider. So I teach. A couple of years ago I met this elusive lady, a writer herself. So we live together — cheaper that way plus more convenient. I haven't figured out if we are live-in lovers or just roommates with benefits, but I'm not really asking. It is just comfortable and most days that is enough. The days that it isn't enough are tough ones. Anyway, I invited her to accompany me to the reunion and she said quote, "I had rather have my fingernails pulled out a millimeter at a time over the course of a week than attend one minute of someone else's reunion." I'm fairly certain that means she doesn't want to come. Too bad. You and I could have double-dated again, you talking trash about my date when her back was turned!

The same day as the Boston bombing fifty-five innocent people died in Iraq from five car bombs in five different locations. The world has gone nuts. Makes me relive the insanity of the Vietnam War. You would think that, after thousands of years of pointless warfare, human DNA would have evolved to a higher standard. But we are still sitting perched in our trees, club in hand, drool dripping from our lips, waiting to pounce on whatever passes by. I think I'll go pour another Scotch and put on some Woody Guthrie tunes.

Always unfiltered,

Scotty
Thomas Alexander Scott

• • •

From: Olivia Walker MacLearn
To: Mary Alice Schneider
Sent: Sunday, April 21, 2013 10:45 PM
Subject: "Dear Diary" time again…

Just a quick note, M. This is going to be one of those weeks when paperwork threatens to swallow me. (Wish it would spit me out a bit thinner.) Speaking of which, if I die young enough for old friends to attend my funeral, please instruct the person who embalms me to do a little liposuction first. (There is cash in the top desk drawer if you need to bribe him/her.) I would like to be laid out really in tight slacks and a plunging V-neck sweater. Will amuse me to watch the reactions while I float about "up above" — fingers crossed on that one.

I heard from Rich again today. We are writing more regularly, but I feel we are becoming more formal — not really the right word but it will have to do for now. I need a merlot and some mindless television.

Oh, I have also heard from Scotty a number of times. Our conversations are definitely not becoming more formal! He was and is a hoot! Liv

• • •

From: Rich Stapley
To: Olivia Walker MacLearn
Sent: Monday, April 22, 2013 10:58 AM
Subject: Scotty

Liv, Meant to ask you in the last note — you mentioned Scotty. I should check in with him; it's been years. Can you send his email address? No hurry. He has done without hearing from me for 30 or more years and can probably survive a few more days. Thanks.

If he's going to this reunion, that would increase my interest. Rich

• • •

From: Olivia Walker MacLearn
To: Richard Stapley
Sent: Monday, April 22, 2013 9:14 PM
Subject: RE: Scotty

The email addresses on the class list from the reunion are supposed to be pretty accurate. The one for Scotty is the same one he uses to email me, so that should work. Liv

• • •

From: Mary Alice Schneider
To: Olivia MacLearn
Sent: Tuesday, April 23, 2013 9:15 AM
Subject: Crazy weeks!

Hi Liv,

I know what you mean about crazy weeks. Both girls are sick with gastro-intestinal kid afflictions and we're expecting some NYC guests for dinner tonight, so today will be madness. I'm going with classic New England diner food, my homemade chicken pie and fruit salad with brownies for dessert. It's pointless to try to impress thirty-somethings from the big city with anything but comfort food. They know too much about haute cuisine.

The young guests, two of Eddie's academic friends, brothers originally from Bulgaria, are so handsome that we have to protect them from predatory women. One is married now, so that's a help. I've always admired their sexiest characteristic, the ability (they are both well over 6 feet tall with wide shoulders) to move large pieces of furniture without breaking a sweat. In fact when Yanov phoned, he asked if I needed any pianos moved.

Regarding your last wishes, If I'm still around when you go to the better place, I promise that you'll be "laid out like a queen," as we heard Sally Bowles sing in "Cabaret" about Elsie, who actually might not have had a view from above, given that she "rented by the hour." Love from Crazyville on the Cape, Malice

p.s. Send more information about this slow epistolary dance you are doing with Rich.

• • •

From: Olivia Walker MacLearn
To: Mary Alice Schneider
Sent: Tuesday, April 23, 2013 9:15 PM
Subject: slow epistolary dance

M, I am going to print out all my emails to and from Rich so I can read them in order and then give you a more reasoned answer, but this has been a busy day so you will have to settle for an off the top of my head answer for now.

Rich initiated our correspondence. Hearing from him rather startled me, and I think I probably read too much into the fact that he wrote. And I believe there was another email — something about our correspondence being not quite dinner and a movie that was kind of flirty for want of a more mature word.

But in truth a number of his emails seem gender neutral. He could just as easily be writing to Scotty as to me. So my instinct tells me this is more of a line dance than a waltz or even a cha-cha. :)

That is probably for the best given the numerous issues that could surface if we were doing a slow dance when the band stopped playing.

Lucky houseguests! I crave your chicken pie! Liv

• • •

From: Mary Alice Schneider
To: Olivia MacLearn
Sent: Wednesday, April 24, 2013 7:27 AM
Subject: RE: slow epistolary dance

Hmm. I was envisioning more of a Tango or perhaps some Salsa if everyone has hips in good form, but it is early days yet. Maybe you have to see each other and maybe I have to read between the lines in his letters. I promise not to look at form unless it impacts content.

The Bulgarian brothers moved through the chicken pie with real efficiency during their short but pleasant visit. Even though we think of them as teens, they're now in their thirties, one, 37, a bit younger than Cassie and the other, 31, a bit older than Amy, and very sharp business men (scientific instruments of course). I get teary eyed when they praise the USA. They grew up in a country that was under Soviet domination and came here for a chance at success. Enormously grateful, Simeon, the older brother, says he never minds how high his taxes go because here he has the chance to achieve which he never would have had in his former life. It made these guys sick to think of the two men who terrorized their new country last week.

Sorry about the grim political rambling. It's just great to see the boys all grown up and doing well. Malice

• • •

From: Guendaline Field
To: Olivia Walker MacLearn
Sent: Wednesday, April 24, 2013 10:12 AM
Subject: Continuing correspondence with Rich

Liv, does this mean I can make you number 58 on the reunion attendance list? I have several other questions, but I will hold onto them for a while. Guen

• • •

From: Olivia MacLearn
To: Guendaline Field
Sent: Wednesday, April 24, 2013 10:45 PM
Subject: RE: Continuing correspondence with Rich

Guen, you can put me on your personal list, but this is not for public knowledge yet, just in case what develops is better put on ice. :) Liv

• • •

From: Olivia Walker MacLearn
To: Mary Alice Schneider
Sent: Wednesday, April 24, 2013 11:02 PM
Subject: RE: slow epistolary dance

Salsa, huh? Were you thinking mild, medium, or hot? (Sorry. I fear my sense of humor has taken a turn for the warped.)

We need to find time for you and Eddie to visit. You can red-line Rich's emails while I consume merlot. Liv

• • •

From: Mary Alice Schneider
To: Olivia MacLearn
Sent: Thursday, April 25, 2013 10:12 PM
Subject: Hot Salsa

Eddie and I would love to visit you. Getting off the Cape for anywhere but Boston right now would be a thrill and nobody loves redlining emails more than I do. Also nobody enjoys Merlot more than Eddie, so he is ready to travel.

Sitting by a pool is his idea of heaven. I guess we love whatever we don't have. All those years on Cape beaches make him long for water with nothing remotely questionable in it. The bottoms of his feet are a testament to all the barnacles he has jumped on getting off his windsurfers and my favorite childhood memory involves getting nipped by a big blue crab that my mother later served me. Ah, the circle of life. Don't tell my vegan friend Angela about this. She nearly fainted when I offered her local honey for her toast. It appears that I have been exploiting bees. Malice

• • •

From: Guendaline Field
To: Olivia Walker MacLearn
Sent: Friday, April 27, 2013 3:27 PM
Subject: Ancestry.com

Liv. It just occurred to me that I have not shared with you how I found you. My biggest problem in running searches through the various people search sites was that I didn't know your married name. For weeks I searched hoping that some source could find a reference in your maiden name that would give me a clearer track.

I have been researching my family on Ancestry.com for a couple of years. Feeling frustration and being a bit giddy I typed your name in and searched. You were there! You were in a list of descendants from Charles William Walker. My earliest ancestor hit these shores in 1789. Your family beat ours by thirty years. At any rate your name was listed as Olivia Walker MacLearn. I found you! With the married name you popped up all over the place!

• • •

From: Olivia Walker MacLearn
To: Mary Alice Schneider
Sent: Friday, April 27, 2013 10:15 PM
Subject: RE: Hot Salsa

As if by your command, M, Swimm Pools is on the schedule to open the pool next week. However, unless the weather changes drastically, it will be polar bears only! (Does Eddie count as a polar bear?)

Question: do you have an account with ancestry.com? I am a little nervous about how much info is on their site, as apparently that is how Guen found me. Although maybe it is just that she found me on that site under Walker, and then, after learning my married name, as I believe she expressed it, all sorts of information popped up! That could be problematic. Liv

• • •

From: Mary Alice Schneider
To: Olivia MacLearn
Sent: Friday, April 26, 2013 11:24 PM
Subject: RE: RE: Hot Salsa

Eddie, who has a good deal of polar bear in him, rejoices in the knowledge that the pool people are on the job and will follow us anywhere if you throw in some Merlot. I'm more of a sit by the pool and read type as you know.

We definitely don't have any dealings with ancestry.com as we are well aware of the horse thieves, bootleggers, illegal aliens (my English grandpa for one) and various other miscreants who came before us and have no particular urge to share this information with the world.

Eddie won't even let us be on any social media because he says the bright back room boys who work with him see social media as a portal into the life of anyone foolish enough to participate in this latest form of letting it all hang out. Cassie disregards all his warnings and often fills me in on who is doing what with whom. It's shocking how forthcoming and generous with photos some of our college age relatives are about their activities. One can only hope their future employers don't go looking at their pages online.

With fond thoughts of lounging poolside, Malice

• • •

From: Olivia Walker MacLearn
To: Mary Alice Schneider
Sent: Saturday, April 27, 2013 11:02 PM
Subject: Home is looking so good!

M, I thought this jaunt would never end, but I'm finally back at my hotel after the last of the numerous meetings and dinners to check on the smaller charitable offices and to promote our next big financial push. All worthy endeavors but tiring as one has to be charming and knowledgeable and humble and confident, etc.. I'll be home late tomorrow. We need to talk about Guen's email. I'll forward it to you when I get home. Time to sleep! Liv

• • •

From: Mary Alice Schneider
To: Olivia MacLearn
Sent: Sunday, April 28, 2013 8:54 AM
Subject: RE: Home is looking so good!

You're a freaking saint. Don't know how you do it. Grace under pressure has always been yours, but definitely not mine. Eddie and I are fully into scut work this weekend, cleaning up the wrap around screened porch so that when their renovation starts and the foursome moves in the kids will have a safe play area. One of the bad features about living on Buzzard's Bay is that Buzzard's Bay is right there in plain sight, tempting the pre-schoolers to explore. They'll be able to watch it from the porch, screen door locks in place, and stay out of trouble I hope. When my life guard certification expired in '68, I heaved a sigh of relief, but I've never given up watching every kid in sight from the beach or on a boat. Eddie's sister's kids, so much older than ours, were born Kamikazes and I spent forever guarding them in all situations involving water.

Eddie also accuses me of having a teacher's herding instinct whenever we go anywhere in a group and I admit to it, but he should know why. Back in '69 I lost two kids on a field trip to a showing of Zefferelli's "Romeo and Juliet" in Boston. They showed up a few hours later back at our school, explaining that they'd gone to Dorchester to complete a drug deal, in their opinion an honest excuse. It isn't just the precious memories that linger, I guess. Lately I've been dredging up a lot of bad ones. To happier thoughts! Malice

• • •

From: Olivia Walker MacLearn
To: Thomas Alexander Scott
Sent: Sunday, April 28, 2013 2:53 PM
Subject: Did Rich email you?

He said he was interested in reconnecting with you, and I haven't heard from him since he asked for your email address. Should I be looking for a good defense lawyer for you?

I'm sitting in the Delta club waiting for my flight back to LaGuardia after a multi-day jaunt to numerous headquarters of some of the smaller charitable organizations with which we work. I am so ready for a long soak in the tub, a merlot, and Revenge — the television show — a clarification I feel I need to make after causing Mary Alice to fantasize that I was up to no good last time I mentioned looking forward to Revenge.

I still need to absorb the tale of wife #3. And about your current roommate — is she old enough for beer and pretzels? Liv

• • •

From: Olivia Walker MacLearn
To: Richard Stapley
Sent: Sunday, April 28, 2013 2:45 PM
Subject: Did you ever get in touch with Scotty?

I know he is an important factor in your interest in attending the reunion.

I have been corresponding with Scotty and also with Guen. I have really enjoyed getting to know both of them again. Funny how little people seem to change. I did not know what life had in store for either of them, so all of that has been news, but their personalities, idiosyncrasies, value systems, etc. seem pretty much unchanged. I look forward to hearing what you think of that, at least in regards to Scotty, as you did not know Guen all that well.

I'm sitting in the Delta club waiting for my flight to LaGuardia after a five day jaunt from one charitable headquarters to another. Good meetings though so (somewhat) worth the exhaustion. I eagerly anticipate a long luxurious bath and Revenge — the television series, not actual revenge. Liv

• • •

From: Olivia Walker MacLearn
To: Mary Alice Schneider
Sent: Sunday, April 28, 2013 10:30 PM
Subject: Home!!!

M, I am home, bathed to the point of being water-logged, and ensconced in my bed! I can feel my eyelids closing.

I just forwarded Guen's email to you, the one where she writes about all sorts of information popping up about me. She is probably the most analytical of my Morrison friends, so she is not likely to skim over anything without pausing. Sigh... Liv

From: Rich Stapley
To: Olivia Walker MacLearn
Sent: Sunday, April 28, 2013 11:49 PM
Subject: Revenge

A dish best served cold, is it sweet, or is living well the recipe?

I did get a note from Scotty, who cheerily backed me against the wall and used his foil to put a scar on both my cheeks. Maybe it was more jaunty than cheery — as if a Morrison sitting room from 1967 had morphed into a Continental pre-WWI gentlemen's library, and he was upbraiding me for the bad form of mistreating his sister, never quite putting me in danger but letting me know that he wouldn't mind cutting a bit deeper and closer to vital organs, smiling and nonchalant the whole time.

And you, Olivia, though not in the room, were the sister he defended, suggesting to me that I shouldn't postpone an apology any longer. I've had a long time to figure out a better way to have treated you that spring — books, movies, plays, homilies and sermons haven't clued me in, but I do know I wasn't kind or thoughtful enough to do it better than I did. There is more than one way to be honest — it's not a virtue that stands alone well — without consideration of the other.

So, I apologize to you for hurting your feelings, for not being wise enough to realize that telling you the way I did was a battering, with nothing clean about the breaking up.

I'm not even doing this well, and I've had more than 45 years to try to get it right.

So, I'll stop now, and wish I could hand you a glass of merlot before disappearing. Rich

• • •

From: Olivia Walker MacLearn
To: Richard Stapley
Sent: Monday, April 29, 2013 8:35 PM
Subject: You had me at Merlot

All joking aside, Rich, thank you, for your apology.

I don't know if there is a good way to break up with someone, and if there is, I don't see how one could know that without the wisdom that comes from years of all that life serves us. But I appreciate that you wish to have done better, and that you would like an edit of that day in April.

For me, if I could have an edit, I would simply wish to erase the fact that there was a time when you knew you were with someone else, and I did not. But there are no edits, only the easing that comes with the passage of time.

So thank you for your words, Rich, and for wishing you could hand me a glass of merlot. No need to hide. I'll even hand you a glass of Zin, if I have the opportunity during the reunion.

Oh, and if you hear from my gallant protector again, please assure him that he can stand down. All is well. Liv

• • •

From: Olivia Walker MacLearn
To: Mary Alice Schneider
Sent: Tuesday, April 30, 2013 10:15 AM
Subject: The simple act of apologizing...

Well, M, after the first decade or two, I did not expect to hear an apology from Rich, but I did. He emailed me late Sunday night, sometime after I'd already fallen asleep. (Good thing. Not sure I would have slept had I read it then. Took me all day Monday to grapple with what he wrote and finally to answer him.)

Some background: A week or so ago Rich asked me for Scotty's email address. Said he wanted to see if Scotty was going to the reunion. Anyway, it appears they emailed and apparently Scotty defended my honor. :) To quote directly from Rich's email, (Note: As this is a direct quote, *me* and *my* pronouns refer to Rich.) Scotty ... "cheerily backed me against the wall and used his foil to put a scar on both my cheeks. Maybe it was more jaunty than cheery — as if a Morrison sitting room from 1967 had morphed into a Continental pre-WWI gentlemen's library, and he was upbraiding me for the bad form of mistreating his sister, never quite putting me in danger but letting me know that he wouldn't mind cutting a bit deeper and closer to vital organs, smiling and nonchalant the whole time."

I think Scotty's anger, after all these years, really affected Rich. He did not apologize for breaking up with me, for which I am grateful! I would have hated to find out that his reason for walking away from what I thought of as a deeply serious relationship was superficial enough to be apologized away. Rather, he apologized for the callous way he told me.

I am not sure how this affects my feelings about seeing him again. So many issues here, the shallow kind – I could use a fun weekend. I haven't had that kind of fun since my friend Hunter and I decided "with benefits" wasn't working. And then there is the truly meaningful issue – if I could rewrite history, would I really change anything that happened? Think about the movie

152

Back to the Future — what would I lose if history were altered? Ian? Holly? The depth of the friendship you and I forged when I returned from Europe and fled to your arms for comfort? I cannot imagine my life without any of those!

Oh my, this is way too serious for morning! I think I'll go grocery shopping instead, where the hardest decisions involve calories and fat content! Liv

• • •

From: Rich Stapley
To: Olivia Walker MacLearn
Sent: Tuesday, April 30, 2013 11:57 AM
Subject: Re: You had me at merlot...

Liv, a lovely and generous reply from you. Thank you. And If you want to not talk about it more, you'll have lots of chances if you go to the reunion.

Last night I watched a documentary I had taped some months ago — *Ethel* — Rory Kennedy's look at her mother's life. (Rory was born six months after her father's death.) She and several of his sibs talk about their mom and the family, Rory interviews Ethel, and there are lots of home movies. (Even in the 1940s, rich people had excellent movie cameras and knew how to use them.)

Several things struck me: Bobby talked to people while campaigning the way no politician talks these days, down-to-earth, unscripted, direct, formulating his answer as he talks. (Plus, he talks about poverty and unemployment as his responsibility to alleviate.) And, after his brother's death, he retreats into himself for six months and reads poetry and philosophy and thinks about things, emerging with a political and social conscience intact. Quite amazing — who talks about Aeschylus?

My favorite moment though was near the end when Rory and the younger children tell Ethel that she shouldn't give their father credit for how they turned out because she raised them. She says, no, they were raised with his values, the ones she chose to emphasize.

Quite extraordinary — you might enjoy it as a piece of our history.

I still have a framed bumper sticker — "Robert Kennedy in 1972." They were given out in L.A. during the 1968 primary campaign. I don't understand why. Enough.

Cheers,

Rich

• • •

From: Olivia Walker MacLearn
To: Richard Stapley
Sent: Tuesday, April 30, 2013 7:58 PM
Subject: RE: RE: You had me at merlot...

OMG, Rich, I too remember how different politics were then. Was it? Or were we just less bombarded by the negative? (Or was I just naive?)

Have you been following Joe Kennedy III at all? (He's new to the U.S. Congress from Massachusetts.) I attended a couple events when he was campaigning. He has youthful innocence and energy, combined with a commitment to aiding those who need help, and of course that Kennedy mystique.

Okay, I am going to let Guen know I'm signing up and as you suggested, we can "not" finish talking about the breakup over a merlot and a zin. Liv

• • •

From: Rich Stapley
To: Olivia Walker MacLearn
Sent: Tuesday, April 30, 2013 10:28 PM
Subject: Your work, besides evaluating merlots

Liv, I just logged on to send a postscript to my earlier note to ask you to walk me through one of your charity events, from the idea to handing a gigantic check to a struggling organization, and there was your promise to have Guen save you a place at the reunion. Great news for all of us who feared a dull weekend. Plus, Scotty and a few others now have no excuse.

As for Joe Kennedy III — didn't know about him — although his dad is one of the Ethel and RFK children who talk about their mother (*mummy* they each call her) in the documentary. Just looked him up; he's building the resume of service: Stanford, lacrosse, roomed with Jason Collins (do the connections never stop?), Peace Corps, Harvard law, prosecutor, now Congress. Holy cow, as the Buddha might say, or is that phrase redundant when the Buddha says it?

Glad to hear that he's for real.

Rich

MAY

"Rough winds do shake the darling buds of May."

–William Shakespeare

Mind Over Mirror

From: Mary Alice Schneider
To: Olivia MacLearn
Sent: Wednesday, May 01, 2013 9:37 AM
Subject: RE: The simple act of apologizing

Liv, I'm two emails behind and my head is spinning, not just from the allergy meds. There must be some law that says all the Cape pollen gets released in one mad burst in late April/ early May. If I say anything irrational, just chalk it up to the meds. It's a good thing you can't hear my annual Ursula the Sea Witch voice, which is all I have at the moment. Josie accused me of faking the voice, so I assured her that all I wanted was HER voice, giving her quite a turn. Grandpa Eddie said all I need is to kiss a prince, so I guess the voice will stay for a bit.

First, Guen has not turned out to be psychic after all, which is good news. I had no idea that ancestry.com was so invasive. We should be able to keep our horse thieves under wraps if we wish.

On to the real meat and potatoes. I just love Scotty. Good for him, defending the fair maiden after all these years. How well I remember those girls' dorm sitting rooms and all the sexual tension they contained. Rich deserves a sabre scar or two for his behavior. Remember my Mom's old maxim (one of far too many). "Time wounds all heels." Callous? Ya think???

You are lucky not to have read the letter before going to bed or you never would have slept. Really, you must "have it out" with Rich one of these days or erase him from your slate forever. (How dated is that metaphor in an era where dial phones and chalk boards reside in museums?)

Still, the basic human emotions stay the same or why would the poets of long ago still speak to us so clearly. For me Emily Dickinson is as fresh as today. In fact I plan to read some of my favorites when the kids go home, just to set my emotional clock once again. We still fall in and out of love, suffer and survive as our ancestors did, only now we blog and twitter about it.

Get out your own epee and have a serious talk with Rich. He needs to hear from you. As much as I try to avoid this topic, there's no telling how much time we all have left and I don't think you would want Rich in the dark forever. He does not deserve to go uninformed into "that good night." Keep me posted, Malice

• • •

From: Olivia Walker MacLearn
To: Mary Alice Schneider
Sent: Wednesday, May 01, 2013 5:32 PM
Subject: Scotty will be so pleased!

M, just to be clear: You love Scotty? Does Eddie know of this change in attitude? (Oh damn, I now have a Jimmy Buffet song stuck in my head — something about changes in altitude, changes in attitude. Well, who knows what a trip south to Kentucky will do for my attitude.)

Relax! I know you are devoted to Eddie and I promise not to make the same joke to Scotty, who really does seem to feel that the right one got away when you rebuffed his advances. (Sadly, even though I am sure you would have been a major upgrade to his three partners in short term marital bliss, I am having trouble envisioning the two of you together. If you hadn't rejected him, I probably would have been visiting you these past four decades at the Danbury Women's Prison after you lost your argument for justifiable homicide!)

More later. I am in the mood for an "early bird special" dinner. If I can hold out another twenty minutes, I can run over to Finalmente, and by the time I have sipped some red and nibbled some bread, the non-elderly diners will begin to arrive and I can enjoy my dinner in the company of others. Liv

• • •

From: Guendaline Field
To: Olivia Walker MacLearn
Sent: Wednesday, May 01, 2013 6:08 PM
Subject: Tentative Schedule

Liv: I am delighted that you are at least considering the reunion. I will very gladly put you on my personal list.

I have come to the conclusion that an off year reunion has many benefits. For one thing we are getting wonderful attention from the alumni office. We are the only focus and they have been so very helpful. Here is the tentative schedule which must be firmed up this week. On arrival we will have a cocktail party at that wonderful old hotel downtown (Lincoln Hall). That will give us a chance to "break the ice" and start getting to know each other again. Several of the faculty as well as staff will attend and circulate to answer questions about what is going on at our old school these days.

The alumni staff recommended a luncheon at a local casino that just opened outside town. This would be followed by time to "enjoy" the gambling center. I am told the restaurant at the casino is very nice. Do you think our classmates will be offended by including this function? One of my friends loves going to horse races at her reunions so I am hopeful this will be acceptable and not offensive.

Saturday night will be a dinner event hosted by the current President. The chaplain has also offered to hold a religious service in the old chapel where our convocations were held. The reunion would end on Sunday with a brunch.

Any thoughts? I need to finalize the arrangements by Friday. Guen

• • •

From: Olivia MacLearn
To: Guendaline Field
Sent: Wednesday, May 01, 2013 6:16 PM
Subject: RE: Tentative Schedule

Go ahead and add me to the official list! (How is that for a devil may care attitude?)

Your events sound absolutely perfect! And seriously, if someone has an objection to the casino, they can just have a drink and chat with friends. I think it sounds quite enjoyable.

So, great work, Guen, and thanks for finding me. I am excited to see all of you again! Off to dinner. Liv

• • •

From: Guendaline Field
To: Olivia Walker MacLearn
Sent: Wednesday, May 01, 2013 6:30 PM
Subject: RE: RE: Tentative Schedule

Yes!!! That's the kind of devil may care attitude I like. Guen

• • •

From: Olivia Walker MacLearn
To: Mary Alice Schneider
Sent: Wednesday, May 01, 2013 11:24 PM
Subject: into the night…

M, how many years has it been since we last sat by the fireplace and debated full disclosure?

Ian and Holly never budged from their position that people disclose too much and nothing good ever comes of it. Eddie always added something scientific, inevitably causing one of us to call for a drink refill break, which was probably his intention. You and I went back and forth, no rock left unturned, no thought unanalyzed.

This time, with no further effort to support my decision, I think I am inclined to stand firm with Ian and Holly. So there will be no full disclosure for me, unless of course Guen really did find "all sorts of interesting info" on Olivia Walker MacLearn as she wandered through the net. We will see, I suppose. Liv

• • •

From: Olivia Walker MacLearn
To: Thomas Alexander Scott
Sent: Thursday, May 02, 2013 10:19 AM
Subject: Wives and Live-Ins…

Scotty, I've been pondering your marital choices since your first email, but this last email really got to me.

You have joked about Mary Alice being the one who got away. I know M was not the right match for you. Most likely one of you would have ended up six feet under and the other incarcerated. :) But M set the standard for the type of woman I always imagined you sharing your life with, and after reading your comments about Wife #1's multiple orgasms with multiple men, I cannot understand how you were involved with, let alone married to, a woman like her. You deserve so much more than that.

No comment on Wife #3. Maybe someone like Wife #2 only with a bit more in common? As you say, you learned something of value from that relationship.

I suppose your current live in might have merit. Her reunion comment sounds like something M might say to be funny, but M would go anywhere with Eddie, so the question is: would this current woman go anywhere with you if you really needed her to? If not, I shake my head, mystified because you are such a prize.

So, Scotty, on our agenda for discussion: Why does Scotty choose poorly when it comes to women? And after we solve that: After all those years of mature behavior, is Liv really only interested in a quick roll in the hay with Rich? (Seriously, all esoteric issues aside, how comfortable could sex in the hay be?) Liv

• • •

From: Olivia Walker MacLearn
To: Richard Stapley
Sent: Thursday, May 02, 2013 11:27 AM
Subject: Pheeling Philosophical…

Rich, I meant to ask you, but was seriously sidetracked by your description of Scotty as a WWI defender of my honor: How did he seem to you, aside from still angry about our breakup? Does it feel as if you've been friends forever?

Guen seems exactly the same as I remember her. With Scotty it is as if we never stopped talking! I still tell him things and afterwards think, "Holy cow! Where did that come from?"

I've not corresponded with Gloria. Knowing her as I did when she, Guen, Scotty and I were the gang of four, I am sure she was the most hurt by my decision to completely vanish. You would not know this, I suppose, as you had no reason to try and contact me, but immediately after graduation I chose to disappear, to symbolically enter witness protection, go dark, sever all ties, etc…

I imagine Gloria and I will be cordial when we see each other at the reunion, but I am pretty sure that if she and I are to truly recapture our close friendship, full disclosure of my reasons might be necessary. However, I think disclosure often comes with more negatives than positives, so I am not a fan. Suppose, for example, I asked you to tell me why Susan seemed a better fit then I was in the spring of '67. (Trust me, I am <u>NOT</u> asking that!) Your answers might satisfy curiosity, but wouldn't disclosure open more wounds than it would heal? Aren't there things people are better off not knowing? Isn't the call for full disclosure often just Pandora's Box flirting with whoever passes by? Liv

• • •

From: Mary Alice Schneider
To: Olivia MacLearn
Sent: Thursday, May 02, 2013 5:30 PM
Subject: RE: Into the night…

Wow again! So what are you and Rich going to discuss? Child rearing??? Charities? Business? Favorite recipes? Talk about the elephant in the room!

My ethnicity is showing I guess. Eddie says that although I have a lot of the Anglo blood, my Italian always comes through with disclosure issues. I go into a safe zone, seeing Grandpa Giofaso at the Sunday dinner table, a jug of wine beside him and his much younger second wife heaping up plates for all of us. In his heavily accented English, Grandpa says: "So tell us about your problem, Vinnie (or Carlo or whoever) and we'll see what we can do about it." By contrast I can see my father's or my mother-in-law's clan calmly watching Cousin Hugh or Edwin or whoever throttling his wife in full view and then answering any questions about how their marriage is going with "Just fine, thanks."

The biggest challenge always came at funerals when both sides watched me for signs of going over to the enemy. Aunt

Teresa, Mom's voluptuous younger sister, expected at least fainting and rending of hair while Aunt Jenny, Dad's older sister, would purse her thin lips below her wispy perm and expect the stiffest of upper lips on all the family. She was no doubt thinking of the extent of the hors d'oeuvres or the limits of the liquor cabinet.

It's a good thing that you and I go 'way back because here I go letting it all hang out again. I'd seize the SOB by the throat, tell him all, and laugh at him for having missed the best years of his life which he has no whiff of a right to try to reclaim at any level. Good, sensible, scientific Eddie would say "So you still have some anger toward Rich?" Damn straight I do. That last year before Eddie and I married when you and I lived together on the Cape, you were the grown-up and I was the helpless kid friend, trying to make things right in my clumsy way. Now I feel more grown up, in fact older than dirt. But being old gives a woman a chance to say what she thinks. Maybe I can start wearing purple and a red hat that doesn't suit me. You get the picture. I just don't want any friends getting hurt.

Don't ask about the nasty well fed house dog that steals my wild pets' food. Our next door neighbor, who tolerates anything I do, thought I had lost it when he saw me pursuing the shifty beast around our shared back yard. I'm a pretty good broken field runner for a "girl" my age. The dog knows it now. I love to rant.

Malice

• • •

From: Rich Stapley
To: Olivia Walker MacLearn
Sent: Thursday, May 02, 2013 8:41 PM
Subject: A philanthropist's philosophy

Scotty was better than fine. He writes like he's in the room talking in his animated way — gestures, his whole body somehow jumps off the cyber page. How does he do that? There's melancholy, too, but who looks back without regrets? As to being friends forever, we picked up the conversation as if he'd come back from the kitchen with another beer.

I didn't know anything about your severing ties after graduation. I don't remember that it came up at the one reunion I went to, but maybe I was studiously avoiding asking about you, and figured if no one brought your name up, it was them acknowledging that reporting news about you would be a kind of minor betrayal, unless of course it would be to remark that I must have seen your picture in the recent SI swimsuit issue or your wedding photo in the Times when you married that multi-billionaire whose establishing a foundation to dig wells in African villages. The old "breaking up with you was the best thing that ever happened to her/Eat your heart out, bozo" report.

Which reminds me that I would like to hear about philanthropy in a post-Great Society, but I think I will step away, at least for now, from saying more about spring '67. "It wasn't you, it was me." "It wasn't you, it was us." Maybe the word you use, 'fit,' is the right one – "it wasn't you or us, it was that." I don't know. I'll keep thinking about it.

And my guess is that Gloria will be fine, without explanation. You stayed in the kitchen until the Merlot was drinkable, but now you're back. Rich

• • •

From: Thomas Alexander Scott
To: Olivia Walker MacLearn
Sent: Friday, May 03, 2013 1:33 AM
Subject: RE: Wives and live-ins...

Liv, Hell yes, the Forbidden One emailed me. And if he has suddenly fallen off the radar, I had nothing to do with it. Well, I might have had a little to do with it. I was only fifteen words into my response to him when I called him an asshole. I know, I know, it was a profound display of self-restraint. Thank you, thank you, I bow to your applause. Unfortunately when you vow never again to speak to a particular person, you forfeit the opportunity to curse them adequately. I was about to launch into a lengthy, tardy tirade when my scruples made an unexpected appearance. Sad to say, fairness has a way of interfering with one's grudges. So I tried to be fair with my comments. However, I did tell him that comparing the depth of your soul to that of his little frosh Susan was like comparing the Mariana Trench to a rain puddle. A little harsh maybe, but that's certainly the way I see it.

You ought to be glad you didn't wind up with Rich Stapley. He described his life up to now as "dull and pedestrian." In response I told him that mine was more like a ride on a spectral roller coaster with no tracks. Lots of scary and sublime surprises, dizzying heights, life-sucking lows, and the hope of getting through it all without throwing up too much. So, see, Walker, you would have had more fun going along on my ride than plodding along his path! Or maybe you came out better than both of us since you found a true lasting love, even though your great joy also brought you great pain. It doesn't hurt as much to lose somebody to whom you never quite gave your whole heart. I guess. Never having had that "true lasting love" experience kind of limits my credibility in this discussion.

Little did I know when I responded to Stapley that I was unleashing a Frankenstein tekkie-monster. He wrote back! And then without any response from me, he wrote again—at 3:00 AM! I'll spare you all the gruesome details of his defense except that he claims some credit for sitting "down with Liv right away when I realized that feelings for Susan were over-whelming me." He seems, at least to me, to think that the whole problem was not in the breakup itself but in the way he handled his confession to you – ham-handedness, he called it. As if better wording would have somehow made everything rosy and right, sad but understandable. He asks that he be sentenced to Purgatory, not Hell, but, as far as I'm concerned the jury is still out on that one. Each email from him seemed to sink him deeper and deeper into the hole he had already dug for himself, till all I could see was his hand waving an alibi that was tissue paper thin. After his first email I was ready to reconcile things between us. After his third, I feel less kind and less need to be fair.

But then I see my own reflection in the mirror of his sins, and I realize that he was with you longer than I was with two of my wives. So there's that chunk of humility for me to swallow. If I see him at the reunion, I will be chatty and polite but rather closed. And I want to reconsider my suggestion that you hop into the sack (which is much more comfortable than hay) with him as a way of tossing defiant spite at Life's limitations.

All of which leads me back to your most recent comments concerning my lack of discrimination in matrimonial partners. No, Wife #1 was nothing like Malice; in fact she was nothing like anyone I had ever met before. To understand what little *thought* actually went into the choosing, you have to revisit the times. The early 1970s, a war with no purpose grinding out a procession of body bags from the jungles of Southeast Asia, the rise of anti-authoritarianism, disillusionment, open marriage, constant cultural cave-ins, free love, escapism, "if it feels good, do it," sex, drugs, and rock 'n roll, and above all fatalism, "live for the moment." I was where I didn't want to be, doing what I didn't want to do, having no choice in any of it, and looking for comfort anywhere I could find it. I think she was my way of flipping the finger to society. We took what we needed from each other and were satisfied with that. There was very little risk and lots of risqué. It was a haven for me from a world that I could no longer understand or respect. And I'll tell you this, Liv, I would have stayed in that cocoon forever. She was the one who informed me one hot Texas day, without an ounce of animosity, that she had decided to move on. I let her go without resistance because that was our deal. But in a real way I have never let her go. Many times I have wished I could retreat again into that hot, uninhibited, Bacchanalian haze. But Life raps on the desk and demands my attention.

I have left out one other motivating factor for that first ill-fated selection. Hang on to your hat here. I was adrift without an anchor in those days. Part of it was "the world," part of it was melancholia after the incredible high of college, and (no guilt being thrown here, just fact) part of it was that my best bud, my kindred spirit, my anchor to reality just simply vanished off the face of the earth. Every unanswered letter I sent you, every phone call with buzzing silence on the other end, spiraled me down the rabbit hole with nothing to grab onto. I'm not blaming you for anything; I'm just telling you how it felt. I gave up after the void stretched to three years. I can remember the very day that I called off the search and just tucked you into the best room in my memory. You will notice I have not pressed you now upon your reappearance as to where, what, and why. But Grace Slick advised in her acid-laced song, "Go ask Alice." So, "Alice," I'm asking.

Exhausted by the effort of this email, I'll save your other questions for the next one. One last thing, I would like to know where, what, why, but just having you back is worth more than any explanation.

The Great Scott retires to bed,

Scotty
Thomas Alexander Scott

• • •

From: Olivia Walker MacLearn
To: Thomas Alexander Scott
Sent: Friday, May 03, 2013 9:39 AM
Subject: words fail me…

This was one of those mornings that started with a less than ladylike comment as I stared at the scale. Three Asian meals in three days and four pounds back on the scale. Soy sauce sodium. Happens every time, so I know it's coming. And yet every time I get weighed anyway.

I sat down to breakfast after carefully checking the sodium count on everything. Good Morning America was playing in the background as I powered up my iPad. A female voice caught my ear: Jennifer Finney Boylan was telling her story, the story of a man turned woman after marrying and fathering two sons. She told that story as she sat on the couch with her wife of twenty-five years and one of their sons, just six-years-old when Jennifer faced the truth of who she was, and now in college. Theirs is a story of being true to oneself, of love that can stretch to encompass the unexpected, of believing that leading a life that is a lie is unacceptable if one is to properly parent. I could taste my extra salty tears before I was aware they were flowing, good tears, the kind that come when glimpsing the best humanity can be.

Then I clicked on the little envelope that has become as much a part of my morning routine as the two cups of coffee I sip with something akin to passion, and I discovered your email, written in the wee hours of the night, sitting in cyberspace, patiently awaiting my waking.

I read as I sipped, until I reached your final words. I think I set my coffee cup down before the tears came again. Not good tears this time. No, these were tears of regret for hurting a dear friend; tears of shame for not realizing how much it would; and mostly tears of sadness for the years we both lost because I took the road that seemed my only choice, when in truth it was not.

You deserve to know the where, what, and why, and I will do my best to explain. I will write again before I sleep tonight... Liv

• • •

From: Olivia Walker MacLearn
To: Mary Alice Schneider
Sent: Friday, May 03, 2013 11:12 AM
Subject: Full disclosure wins the day…

M, I cave to your wisdom that the time for disclosure has come, but oddly not because of Rich.

Scotty wrote me the dearest email. He told me how it felt when I disappeared, and his words finally broke through my own self-centered view of the past. So I agree with you, at least as to telling Scotty, who deserves to know why I turned my back on his sweet friendship, and once I cross that bridge, maybe Guen and Gloria deserve the truth as well — but I am not quite yet ready for that.

I am still not sure that telling Rich is either wise or kind, not now, perhaps not ever. But for now I need to be brave and begin. It is time to dismantle the web I wove. Liv

• • •

From: Guendaline Field
To: Olivia Walker MacLearn
Sent: Friday, May 03, 2013 12:33 PM
Subject: Reunion Schedule

MORRISON COLLEGE CLASS of 1967 SPECIAL REUNION

Friday, May 24
Registration and Cocktail Reception
7:30 p.m. – 9:30 p.m.
Mary Todd Room
Lincoln Hall Hotel

Mind Over Mirror

Saturday, May 25
Lunch
11:30 am – 1:30 pm
The Gratz Gaming House
1780 Old Holley Road
Casino opens at 1:00 pm

Cocktails and Dinner Hosted by Morrison President
Dr. Marvin C. Wright
6:30 p.m. - 8:30 p.m.
Morrison College
President's Room

Sunday, May 26
Church Service Morrison's Morgan Chapel
9:00 a.m.

Brunch
10:30 a.m.
The Alumni Offices Dining Room

Thanks to generous and anonymous classmate donors there will be no charge for the cocktail hours. Lunch is $20.00 per person and dinner is $27.00 per person. The Alumni Office is graciously covering the cost of the Sunday Brunch. Payment for your selections will be made as part of registration on Friday.

• • •

174

From: Olivia MacLearn
To: Guendaline Field
Sent: Friday, May 03, 2013 12:45 PM
Subject: Perfect!

Just wanted to send along a quick, well-deserved compliment. Great work pulling this together. Perfect event choices! Liv

• • •

From: Olivia Walker MacLearn
To: Thomas Alexander Scott
Sent: Friday, May 03, 2013 9:27 PM
Subject: You might want to pour yourself a double.

Well, Scotty, it has been an AT&T kind of day. I've checked in with those with whom I've debated the issue of, as Mary Alice calls it, "full disclosure."

Ian is still against it. (No, I do not think he talks to me from the great beyond. I just remember how often he huffed his disapproval of the idea and can't imagine he would have changed that opinion.) My theory is that the Scots are even more stiff upper lip than the English when it comes to talking about troubles. Ian and his relatives could have written most of the sayings we all associate with the British: What's done is done. Keep calm and carry on. All good things must come to an end, and so forth.

Holly always sided with her dad, but her reasons were more personal than philosophical. She worried that I would fall apart if I revisited those two post-graduation years.

Eddie and M usually straddled the issue: On the one hand, but then you have to consider... Eddie, always the scientist, still does, but M changed her mind after Rich reentered my life, arguing that he should know what happened to me. And that change in her opinion sent me directly to decision-hell. Right up until your email I was stubbornly set on non-disclosure. Disclosure seemed to me to be Pandora's Box, and I was not expecting hope so much as fearing pestilence.

But then, these 46 years later, your email helped me see my decision through your eyes, through your confusion and disappointment, so I knew I needed to come clean. I am not sure I can share this with anyone but you, not even with Guen and Gloria. And Rich? I don't know. But that is a problem for another day. For now, I need to begin the tale of Liv on the Lam.

My parents' lives, as I am sure you well remember, were filled with servants and luxury. They traveled and partied. They mostly out-sourced parenting to nannies and tutors and various experts who tried to teach us sports and music and grace and such. It worked for Colton, the Yalie, the Glee Club member, the pheasant hunter, the golden boy. He was their one true joy as parents. Me, not so much.

The two years Rich and I were together, I was gloriously happy. Rich stood for everything my wealthy conservative family disapproved of. He was a liberal anti-war type long before I knew what those terms really meant. The few times he interacted with my parents, dad practically foamed at the mouth over Rich's view of Vietnam or the poor or unions. I loved how his views annoyed them.

When Rich dumped me in April, they were delighted. Good riddance to bad rubbish and all that. Their reaction was expected but it still was difficult. And so when they offered me a trip abroad after college, I jumped at it, if for no other reason than I would not have to be with them, to hear their "we told you so" lectures.

And then at the very end of May, a week before graduation, I had the flu. Remember how crappy I felt, and how you all said it was my body purging itself of everything Rich? Only it wasn't the flu. About the time I started to feel a bit better something pecked at the corner of my mind. And as I was jotting final graduation activity times on my calendar, I realized what it was. The last time my period was marked on my calendar was the 21st of March.

Thanks to the lack of available birth control in the 60's, at least in the mid-West, Rich and I had relied on condoms, and now and then we did not bother using one, because it was early or late in my cycle and we thought if it worked for the Catholics, it should work for a nice Presbyterian girl as well. And it did. For two blessed years it worked. But one damn time it failed — just a week or so before Rich told me about Susan and asked for his pin back, our loosy-goosy approach apparently failed. And by the time I knew for sure, I was packing for Europe and for all I knew Rich and Susan were skipping through the meadow singing: "going to the cha-peal and we're gonna get mair-air-aried."

Talk about stress! The 60's were a bad time to be unmarried and pregnant. But unmarried, pregnant and without a potential mate at the other end of the shotgun was even worse. My parents were horrified. I had failed them even more than usual. Worse than being un-athletic and tone deaf. Worse than not applying to Smith.

So a promise was demanded and agreed to. No one would be told. I would enjoy Europe in luxury for six months and then I would be checked into a "wonderful place" where I would give birth and relinquish "it" to a couple of infertile commoners.

Best laid plans and all that. In early November I was trying to get comfortable with a baby rolling about and kicking at my stomach, and I began to gently massage what now would be called my baby bump, trying to calm the child so I could sleep. And I whispered to the little creature that life would be better without me there to remind everyone that there was no father. Only the more I talked, the less better that idea sounded.

Early the next morning I called M and at her hello I shouted my dilemma: I cannot give up my baby! What should I do? Tell me what to do!

"Come home," she said. "Come to the Cape. We'll do this together." And we did. She postponed her wedding to Eddie, who was already in grad school in Boston, and we made a nursery and practiced Lamaze breathing. And for the first time, I began to feel that I was doing what I should do, that I was not "in trouble" but simply with child.

When Holly was born that Christmas Eve, M was with me to remind me to breathe, and to declare that I was strong and brave and would be a wonderful mother. And days later Eddie was there to drive us home to the house on the Cape, a house that I rented six months later, when Mary Alice and Eddie tied the knot and moved to Boston. And there I lived and raised Holly alone until one fateful spring day, when Holly was not yet a year and a half. I left her in the care of a sweet neighbor to bike to the local diner for lunch.

I guess I've already told you the story from there. I was distracted by some flowers, almost biked right into Ian, and we talked for hours. Of course I omitted the part where I introduced Ian to Holly that very day. I've always said he fell in love with her first, then me. Nothing could have pleased me more.

Holly assures me that she feels no threat from Rich learning about her, because Ian was her dad from the day he first held her until the day he died. She told me when I talked about coming to the reunion that she was afraid I would see Rich and that the memories would be difficult. She worried about my heart being broken again. When I asked if she felt at all curious about Rich, she made a little noise, rather like a colt calling to its mom, and said: Why on earth would I?

I know this doesn't really answer why I dropped out of sight. I suppose because I felt stupid, and flawed, and well, just really stupid. And as dumb as this sounds, even to me, I was afraid Rich would find out and somehow that thought horrified me. The thought of Rich talking with Susan about whether it was even his, and if he owed me anything made me feel shame. As if their questioning if I was "sleeping around" would brand me as that kind of girl. (The 60's were not exactly the decade of the woman.)

So flawed reasoning or not, that is why I dropped out of sight. But why did I stay out of sight? I don't know. Perhaps my sense of having done the right thing was more fragile than I admitted. Perhaps part of me believed my angry parents, who when they learned of my decision to keep Holly, declared me unfit to make decisions that a poor fatherless child would be forced to live with. Perhaps I was afraid they were right and you all would think less of me for not leaving her with the couple who could provide her a name and a proper family.

And then I met Ian, and mom and dad embraced their new worthy son-in-law, and they told all their friends that I'd fallen in love and married in Scotland and came home with my well-heeled wealthy husband and our beautiful daughter. And I let their lie define my life, so that Holly would not be tarnished by my mistakes.

As you once asked me, dear Scotty: Do you still think kindly of me? Liv

• • •

From: Olivia Walker MacLearn
To: Mary Alice Schneider
Sent: Friday, May 3, 2013 9:49 PM
Subject: Done

Okay, M, I've sent Scotty an email with full disclosure as best as I can tell it. Now I just wait... Liv

• • •

From: Mary Alice Schneider
To: Olivia MacLearn
Sent: Saturday, May 04, 2013 12:03 AM
Subject: RE: Done

At LAST! I'm thrilled to hear that you have finally come clean with Scotty. Poor thing. He was your confidant all those college days and then he thought you had dumped him. Point of view is such a big issue in literature and in life. Every time I get in a mess with someone, I force myself to see it from the other person's point of view and it really helps. Sometimes, of course, I turn all bitchy and just say "Screw it!"

Only five or so years ago, Eddie and I had a reunion with my three roommates and their husbands and they blew me away with apologies for being jerks and wasting my time. I had been thrilled to have girl friends, but they thought I was so studious that I secretly rejected their fun-loving tendencies. I felt a huge rush of love for them and guilt for being such a grind, but they did not know how hard I was working to be worthy of Eddie. Diligence became an obsession for me and I never missed a class or handed in anything late. My roommates and I had to be over 60 to tell each other the truth. What a world.

But over 60 is still young these days. We may have a lot of life left, so why not be honest about it? Holly's dad will always be Ian, but maybe she deserves to have a look at the sperm donor before he moves on to the next world if there is one. There's a whole school of research out there now about how powerful first love is. People our age are reconnecting with their first loves, especially after death or divorce. After my cousin Bella's first husband died, she reunited with her first big relationship (he had, in fact, been the roommate of the guy to whom she was married for 45 years and by whom she had four children), and married Frank on what would have been her 50th wedding anniversary with Stan. Strange, but they're very happy.

Here's one for the books too. A girl who had had a "thing" for Eddie back before there was air found him on the internet just before our 40th HS reunion and wrote to him at our shared email trying to rekindle a spark that had never existed for him. He said, "Knock yourself out; you're the writer," so I dashed off a long and chatty letter to her, full of subtext of course, and oddly we never heard from her again. Our daughters got the giggles when they read the pleasant note full of family details and expressions of happiness at hearing from an old friend after so many years. The subtext was full of "Remember me, you mean girl from the better part of town. Well, I got the prize, the guy with the brain because he likes them bright no matter where in our narrow-minded town they live." We did actually see her at the reunion and she was a vision in cranberry, so apt for the Cape. Even her hair was cranberry as were her stockings. She looked like a juice ad.

You know what I love about getting old? It's finding out that all the feelings we thought we had invented when we were young are ageless and timeless and still here to drive us mad. We can lust and love and hate and connive with all the passion we felt in high school, perhaps with more now that we know our time may be growing short. What is stopping us? Is it the fear of some sort of disgrace? Hell, no! I will chase bad dogs with sticks through my yard and tell off my enemies if I want to. I will admit terrible truths to myself and to others if I think they need to hear them. If I love people enough, though, I might spare them. It remains an option.

Oops. I appear to be ranting. You have energized me with your "coming out" after all these years and I feel young again. Who knows what wonderful things are out there waiting for us. We can "shine in use," not "rust unburnished" like so many we both know.

Do keep me informed about whom you plan to tell and when. I'm such a spectator, but it was wonderful to be a cast member in your life back when we were young and beautiful and did not realize it. How foolish and lucky we were. Malice

• • •

From: Olivia Walker MacLearn
To: Mary Alice Schneider
Sent: Saturday, May 04, 2013 10:43 AM
Subject: She looked like a juice ad…

M, on a morning when I woke feeling exhausted from my walk down memory lane as I composed Scotty's email, your story of Eddie's admirer in her cranberry colored outfit was the perfect antidote! You do have a way with words! Liv

• • •

From: Mary Alice Schneider
To: Olivia MacLearn
Sent: Saturday, May 4, 2013 12:02 PM
Subject: Cranberries

Glad to hear I made you smile. I'm still hiding out from the pollen, but I did manage to get out for some grocery shopping which I have always found therapeutic. Some deep need drives me to plan meals ahead and stockpile food staples. Eddie accuses me of going to a store to stock up before the hoarders get there. This need probably dates back to my childhood when the hurricanes would hit and my mom fed and housed the neighborhood, all the folks from the low-lying areas because our house was on just high enough ground to escape the water. She'd make vast pots of pasta and serve it with Grandpa's jug wine by candle light because we always lost power. People would sleep fully clothed, but with shoes off in front of our fireplace. Being a kid, I was always fascinated by the orangey tint their brown leather shoes gave their socks after the damp did its work.

It's strange how lately I can remember childhood with new clarity, especially those moments of crisis or joy.

I guess we both have some refreshed college memories now that you're sneaking up on that reunion. As exciting as it is to anticipate, when it is finally over we will have all the enjoyment of deconstructing it for ages. I want to know EVERYTHING, so take notes if necessary. Photos would be nice too. In all the anticipation of your reunion, Eddie and I have nearly forgotten our 50th HS event – probably a big yawn, but we'll go. Maybe Miss Cranberry will make another appearance.

Malice

• • •

From: Olivia Walker MacLearn
To: Richard Stapley
Sent: Saturday, May 04, 2013 4:19 PM
Subject: Reflections

No SI Swimsuit Issue, Rich. We could not agree on terms. Ha!
I wish. My last skimpy swimsuit was bought when I was still in
college.

Ian was wealthy. Cannot deny that, although multi-billionaire
might be a bit of a stretch. Your comment did make me think
though that it was rather ironic that I ended up in similar
financial shape as my parents. Not with the same lifestyle
though! Ian's and my home was beautiful to be sure, and its
location heavenly, but it was a real family home. No nannies
or tennis courts or horse stables or such.

I agree about not trying to figure out why you and I ended,
but I find myself thinking about why we started. Was it your
politics and your war views that intrigued me — views directly
opposite to my parents'. Was it sex? We came of age in a time
when we had to learn most everything first hand. Television
and movies were circumspect about all things sexual. Many
of our parents believed in "what they don't know won't tempt
them." Of course we lasted nearly two years (practice makes
perfect?) so either we were slow learners or we were about
more than sex.

Just in a philosophical mood I guess. Scotty got me reflecting on the years following graduation. For him there is a
need to understand my withdrawal from my friends. In trying to meet that need in my dear friend, my own understanding has become a bit clearer.

Well, I meant to just send a funny SI comment but I seem to have written more than that. Ignore all but the first paragraph if you wish. Liv

• • •

From: Rich Stapley
To: Olivia Walker MacLearn
Sent: Saturday, May 4, 2013 6:13 PM
Subject: An astronomer observes

Shakespeare on the marriage of true minds: "It is the star to every wandering bark, whose worth's unknown, although its height be taken." So, I'll toss caution out the port-side window of the Hubble and venture this comment, then probably lapse into a moody but neither unattractive nor truculent silence: I think what you and I had was a relationship that evolved — you know, evolution, improvements over time, enjoyment then friendship then romance. What Susan and I experienced was the Big Bang — from zero to infinity in a nanosecond. Evolution is probably better in the long run, but tell that to a callow youth who thought he was a mature man. Hawking meets Darwin for a WWF cosmic smackdown.

As for sex: any man who lives long enough (outside a monastery) is embarrassed by his early sexual life — chagrined, humiliated, disconcerted, vexed, and distressed (thesaurus in hand). Embarrassed and humiliated probably cover it sufficiently. I had no clue what I was doing, and your putting up with me was either a classic "oh honey, I had fun" pat on the head or you were clueless as well.

We were certainly more than about sex, and I most assuredly qualify as a slow learner (worse than slow because I didn't realize I knew nothing. "Cock-a-doodle-do" strutted the rooster). So, a belated thanks for not putting out a cigarette on my chest whenever I asked Hemingway's eternal question, "Was that good for you?"

As long as I'm talking about sex, I'll break another taboo and talk about money: did Ian bring a pile to the marriage? I wouldn't be surprised if he didn't and that you had a hand in many of his smart business decisions.

Glad about the house; not surprised about that either. You're right — there are family houses and there are estates that aren't. Rich

• • •

From: Thomas Alexander Scott
To: Olivia Walker MacLearn
Sent: Saturday, May 4, 2013 10:14 PM
Subject: RE: You might want to pour yourself a double…

Liv, my precious Liv, hurt was the first thing I felt when I read your story. Not my hurt, but yours. I saw you, young, alone, isolated by the circumstances, bewildered. I swear to you, Liv, it took every ounce of control I had not to grab my laptop and hug it to my chest as if it were you, as if I could reach back across the decades and comfort you. It just kills me that you went through such pain and I wasn't there to help. You know, at least I think you know, or certainly I want you to know, that if you had called me, I would have dropped out of grad school, hocked the old Impala for airfare, and come to you. We would have hidden in hamlets and bounced from borough to borough defying the Selective Service bloodhounds to find us.

But that's all "would have" stuff. The incredible part of your story is that there were so many real-life heroes — and so few villains. Our daring Mary Alice, of course, acted bravely because that's who she is and that's what you do when someone who is part of your own self hurts. And Ian, Ian was a gift. I'm too much of a realist, too steeped in logic, to believe that some Beneficent Chess Master moves us measly pawns to the safe spaces, to the greenest grasses. But then I hear your story and I crack open my logic just enough to believe that Ian was a gift from Someone to you and Holly. Suddenly I realize that I haven't paid enough attention to him in our emails. And Holly, Holly is a true hero (I hate the word heroine; too many bad associations for such a grand thought) in loving her dad and you and the wonderful hand that life dealt her. And I agree with her, why should she be curious about Rich; Ian was her dad. She may not carry Ian's DNA but she carries the imprint of his love. I would trade the former for the latter any day of the week.

But the greatest person in your story is of course you. Just when I thought that my regard for you could never be greater, just when I thought I had placed you on the highest pedestal available to mortals, you share your story and my esteem for you just explodes into a whole new dimension. Do I still think kindly of you, Liv? I stand and cheer you. I lift the eternal cup to toast you. I bow down and hug your ankles, so proud to be in your presence.

Having heard your story of the lost years, I don't deserve to be able to say I forgive you for the separation, so I won't. I never did harbor the first grudge or ill thought toward you. I could never do that. Besides, what I went through – the loss, the lostness – carved me into the guy I am today. I may be pretty pathetic in a lot of people's eyes, but I kind of like me. So without the word "forgive" ever in play, I will tell you not to worry; it all came out okay.

And Rich? I don't know. The things about him that you appreciated make me remember the Rich who was my friend. But in a way I don't think he deserves to know. I don't count him as a villain in your story (only your parents warrant that title). And who knows how he would have responded if you had told him at the time? Yet there is a tiny twinge when you say that you and Rich made unfortunate love (and, consequently, lovely Holly) just a week or so before he took back both his fraternity pen and his pent-up fealty. As you had stated before, his relationship with Susan had to have begun long before that revelation. Still… So, I don't know, flip a coin? I can't tell you what to do or whom to tell. What I can say is, screw Rich, you told <u>me</u>! And I love you all the more for it.

You will laugh when I reveal to you that I was watching the new version of "Les Misérables" when I opened and read your email! Fantine and Liv, honest to God, as I sat there, I felt like the fabric of the universe was shredding. I vow never again to open anything you send me while a tragedy is playing on my tube! By the way, for what it's worth, I like your story better.

Always receptive,

Scotty
Thomas Alexander Scott

• • •

From: Olivia Walker MacLearn
To: Thomas Alexander Scott
Sent: Sunday, May 05, 2013 12:12 AM
Subject: RE: RE: You might want to pour yourself a double...

I cannot think of how to express what I am feeling right now after reading your email. I thought of writing nothing for fear of saying the wrong thing. But that did not work so well in the past, so I will just do my best.

What I've missed the most over the past decade or so is not sex. (Don't get me wrong. I do miss that!) Rather, it is the incredible feeling of being held in the arms of someone who knows you inside and out, good and bad, and still loves you. The person in the middle of the night who gathers you close and tells you, "Everything is okay. It was just a bad dream. I've got you." Your words are like those arms. Good night, dear friend. Sweet dreams. Liv

• • •

From: Olivia Walker MacLearn
To: Thomas Alexander Scott
Sent: Sunday, May 05, 2013 9:02 AM
Subject: the dark side :)

Well, Scotty, it's morning and with a big chunk of secret gone, my shoulders feel gloriously lighter. I know I was too gushy in my response last night to the kindest, most loving email I've ever received, but I figure if anyone can parse my words, it is you, so I've decided not to worry.

I also decided you would enjoy knowing that your sweet words saved me from having to send you an apology email this morning. (When your email arrived last night, I had not yet done what was going to create the need for that.) Explanation follows:

At the moment you email arrived, I had just finished Googling the title of a song from (with apologies to Tom and Nicole) that incredibly stupid movie *Eyes Wide Shut.* I thought the title was "I've done a bad bad thing," (which would have been a perfect subject line for my email to you) but actually it seems it was "Baby did a bad bad thing."

Hold on to that thought. Now back to why I would have had to send an "I'm sorry" email to you.

A while ago, after his communication with you, Rich sent me an apology for breaking up poorly. I know his reason for apologizing bothered you, and perhaps it should me too, but actually I appreciate that he does not regret falling for Susan. To me that offers hope at least that one meaningful thing was given up for another.

Anyway, in the next email or so we agreed to buy each other a glass of wine at the reunion and not talk about it any further. That made sense to me. However, Mary Alice had started suggesting that I tell Rich about Holly. You and I both know how much M cares about me, so I figured her reasoning was that if in the near future Rich got hit with a bus, I would head right down Shouda Road on my way to Guilty Court for not having told him. So in trying to decide if I should/could tell, I think I was trying to connect a bit more, to better understand Rich now and then.

191

So I wrote some thoughts in an email to Rich — not about why we broke up, but about what brought us together in the first place. Along with other reasons, I included sex, with the following statement: "Of course we lasted nearly two years (practice makes perfect?) so either we were slow learners or we were about more than sex."

He wrote back yesterday afternoon, reflecting on how our relationship had evolved "improvements over time, enjoyment then friendship then romance," but that with Susan it was like the cosmic Big Bang. He also thanked me for putting up with the learning phase of his sexual life, remarking that he was probably clueless about just how much he needed to improve, and he reflected that I was either kind or also clueless.

Perhaps if he had left out the Big Bang part I might have reacted more maturely to the rest, but instead I indulged in a fiercely written reply, which I thankfully refrained from sending! (Had I sent it, the "I did a bad bad thing" apology email to you would have been necessary so you would not be confused when Rich shunned you at the reunion — or worse.)

For your amusement, before I hit delete on the draft of an email I will never send to Rich, I thought I would share the relevant part with you, with my apology for ALMOST telling a whopper of a lie about us without your knowledge or permission! Here it is verbatim:

"Rich, you were not all that bad at sex, and I was not clueless, so I can be a fair judge of that.

I probably would have been clueless but one dateless night, after boring television and a couple rum and cokes, Scotty and I decided to play strip poker. It was silly fun at first, a shoelace, a sock, but as that game often does, it progressed to a different kind of fun. That night I learned what it was like to move ever so slowly to a state of delicious excitement only to change direction and begin all over again. Talk about a big bang! I never did ask who taught him his moves, but dear lord he was an incredible lover.

That was, of course, before I was dating you. I never would have sex with two people at the same time. That's just wrong."

Are you laughing? I hope so, because I'm blushing and that always made you laugh. And now, dear friend, I will hit delete on the bitchiest email I've ever written, ever so thankful I did not send it! Okay, delete is done and I am back from the dark side! Liv

• • •

From: Olivia Walker MacLearn
To: Richard Stapley
Sent: Sunday, May 05, 2013 5:44 PM
Subject: RE: An astronomer observes

Shakespeare on vengeance: Temper thy thoughts oh vengeful woman, less they ink themselves forever upon his memory. (Skip the Google search. I made that up.)

In 2013 parlance, I have decided to delete the explosive Big Bang email I wrote last night in response to yours. After all I asked the questions you answered. Besides I am not even certain which of your comments sent me shrieking into the night.

So here are new topics for your (cautious) consideration: Should we still plan to tip a glass of our respective choices in wine? If we do, should we stick to civilities or allow deeper topics to develop?

Also, if you are feeling brave (or foolish) will we meet as strangers? Old friends? Ex-lovers? Frenemies? Inquiring minds want to know.

Oh and in answer to your money question: Even if I disregard Ian's ancestral castle and grounds, his net worth makes my family look like paupers. Liv

• • •

From: Olivia Walker MacLearn
To: Mary Alice Schneider
Sent: Sunday, May 05, 2013 6:09 PM
Subject: Effects of the Big Bang Theory

M, I forwarded a copy of my most recent email to Rich. I will NOT forward his email, the one that inspired mine. It would annoy you way too much. I though you would particularly enjoy my made up Shakespeare quote — done because he began his email to me with a real one.

Also Scotty received my full disclosure email and sent the sweetest reply. I am really sorry I did not tell him decades ago. He would have been a wonderful, if slightly wacky, uncle to

Holly as she was growing up. I am so thankful to have his friendship. Liv

• • •

From: Thomas Alexander Scott
To: Olivia Walker MacLearn
Sent: Sunday, May 5, 2013 11:34 PM
Subject: Re: the dark side…

Dear Darth Liv,

I love the song, "Baby did a bad bad thing!" Chris Issak is one of my favorite singers. And I won't describe my feelings about Nicole Kidman lest drool begin flowing from this email all over your computer. So with that song playing in my head, I read your email and was in stitches! And your admitting to me that you were blushing did make it all the funnier!

First of all, (even though I am mentioning it second) your email last night was perfectly worded and lacked any semblance of "mushiness." You wrote what I yearned. So, perfect.

Next, feel free to lie about me any time you want, especially if I come off as the studly sex pistol. Did we ever play strip poker? If not, why not? If so, did you make sexual advances on me after I passed out? I won't ask who won your hypothetical game because it sounds as if we both did! But really, feel free to lie about me; I do it all the time. You should read some of the resumes I have submitted. I would think that excessive creativity is a virtue when one is applying for a writing job!

Thirdly, or wherever we are in this miss-numbered email, "the Big Bang??" Oh, give me a break! If she was so absolutely, astronomically perfect, why are they now divorced? Maybe he made one too many sophomoric statements such as his "Big Bang" fiasco. Tell him that if Susan was his Big Bang, he was your Little Sputter. You know your problem, Walker? You are just so damned nice to people. Even when they don't deserve it. "Improvements over time," hell, I would have reamed him for that one too if I were you. Makes you sound like a Cub Scout merit badge. If you really deleted that deliciously stinging email to him, can you retrieve it somehow? I think that one is worth saving, a little ammo in waiting. Send me a copy; I may frame it. I'll use it whenever my whatever-we-are-to-each-other seems less than enthusiastic about a little recreational coitus.

Sixthly (who cares by now?), Heaven forbid that Rich gets hit by a bus. A large sedan, okay. Maybe a Hummer even. But so what if he did? You think that he needs to know about Holly before his untimely death and I ask you: Why? For what purpose? Toward what end? Holly, though as yet invisible to him, has made no difference in his life and he has certainly made no difference in hers beyond the sperm contribution. So why have any guilt on your part about his ignorance?

And lastly, since I am hunkered in a Hampton Inn in Houston with an early wake up call to participate on a panel for a writing class at Rice, I kind of like the view of Liv from the dark side. I intend to climb into bed softly singing with a snarled-lip stammer on my "B's", "Buh, buh, buh, Baby did a bad, bad thing" and fall asleep with a smile on my face.

Your evil twin,

Scotty
Thomas Alexander Scott

• • •

From: Olivia Walker MacLearn
To: Thomas Alexander Scott
Sent: Monday, May 06, 2013 10:15 AM
Subject: RE: RE: the dark side…

You are probably on stage educating young writers as I type, so I will keep this short: Thank you for not adding "er" to Darth Liv.

• • •

From: Mary Alice Schneider
To: Olivia MacLearn
Sent: Monday, May 06, 2013 10:43 AM
Subject: RE: Effects of the Big Bang Theory

OOH! I want to know the quote with which he started. Plleeease…. (hear me whine). Please don't let it be the "Hell hath no fury" one or I will have to have him iced. You should have let the creep try to find the source of your made-up line.

So you might tip a glass as what?? I sort of like ex-lovers, but frenemies sounds OK too.

Do warning bells go off over his obvious interest in your net worth? I love that you set up a little ratio example for him to begin to comprehend the relative wealth of your family of birth to your family of marriage. Let us hope he has no designs on your swag. Perhaps I have watched too many episodes of "Downton Abbey," but now I'm suspicious that every man who appears before one of my widowed or divorced friends may be a gold digger.

You are sailing into some dangerous waters. We were both lucky to marry the right man, but when I see some of the gruesome marriages that somehow last and some of the awful second marriages that are appearing with shocking regularity, I fear for the rationality of our gender (too Jane Austen?). For a woman who never married or did more than steal a kiss in a garden, Jane had a lot of sense. I wonder what she would think of our world. Along the same line, a cup of tea with Emily Dickinson would be enlightening for all of us. She knew about unfulfilled longing. That's for sure.

I would love a peek at Rich's letters, but I'm overstepping on this wish. Malice

• • •

From: Olivia Walker MacLearn
To: Mary Alice Schneider
Sent: Monday, May 06, 2013 11:35 AM
Subject: RE: RE: Effects of the Big Bang Theory

Because you whined "Plleeease" so nicely, I will send the quote, but not the rest of his email, which certainly would send you to the freezer for a bag of ice cubes. What? Slight misinterpretation of your threat?

Shakespeare on the marriage of true minds: "It is the star to every wandering bark, whose worth's unknown, although its height be taken."

I confess to having no idea what the quote means, but then you majored in Lit and I majored in math and minored in boys. (Some youthful decisions really should come with mulligans.)

Oh and Rich was so far to the left when we were together that his most likely temptation would be to transfer my funds to the state of California, earmarked for schools and soup kitchens, so I think we can shelve any gold digging concerns. :) Liv

• • •

From: Mary Alice Schneider
To: Olivia MacLearn
Sent: Monday, May 06, 2013 1:15 PM
Subject: Shakespeare

This one I actually know by heart because I recited it at our first daughter's ill-starred wedding. It's from Sonnet 116, "Let me not to the marriage of true minds admit impediments." He's referring to love, which we set our sails by but which we do not entirely understand. If he starts hitting you with the line "Love's not time's fool tho rosy lips and cheeks within his bending sickle's compass come," tell him to sit on it. Malice

PS The conceited creep may be thinking of the concept that love does not "bend with the remover to remove," assuming that you continued to love him after he screwed you over (note the ending with a preposition — I must be really miffed).

• • •

From: Guendaline Field
To: Olivia Walker MacLearn
Sent: Monday, May 06, 2013 12:10 PM
Subject: Final Count

The Hotel and Casino are being very nice about pro-
jected attendance but I am trying to give them a fairly
good figure on the meals. Will there be anyone with you
at the reunion? To my surprise almost everyone will have
a spouse, child, significant other or quest. We will have
over 100 in attendance if all goes well. Can you believe
it? Guen

• • •

From: Olivia Walker MacLearn
To: Olivia Walker MacLearn
Bcc: Thomas Alexander Scott, Mary Alice Schneider

Sent: Monday, May 06, 2013 12:29 PM
Subject: Plus One

Okay, M and Scotty, I figure if I angst myself through two discussions, (I know that's not a verb, but ever so appropriate.) I
will have to be off caffeine for like two years, so I am writing
one email, which I will blind copy to both of you. That way I
can receive back two emails filled with wise words for the cost
in stress-currency of only one email sent. It's kind of how a
pyramid scheme works I think. Or maybe just the opposite?
No matter.

I just received an email from Guen, who wants to know if I am bringing anyone to the reunion as it appears everyone else is bringing a "spouse, child, significant other, or guest."

Who brings a child to a 46th reunion? Well, perhaps Colton, because he thinks his current toddler screams impressive sperm, but other than that? Now if Holly had a birthmark of the state of Arizona on her neck it might be worth dragging her along to provide an interesting ice-breaker when I first see Rich, but otherwise I am stuck with no spouse, no significant other, and a friend (yes, M, I do mean you) who cannot be invited because she surely would be the guest from an Agatha Christie novel. (Dim lights. M exits stage right. Rich falls to stage floor. Loud screams as curtain is lowered.)

I am too old and too busy trying to figure out how to look young for this plus one nonsense! Liv

• • •

From: Olivia MacLearn
To: Guendaline Field
Sent: Monday, May 06, 2013 4:16 PM
Subject: RE: Final Count

Guen, I will be coming unaccompanied. If Scotty's significant other does not attend please feel free to seat the two of us at the children's table since it does not sound like there is a need for a singles table. :)

You have done such an incredible job setting this up. Liv

• • •

From: Mary Alice Schneider
To: Olivia MacLearn
Sent: Monday, May 6, 2013 6:55 PM
Subject: RE: Plus One

You got that right about the Agatha Christie move on Rich, but I probably wouldn't do the dim lights thing. I'd just poison his drink or something.

You're also right about bringing a child along. At our age, for goodness sake, how old is a child? Our kids are getting old. Our son has been abusing Viagra for years by way of an example. Says he doesn't need it except for when he's drunk. Let's not even go down that path. Maybe you could take him to your reunion. Just kidding.

Don't even for one minute worry about the "young" issue at a forty-sixth reunion. Everyone will be OLD. And if they don't for some reason look old it will be because they have had everything carved off, sucked out, Botoxed or replaced. They will look like those Japanese figures of horror, the Mujina, the terrifying creatures with a face that has no features. Some of the women at our country club have almost no facial expressions. One whom Amy pointed out to me at the pool has no belly button, just like the gator in Disney's "The Princess and the Frog." Apparently she had a botched post baby tummy repair and they didn't get the navel right. They didn't get it at all. She should have stuck with a one piece, but what do I know.

Be sure to keep track of all the dapper dudes who show up with trophy wives and stories of the joys of fatherhood. They're my faves. I love watching them stride around on the Cape in the summer pushing designer strollers full of designer babies. A mean little voice says their wives are getting it on with the pool boys, exterminators, renovators (pick one or more or add one of your own). It's miraculous what men believe about themselves as they age. Women, at least, if they're with younger guys, have few delusions about what the guys see in them. A very wealthy divorcee friend tells me that young guys are better than any exercise class she has ever taken.

The general practicality of women reminds me of that scene in "Romeo and Juliet" when she asks him how he got into the garden. He says "With love's light wings did I o'erperch these walls, for stony limits cannot hold love out," and she says, referring to her dad and uncles "If they do see thee they will murder thee." I used to use this as an example to the kids of how boys are really much more romantic creatures than girls, or perhaps more delusional. Again, pick one.

I'm not too worried that you will take a stupidly romantic route on this reunion. You're SO driving this bus. Just stay in that seat and do what you want. You've got your health and your looks, your sense of humor is intact and you don't need a man to take care of you. If anyone tries to show you something you've never seen before, you can donate it to science.

Ranting as always and still got your back,

Malice

• • •

From: Rich Stapley
To: Olivia Walker MacLearn
Sent: Monday, May 6, 2013 7:34 PM
Subject: Ink themselves…

The Shakespeare quotation is done well, Olivia. Should have known that someone with a Shakespearean name could speak Renaissance. Tattoo removal is no fun, so thanks for the favor. And, sorry I sent you shrieking into the night. You warned me to leave well-enough alone.

I hope we can meet over wine (if the prospect ruins your vision of the reunion, I can stay home). And I certainly don't mind deeper topics, but maybe the less said of the me of 46 years ago, the better. Surely, life experience and thinking about time and what's in store would make for better conversation — as would just sharing a meal and a walk with people we haven't seen, but who meant a lot to us.

We should meet as friends and ex-lovers, not just civil but connected by the intensity of how people live when they're the age of Romeo and Viola and all those other lovers, star-crossed and starry-eyed. Please not frenemies, which sounds like something for the tent of the class of 2003 (we're not overlapping their reunion, are we? If we are, I suppose Scotty could cruise by looking for a trophy wife. Well, the class of 1983's tent maybe).

For me, it would be a chance to talk to you and other friends about what more than 40 years has made us into, how we're different, and what we want to do with the-probably-no-more-than 20 years we have left to enjoy most of our faculties. I'm no Imogen Cunningham (book of portraits she started taking at age 90) or Manoel de Oliveira (more than 100 and still making movies) — by my late 80s, there won't be much left of me.

Maybe I'm minimizing the hurt I caused, but I still imagine conversations with you and Scotty and others that I can have with only a handful of people. So, I'll scare up a bottle of California Merlot to bring, just don't break it over my head while christening me the USS Bozo.

Rich

• • •

From: Thomas Alexander Scott
To: Olivia Walker MacLearn
Sent: Monday, May 6, 2013 9:23 PM
Subject: RE: Plus One

Lone Walker,

So the other night I reconvened a plea bargain session with my rent-and-sex sharer and promised more than I could ever actually deliver if she would accompany me to the reunion. Her reply: "I would be glad to have a whole body photo taken and a life-size cardboard cutout made for you to take to your precious reunion so you can just move it into place beside you as you mingle — since that is all I would be doing if I went! Better yet, I will purchase a life-size cardboard cutout of the bosomy model Kate Upton and paste a picture of my face over hers so that your college cronies will drool over their "vert gallant" classmate. Without pausing to think (a nasty vice of mine), I replied that the sex would be about the same either way. She then suggested that I go off and have intercourse with myself, although she said it much more succinctly. And the evening deteriorated from there.

So here are my suggestions for both me and you, us non-plussers:

We contact a local modeling agency near Morrison and hire glamorous escorts as fake friends. Nobody will notice because reunions are full of fake friends anyway.

You go with Rich and I will contract with a different kind of escort service and hire a date, instructing her to dress appropriately for the "Least Fabric Worn to a Reunion" prize.

You go with me and let everybody wonder if we are reunited best buds or just two desperately alone classmates who hooked up to save face.

I take a llama and let everybody guess what the hell that means.

Actually, I kind of like the first half of number three. Ahem, ahem, dear lady, (this is me bowing from the waist swishing my feathered hat off in my right hand) could I have the honor of your presence at the upcoming gala at the palace? Seriously, I would like to be with you that evening in whatever capacity you or anyone else want to name it. If Rich offers and you decide to accept his offer, I would of course understand.

But I must warn you how sticky it is to slow dance with a former lover whose busted nose and lip are bleeding profusely.

At your beck and call,

Scotty
Thomas Alexander Scott

• • •

From: Olivia Walker MacLearn
To: Mary Alice Schneider
Sent: Monday, May 6, 2013 10:43 PM
Subject: RE: RE: Plus One

Well, M, I am not sure whether to laugh or cry after reading
your email! Love the belly-button story. I've heard a few post-
fix horror stories, mostly concerning Botox, and one woman,
who had her breasts lifted only to lose sensation in both. Her
husband is ecstatic, but she feels like a vegetarian dining
nightly at a renowned steakhouse.

However, this talk of everyone being OLD is depressing! I
don't feel old when we hang out, and certainly not when I read
Scotty's cheeky emails. Hell, M, if your description of my college reunion crowd is correct, if everyone's going to look either
like Grandpa and Grandma Moses or a Japanese horror figure,
I don't know if I even want to attend. Although I did write Glen
to tell her to seat Scotty and me together (assuming his current
live-in keeps to her no-reunion stand) at the children's table, so
maybe I'll just buy a walker and go anyway. Liv

• • •

From: Olivia Walker MacLearn
To: Thomas Alexander Scott
Sent: Monday, May 6, 2013 11:12 PM
Subject: One plus one...

So, Scotty, how was the writing class? Did you wow them? Do
you teach at other universities often or are the home professors
too annoyed when their students ask if you can just stay on?

I just reread your Darth Liv email from Sunday. I'm so glad my blushing still provides added amusement. Sadly I do not remember a real strip poker game t'ween thee and me from ye olde college days, but I do remember your voice. I would have liked to be a fly on the wall when you crawled into bed singing "Buh, Buh, Buh, Baby..."

Okay maybe not a fly. Ewww. Gross. But you did create an image that stayed with me.

By the way I emailed Guen, even before your gallant offer to accompany me. Cheeky, aren't I? (I would be delighted to plus one with you by the way, although doubling with twin llamas is tempting.) Actually I told Guen that I was coming alone, and that unless your significant other changed her mind, she could seat the two of us together at the children's table. (I wonder if I should clarify about the table. People take my jokes seriously way to often.)

Drive safely on your way home. Tomorrow? Wednesday? I am feeling oddly sad tonight, without identifiable reason. Oh well, as Annie sings: the sun will come out tomorrow! But tonight would be a good night to hide in a couple strong arms. Liv

● ● ●

From: Olivia Walker MacLearn
To: Richard Stapley
Sent: Tuesday, May 07, 2013 11:33 AM
Subject: Reboot

I have begun to reflect on how I have communicated with you over the past weeks, and why. Partly this is in reaction to your last email, which felt more "real" than our communication has seemed at times, but partly the reflection beastie has been rearing its impudent head ever since Scotty asked me if I would be willing/able to tell him why I disappeared from his life after graduation. I guess in a way I left him as abruptly as you left me.

Most friendships, even the very close ones naturally fade a bit after high school, college, job or marriage changes, moves, etc.. But it is a natural movement away from talking every day, to a couple times a week, to long phone calls once a month, to annual Christmas letters. That is not what happened with Scotty or with my other Morrison friends. The years after we ended our relationship were a difficult, confusing, life altering time for me, and unfortunately when I left Morrison, I shut out most of the people I should have clung to. I simply disappeared. No forwarding address, no Christmas card, no birthday flowers. Only Mary Alice remained in my life.

When I heard from you some weeks ago, I was at the end of a time that should not be in any way thought of as lonely or isolated. I enjoy wonderful family times with Holly and my son-in-law and granddaughters. I have a remarkably decent relationship with Colton as long as we avoid talking about Obama, guns, immigration policy, taxes, well, you get the picture. My dad is still alive and rocking it at a posh assisted living community in the Hamptons. I see him for lunch now and then, and since I no longer live to annoy him, our time is mostly always good. And I have many CT friends and a "second family" with Mary Alice, Eddie, and their kids and grandkids.

However, these past dozen or so years have been lonely when I close the door and turn out the lights, as so many singers croon. So I think for a brief time, after the initial panic of hearing from you eased, at a sub-conscious level I began to envision a relationship mulligan, and when the spark of talking with you did not flash into a rip roaring campfire, my inner teenage instincts took over.

That said, for now I suggest rather than a relationship mulligan that we declare an email mulligan. And I propose that we share your bottle of California Merlot simply as two ex-lovers, because we were that, whatever lover means in reference to two people as young as we were at the time. For me it would be impossible to meet as friends because of the way we ended. Perhaps we will become friends. I think I might like that, but only time will tell.

And finally, Scotty needed full disclosure, as Mary Alice calls it. Facing my fears and sharing the truth of those post-college years with him was as much a gift to myself as it was to my dear friend. Whether you and I ever talk about that time, about the why and where of my disappearance, is debatable. I suppose, like the question of our friendship, that too remains to be decided. Liv

• • •

From: Rich Stapley
To: Olivia Walker MacLearn
Sent: Tuesday, May 07, 2013 7:30 PM
Subject: Mulligans

Liv, only in the past day or two did I understand that your retreat from Morrison friends might have been a result of my breaking up with you. I'm so sorry. I can still remember how my chest felt leading up to telling you — some combination of being about to burst and being in a vice. I was in such haste to get rid of the feeling that I didn't figure out a way to talk to you about what was going on. I'm sorry it was unbearable, and I'm glad that Mary Alice has stayed close to you.

Pause, chagrin, bow slightly, reach out to touch you at the top of your left arm — I'll take the mulligan. If you want, give me a day or so, and I'll start.

The bottle of Merlot may already be breathing. Inhale. Exhale.
Rich

• • •

From: Mary Alice Schneider
To: Olivia MacLearn
Sent: Tuesday, May 7, 2013 10:59 PM
Subject: Old…

I like the walker idea. You can toss it away about halfway through and claim to have been cured, then convince others to join your newly founded religion. Just a thought.

Seriously, you don't feel old? I don't exactly think old, but I definitely feel it and so does Eddie. We still accomplish a lot, but everything we do seems to take longer than it did before and to hurt more. We look old too. Sometimes when we walk past a shop window I see my mother and his father reflected in the glass. Creepy. It's especially so because the longevity in my family comes from my father's side and I'm hoping to have inherited some of it.

Then again, I do the work of a thirty year old, taking care of two little ones for forty plus hours a week. Maybe that's the source of the "old" feeling. All the women I hang out with are young enough to be my daughters and want me to adopt them. They like the idea of knowing their "mother" would be in charge of their kids. Also I cook and fold laundry.

As for Eddie, he's the only guy in our neighborhood who does his own lawn and garden work. His hard work generates one of the oddest phenomena we've seen, the well dressed migrant tomato pickers, neighbors all, who arrive nightly on the bus from Boston (a nasty hour plus ride) and stop by our garden to pick some fresh tomatoes on their way home to dinner. One night he spotted three at once, their jackets draped over brief cases while they picked their way through the plants in their wing tips. He wants to send a photo to United Farm Workers, but I've discouraged him. Massachusetts has a freaky enough reputation already.

OK, so maybe we've not quite reached the fossil category, but it can't be too far away. We're concentrating on keeping our minds sharp, he with his think tank by day and his Sudokus by night and I with endless books and crossword puzzles.

Based on what you've found out, Scotty would be your best bet for a reunion partner, whatever that turns out to mean — this from a woman who's had only one meaningful relationship. It's a good thing I stay out of the advice column business, but I can't resist meddling in your life. Malice

• • •

From: Olivia Walker MacLearn
To: Mary Alice Schneider
Sent: Wednesday, May 08, 2013 9:19 AM
Subject: Walker's walker…

M, I wanted to make sure I had the correct name for what I know as The Telephone Game and I've discovered that it is also called Chinese Whispers. (Be patient. I will get to the point shortly.)

I remember playing Chinese Whispers at Brownies. One person starts by whispering a simple statement to the person to the right. That continues around the circle until the final person says it out loud. The idea is to see how much "factual" information changes when passed from one person to the next. So here is Walker's walker, Chinese Whisper version:

"OMG, Jane! Don't look now, but Walker has a walker!"

"Hey, Ralph, Marcie said to avoid Walker unless you want Bertha to get jealous. She apparently has turned into quite the sweet talker."

"Susie, did you hear about Walker? Jane told me all she talks about is birders. And Marcie is pretty sure that Walker dates a street hawker. Not sure what that is, but it sounds creepy."

"Rich, I don't want to alarm you, but Walker is here and Ralph says she is creepy and is stalking someone. Didn't you two date? Should we call the police and tell them Walker is a stalker?"

At that moment I will toss my walker into the air and yell: "Surprise!" Sadly, given the slight edge the Republicans had in our class, and the current evolution of that party, half the crowd will be packing heat and I'm probably toast.

Off to the bank, the cleaners, and the grocery store. Ah, life in the fast lane. Walker

• • •

From: Mary Alice Schneider
To: Olivia MacLearn
Sent: Wednesday, May 8, 2013 10:12 PM
Subject: RE: Walker's walker...

Given the way my brain is working today, this old brownies game makes perfect sense. Today was a "no relief" day, with the baby refusing a morning nap and the pre-schooler home before the baby's far too short afternoon snooze that ended in a nightmare that put her in a snit for the rest of the afternoon. She doesn't really have language yet, but we're assuming she had a nightmare.

I tried a nice long walk with the two of them in the double Bob stroller, but a storm came sneaking in over the bay and we got back just in time to miss the deluge. Thank goodness for the old porte cochere, where we took shelter. I couldn't have reached the barn in time.

Tomorrow promises to be even crazier and longer, with Amy at a late faculty meeting. That means I'll have to entertain the girls for an hour more than usual and somehow I seem, as the academic year wanes, to be running out of ideas. Perhaps we can go shopping. It's that or the garden center, always a fun trip. Smelling gardenias is better than an hour (i.e. 50 minutes) with the shrink.

Speaking of shopping, what are you packing for the big event?? Even though everything you possess is unknown to your old classmates, that shouldn't stop you from getting a load of new stuff for the trip. You have a good eye for shoes, so I feel sure you'll wow them with your choices. Shoes and expensive but simple jewelry will set off anything else you find. You'd almost think I know what I'm talking about, but I don't. I'm just quoting my cousin who routinely sets me straight about my fashion faux pas.

One last delightful tidbit. Josie has a French class at her preschool with a teacher who speaks with a broad Boston accent that makes a simple "Bonjour" an absolute hoot.

Malice

• • •

From: Thomas Alexander Scott
To: Olivia Walker MacLearn
Sent: Thursday, May 09, 2013 12:07 AM
Subject: RE: One plus one…

My Dear Walker,

Of course I wowed them. The whole idea in a panel discussion is to somehow stand out from the other "contestants," who were all colleagues and friends of mine. So the competition is friendly and strange. We wind up saying the most outrageous things to try to top each other and we play to the egos of the students, trying to out-jargon each other and say things that make no sense but sound profound. It's fun messing with their minds. Then all of us panelists hit the bar later in the evening and total the scores. Of course most Hampton Inns don't have bars (their only flaw, but the best bed in moteldom), so we convened at the Hilton where the endowed professors were staying. Eavesdropping on a conversation between two guys at the bar, I heard one say in response to the question whether or not he was married that he had had a "starter marriage" like a starter house. I loved that description! I think I had three starter marriages! What do you think, Liv? Do you think there is a chance that I might actually marry someone and stick with them "till death do us part?"

I loved your comment about being seated at the "children's table" at the reunion. If people don't understand your humor, f**k 'em. Just keep dishing out the humor you observe and laugh even harder at those who don't understand it. Never try to temper your thoughts or your wit; we have dumbed-down life enough as it is.

I called in sick for classes today and drove instead with a teaching buddy of mine across from Houston to Shiner, Texas, where they bottle the incredible Shiner Bock Beer. Free samples in the tasting room lasted well on into the afternoon and we had to stop at a barbecue joint and a taco stand to get enough absorbent food in our bellies to drive home legally to Fort Worth. It was a little slice of Texas heaven, a state with too many roughnecks and rednecks but also with a plethora of fabulous honky-tonks and roadhouses.

So I am back home tonight, tired and a little tipsy, and my Significant Other is in Oklahoma at a writer's conference. She is a biographical researcher and author and is working on a definitive encyclopedia of Texas songwriters. She has interviewed Willie Nelson, Jack Ely, Jerry Jeff Walker (any relation?) among others. She writes excellently, a master of the language, and always does her homework thoroughly. I take much inspiration from her. I know that she and I have a problem with verbal volatility, but I do respect her craft and enjoy her company when we aren't at each other's throats. I'm not sure if you would like her or not (you seldom liked any of the girls I dated if you will remember), since she is excessively straightforward. But she knows what she wants out of life — which is amazing to me.

So I settle onto the floor in front of my couch with a goodnight Scotch and wish that I had you to lean back between my knees and against my chest like we used to do out under the trees at Morrison or when I would slip past the dorm mothers and into your room and we would talk for hours in that position. We might try that at the reunion — if we can find someone to help us get up afterward!

Arms always open for you,

Scotty
Thomas Alexander Scott

• • •

From: Olivia Walker MacLearn
To: Mary Alice Schneider
Sent: Thursday, May 09, 2013 9:53 AM
Subject: reflection

Oh, M, what a sleepless, angst-filled night I've had!

On my way to bed I checked email on my iPad because I knew Scotty was driving home from a presentation in another part of the state. His email was waiting. He was home safe and sound and what he wrote was regular Scotty banter. And the last paragraph was all stuff he has written here and there already. About how I always would "lean back between (his) knees and against (his) chest," and how we would talk that way for hours.

But sitting there in the darkness of my bedroom, reading that paragraph and the valediction, his words gave me chills. It was as if someone smacked me upside the head and I finally saw the truer picture of those Morrison years.

What Scotty describes is real. It is how the two of us were from midway through our freshman year until that day three plus years later, when I drove away from the campus and his life. He and I never had sex and yet we were much more intimate than sex often was in those hormone driven years.

And more frightening than that comprehension is this: whereas the idea of seeing Rich again seems intriguing, Scotty feels like going home.

So I ask you, M, who really left whom in my relationship with Rich? Or more accurately, was I ever wholly there? Very little sleep and two cups of coffee is not doing it so I may try a nap. Liv

• • •

From: Olivia Walker MacLearn
To: Thomas Alexander Scott
Sent: Thursday, May 09, 2013 10:46 AM
Subject: Your email…

Scotty, I don't know what to write; just that I have to. I am struggling with all sorts of overwhelming memories and feelings and suddenly, after all these years of blaming Rich for leaving me, I am not sure if I was ever really his to leave.

Please don't panic! I'm truly, honestly, absolutely not suggesting anything about the us of today, or saying that we were ever more than best buds, only that the light bulb flashed and I finally got it — whatever it was that we were, the "us" of you and me at Morrison was far more meaningful than the "us" of Rich and me ever was. And because of that, and for all the years of anger, I owe Rich an apology. (And perhaps the truth about Holly?)

Anyway, I had to write quickly, before taking time to figure out what to say or even if I should say anything, because as you know, my inclination is to flee rather than upset those about whom I care. And as I've come to understand in the past couple months, that strategy didn't work out too well for all involved. Liv

• • •

From: Mary Alice Schneider
To: Olivia MacLearn
Sent: Thursday, May 09, 2013 8:20 PM
Subject: RE: Reflecting

Did I not say fairly recently that Scotty might be the one for some reunion carnality? What are you waiting for? Wave your wand, turn Rich into a frog or some other less desirable beast, and get together with Scotty. You are long overdue.

Malice

• • •

From: Olivia Walker MacLearn
To: Mary Alice Schneider
Sent: Thursday, May 09, 2013 8:58 PM
Subject: Carnality

Oh, M, have you ever considered volunteering on a crisis hot-line? You seem very adept at sweeping me at the knees when I am running about in circles. WACK! Plop! Deep breath! Gee, the sky is not falling after all. Guess I might as well calm down and smell the roses.

To be fair, while you did mention getting together with Scotty, I thought you meant for a drink or to help each other figure out how to get those damn plastic nametags to stay on. You were never clear that you meant carnality.

Speaking of which, I rather like your choice of words. Definitely not an overused word. Does not remind me of a Madonna, Taylor Swift, or Justin Bieber song. And it kind of fits our generation too: "Damn it all, Bertha Mae, either you put out some carnality, or I will be forced to get it elsewhere!"

However, great word choice aside, there are some rather gigantic obstacles stacking the deck against that ever happening: Scotty has a live-in relationship with a woman who sounds intelligent and accomplished, and who is probably younger and thinner by a decade or so than I am. Add to that the fact that Scotty and I never had sex, oops I mean carnal activity. That is quite relevant because the whole idea of rounding the bases in a brand new ball park is terrifying!

After all, I have not had much experience with start up sex since I climbed over the crest of the hill. Other than Rich and Ian, thc only sex I've had began in a wine daze following a pity party with my friend Hunter the night after his wife left him. I'd spent two hours that evening looking through old photos with Ian at Happy Haven only to have him gaze across the pile of photos and ask me if we'd met before. Hunter and I were both morose and the sweet release of sex was much needed, but the journey there quite forgettable, and not just because of the wine.

I am sure you remember that Hunter and I did continue seeing each other for a brief time. It was good to have a physical relationship, but it was unfulfilling. I blamed it on our bad start thanks to the wine daze — that is Hunter assumed I naturally appeared half asleep during sex, and therefore made no effort to step up his game, and I was too polite to offer him a roadmap. Liv

• • •

From: Rich Stapley
To: Olivia Walker MacLearn
Sent: Thursday, May 09, 2013 10:22 PM
Subject: Email mulligan…

Olivia, this note may prove that looking before one leaps doesn't necessarily make things better. Ever since your offer of an email mulligan, I've been thinking about you and about how to begin this do-over and the Muse has been silent as the tomb. Notice the clichés. It's time to grab the bull by the horns, fish or cut bait, speak or forever hold my peace (shoot or forever hold my piece), sink or swim, be or not be. Can you tell I'm putting things off? So…

"Remembering Olivia Walker. What was your first impression?"

"I noticed her at freshman orientation. Who wouldn't have noticed her? Hair in Sephardic disarray – what a poet might have observed as a sweet disorder in her dress. A nonchalance as she suggested that people might want to line up there or sign in here or pick up a badge and write their first names in as large a print as possible. Nothing directive, but all of us got the drill, as if we were sheep and she were some sort of magical shepherd commanding us by three-note runs on a Pan flute. Smiling at everyone, but more than that, making eye contact as if to say, 'You're why I came to this school.' And I said to myself, 'Rich, you're in college now. You'll know people like her. THIS is why you came more than half way across the country. There aren't people like her at Arizona State.'"

"Okay, Rich. Did you talk to her?"

"Well, not at that freshman picnic, except to observe, sort of to her, but not directly so that if she didn't respond, I wouldn't be crushed like a bug on life's rough pavement, 'How do people breathe in this humidity?' Just as I said it though, the guy who was talking to her said something witty, and she laughed. My question hung in the air, buoyed by that very humidity, then fell to Earth without making a sound. If a cliché about the weather falls in a forest and no one hears it, does it count against the speaker?"

"Did weeks pass before you had a chance to talk about the weather again with her?"

"Actually, I lucked out. We were in the same Intro to Science class (along with almost a hundred others), and I contrived to sit behind her. At the end of the class I asked her if she was good at science, and if so, if I could look over her shoulder. She laughed and I heard the sublime: earthy and unattainable in the same moment. Damn, that sweet disorder again, but this time metaphysical, slipping away, making further conversation impossible. I was hooked."

Rich, but poor in speech

• • •

From: Olivia Walker MacLearn
To: Richard Stapley
Sent: Thursday, May 09, 2013 11:18 PM
Subject: RE: Email mulligan…

Not poor in speech at all, Rich. Those were very sweetly written memories. I confess to not remembering the picnic all that much. I mostly remember being terrified of the tea. Going to tea with my family was always so formal and I was afraid I would tip my cup or drop a spoon or sneeze or sit improperly or trip or…

I do remember when I first noticed you. It was the first week of junior year, and you were manning a booth in favor of some cause. You were so intensely involved in explaining the issues to anyone who walked near the table. Also you were incredibly cute. Sadly, I think the second fact influenced my infatuation as much or more than the first. Liv

• • •

From: Guendaline Field
To: Olivia Walker MacLearn
Sent: Friday, May 10, 2013 8:20 AM
Subject: Last Minute Prep

In keeping with tradition I have been putting together a portfolio of information on each attendee of the reunion to hand out before the dinner on Saturday night. Most of the class has unloaded all sorts of information on me during our email exchanges but you have been very quiet and when not quiet, terse. Now that you have decided to attend I would like to include some information on you. Frankly, I think your write-up might be the one everyone rushes to first. You are after all the mystery alumnus.

Best way to do this, I think, is to just hit you with direct questions. You can answer what you think is appropriate and ignore the rest. Are you married? If so, tell me something about your husband. While you have said you were at some point a stay at home Mom my internet search finds you at events that would usually indicate a career outside the home. Did you have a career? If so what kind of work did you do? (With all your secrecy I should ask if you were in covert operations. Holly does live in the D.C. area!!) Speaking of Holly, her age would indicate you married immediately after college. That would mean you could have been married for over 45 years. Congratulations. Now the big question: Why did you cut us all out? And, more importantly, why have you decided to let us back in? Why do you think now is the time to associate? Did the contacts from old friends just make things look differently? Did the "water under the bridge" observation simply indicate that you are weary of whatever has distanced you from so many friends for so long? OMG, typing this it just occurred to me that Holly could be Rich's daughter. I won't ask!

• • •

From: Olivia MacLearn
To: Guendaline Field
Sent: Friday, May 10, 2013 12:02 PM
Subject: RE: Last Minute Prep

Oh, Guen, I remember now how you would sometimes just cut to the chase when we were all ignoring the elephant in the room, as the saying now goes.

Information okay to share in your "portfolio:" I left for Europe immediately after graduation and returned that November to spend time with a good friend, Mary Alice, on the Cape. When she married and moved to Boston, where her husband was in graduate school, I rented their house. The Cape is where I met and married Ian MacLearn, a wonderful man, whose beautiful ancestral home is in Scotland. His big heart was firmly rooted in the US, where he was CEO of a very effective charitable foundation. Although I was a stay at home mom, I did help Ian with various charitable events, and I am still involved with numerous charities.

Our daughter Holly grew up on the Cape and after college and grad school she moved to the nation's capital. (Talk about two different environments!) She still lives there with her husband and daughters. After Holly moved to DC, Ian and I bought a winter home in Westport, CT, and enjoyed our Cape home in gentler weather.

Ian became ill about a dozen or so years before his death in 2011, and when we could no longer travel, we sold the house on the Cape. Westport is now my home year round.

Non-Portfolio information for your eyes only: Your unasked question will go unanswered for now, at least directly. I suppose anyone who searches for my information on Google can look at Holly's age and the date of my marriage to Ian and come to their own conclusions. Hopefully that will not be a major discussion topic during the weekend, at least not beyond our group.

I'll write more soon! As I write this I'm smiling at how little we've all changed! (Well, inside at least...) Liv

• • •

From: Guendaline Field
To: Olivia Walker MacLearn
Sent: Friday, May 10, 2013 4:47 PM
Subject: RE: RE: Last Minute Prep

Liv, thanks for the fast response. It is amazing how things seem always to lump at the end of a project no matter how much one tries to pre-plan and organize.

Let me encourage you not to think that people are researching or otherwise seeking information about you. I am the only fanatic in the bunch. Once I get on a trail I am compulsive. The only comments I have heard about you relate to joy in the prospect of seeing you again. There have been a couple of people who expressed relief that you turned up - they had worried that something had happened to you that was unpleasant. Now we will all know that everything has been good. No, not just good, it appears that life, for the most part, has been great for you. Guen

• • •

From: Mary Alice Schneider
To: Olivia MacLearn
Sent: Friday, May 10, 2013 5:53 PM
Subject: your sex life

They'd kick me off a hot line right away for my sinful combination of naughty suggestions and extravagant vocabulary. However, I stand by my advice about you and Scotty. I think this is a circle that needs to be closed. The two of you have been approaching this point for what, about 40 plus years? It's time to get on with it. Then it can be over if necessary. It just needs to happen. If he has a mad case of lifelong (and how long is that on our timelines?) loyalty to his live in lady, then you two can give it a miss, but I'm guessing he is as ready as you are for this eventuality. It's just one weekend. Maybe it will turn into more, but if it doesn't, who cares at this point?

I can still remember walking on a little hill over the harbor with a boy from our high school class on a moonlit summer night (we'd wandered away from a yacht club teen party). He stood there, put his arms around me and kissed me on the lips. That was all and it was enough for me, a perfect gem of a moment that I still remember as if it happened last summer. We never dated. I began dating Eddie and filed away the moment with Ben for future consideration. Maybe this time with Scotty will be a similar moment for you, at a lot more mature level with the sense of "time's winged chariot hurrying near," which Ben and I had never heard of back then. I also expect you two to get a room, since what I imagine you have planned might not work on a small hill above a harbor.

Still planning your sex life,

Malice

• • •

From: Olivia Walker MacLearn
To: Thomas Alexander Scott
Sent: Saturday, May 11, 2013 9:36 PM
Subject: RE: One plus one…

Scotty, I just reread my last email to you. Seriously, I should never write to you late at night. So let me try to clarify, and if needed to rectify.

The picture your words painted of you sitting in front of your couch with your goodnight scotch was more effective than hours of foreplay. Gotta admit that first, because if I try to say only my brain was responsible for my last email, well it just would not ring true. However, I know you are involved with someone, and I should not have reacted that way - I could plead the fifth, but since I only drink wine, maybe better just to say guilty as charged, and commit to repent and do better next time.

That confessed, the crux of what I was trying to say in my frantic late-night response was that almost two years before I began to date Rich and then continuing without change after I was pinned to him, you were the person I shared my thoughts with, my dreams with, fears, excitement, on and on. I did with Rich too, of course, but somehow it was different.

All those hours you and I spent talking, sitting together in ways I never thought to label intimate were indeed exactly that. And I was so clueless to how it might have made him feel, that I would babble on and on about "Scotty said this," and "Scotty said that." So while I do not hold Rich blameless for his involvement with Susan while still with me, I wonder if I too was involved, just too adolescent to recognize anything outside of sex as a relationship and a serious hindrance to having a healthy bond with Rich.

Does that make any sense? I hope so because I seem to be having a hard time expressing what I mean and the reunion is rushing toward us and if I've ruined the chance to see you without you feeling a need to hide, well that would be sad indeed. Liv

• • •

From: Olivia Walker MacLearn
To: Thomas Alexander Scott
Sent: Sunday, May 12, 2013 2:48 PM
Subject: One last babble…

Scotty, I need to say one more thing.

You are right that I seldom liked the girls you dated. I was like one of those fathers who declare that none of the miscreants his daughter brings home are good enough. Thankfully you paid not one whit of attention to my opinion about any of them, so at least I don't feel guilty for spoiling your dating life – cause I didn't.

Anyway, should your current live-in decide to come to the reunion after all, I promise to welcome her warmly with no inkling of disapproval. (You might want to tell me her name, live-in sounds more like an au pair than a significant other!)

Okay, no more emails for now. I hope you are off somewhere celebrating mothers, or if not that, then celebrating life in general. Liv

• • •

From: Rich Stapley
To: Olivia Walker MacLearn
Sent: Sunday, May 12, 2013 3:31 PM
Subject: Mother's Day

Liv, I hope you're with Holly so she can shower you with gratitude and her kids can take you for Nana Walks, deep into the woods.

"Grandma, grandma, what was it like before there was dirt? Were you scared of dinosaurs? What about Elvis - were your parents scandalized?"

Cheers,

Rich

• • •

From: Olivia Walker MacLearn
To: Richard Stapley
Sent: Sunday, May 12, 2013 3:40 PM
Subject: RE: Mother's Day

I get Mother's Day every other year, and Holly and family are with his mom in Florida this year. And even if I were there, neither granddaughter has been young enough for "nana walks" for some time.

Mary, the older of the two, will be applying to college in five short months. She is an enthusiastic young woman. Her sister Jane, who is just turning fifteen, is quieter and reminds me every now and then of her grandfather. Liv

• • •

From: Olivia Walker MacLearn
To: Mary Alice Schneider
Sent: Sunday, May 12, 2013 6:26 PM
Subject: DNA

How was your day? Did you have breakfast in bed and did Eddie fetch your slippers and cater to your every whim? This is Holly's mother-in-law's year for having the kids visit (she is still in Ft Lauderdale) so I decided to drive up to the residences where Ian spent his final years, with flowers for any moms without visitors. Going there always pulls me down, but feels so worth the pain.

And of course everywhere I went I heard the greeting "Happy Mother's Day!" And I would pause just a moment before returning the greeting because how does one know if another is a mother? By that age motherhood cannot be identified by looking tired and disheveled. And I wondered if any of those who looked sad at the greeting were so because they were not moms and were regretting lost opportunities. (Of course it also might just have been because lunch was too cold or too hot or too bland or too spicy.)

That of course got me to thinking about your original idea about Rich not having grandchildren – blaming it on a defect in Susan. But what if the real blame is with me for not telling Rich he had a daughter, a young woman who then had two beautiful daughters — to whom he is, technically at least, a grandfather. Might they have had a relationship? Not in lieu of Ian but in addition?

Which of course took me down the philosophical road to that eternal question: how important is the contribution of an egg or sperm in the designation of parenthood? I think about Baby Richard and Baby Jessica, two court cases and decisions that haunted me those many years ago when they were in the news. I remember seeing both children torn from their adoptive parents' arms, sobbing, terrified, as they were returned to their "birth parents."

I always felt the decisions were wrong, at least for the children. But were they? Did the "real" parents have a claim that outweighed the trauma of removing children from the parents they each had known since birth? Is there some inherent connection that is biological?

Holly and I have been talking about this over the past few weeks, more so the past couple days. She remains completely comfortable with me either telling or not telling Rich about her, as long as I make it perfectly clear to Rich, should I tell him, that she does not wish to have any contact and that she expects him to honor that for her and for her daughters. Both of her girls know that Ian was not Holly's birth father so there is little concern about them being upset, but Holly believes that deciding to know more than he exists is a decision for them to make when they are adults.

Holly amazes me! And I sometimes swear that you were not just her godmother but that some of your DNA rubbed off on her, because Holly has your sensible approach to issues that put me into a tizzy! (Or might that be the part of her that is Rich's DNA?)

I started this whole reunion thing with a simple no-strings-attached adolescent-like desire for a do-over of a love affair gone wrong; but as I pull further away from any thought of reuniting with Rich in that way, I feel a sadness settling in for what he missed and is still missing.

To tell or not to tell; that is the question. Whether 'tis nobler… Holly says to just do what feels right to me. Problem is that changes with the direction and speed of the spring breezes. Liv

• • •

From: Thomas Alexander Scott
To: Olivia Walker MacLearn
Sent: Monday, May 13, 2013 1:21 AM
Subject: RE: one final babble…

Damn, Walker, it's fun getting emails from you!

The silence you have heard has not been me panicking, I
promise. It had some to do with course outline deadlines for
summer semester. I was so far behind that I grounded myself
from reading emails until the outlines were finished.

But mostly it was due to a burst radiator hose on a busy
Oklahoma interstate, an excessively irate Irish female, the
need to calm her down or at least contain her fury when the
closest garage didn't have the right part, and a night spent in
a "Bates Motel" reserved usually for alimony-poor truckers,
the most desperately sleep-deprived salesmen, and one or two
past-their-prime prostitutes. The fact that she refused to lie
down on the bed and insisted on sleeping slumped over the
splintery desk in a rickety chair did nothing for her in the
way of mood improvement the next morning. So I guess it
was panic, which usually happens when her writing routine is
interrupted. But it was her panic, not mine.

I confess that I did peek at your first email just before leaving
to go rescue the deranged damsel. It was all I could do to keep
from dashing off the first words that came to my brain (via
some other body parts) which would not have been helpful to
either of us. So I decided to do what you said you needed not
to do before writing: I decided to think this through. Then,
when I returned with Medusa in tow, there were more emails
from you, each trying to explain the last. I was tempted to wait

a few more days to see what you would say next! Of course now my problem is where to begin with my response.

First of all, HELL YES, what you and I had at Morrison was more meaningful than what you and Rich had! What we had was real, unencumbered by fears and expectations, fearless in fact! While I believe with all my heart what I have just said, I will confess to some modicum of jealousy against Rich – then and now. He and I became friends, but honestly my smile was forced and plastered on each time he described the hot nasties that the two of you enjoyed. (Oh yes, describe them he did, in vivid detail; of course, so did you! His renderings made me uneasy; yours made me...well, if anything had happened afterward, you could have described them as foreplay!) So I loved what we had...and I was envious of what he had. But I suppressed that because my number one goal in life was your happiness, which at that time meant Rich.

Secondly, if you typically write emails that hot late at night, I may restrict you to writing only after midnight. Please don't repent!

Thirdly, now you are looking for some personal failing of your own, some grievous sin you committed that caused the Rich-Liv relationship to disintegrate in the heat of a fawning freshman flirt?? WE were a "serious hindrance" to you having a healthy bond with Rich?? I don't buy that, except possibly that our relationship shed light on what was missing with Rich or, better yet, what was missing *in* Rich. No matter how you hold it up to the light, there is no way you can see that breakup as in any way your fault. Repeat after me: "Hello, my name is Liv, and I'm a neurotic when it comes to my former boyfriend." Nope, old Extra-curricular Rich bears the whole weight of that failure. So, no "Pass Go! Collect $100 (plus info about an unknown child)!" card for Stapley. In my humble opinion.

Now, dropping my tendency to number ideas, I will plunge without caution into your first late-night email when you begged me not to panic at the emotions you were expressing. You said that you were not suggesting anything about the "us" of today. Maybe you weren't actually saying anything about us today, but I thought I saw fantasies fluttering all around the edges of your words. If my vision was correct, then I need to confess that those same wispy what-ifs have been flitting in and out of my head ever since we reconnected a few weeks ago. I have been batting them away, trying to chalk them up to the same old "greener grass" demon that has stalked me all my life. Me panic? Maybe I should be the one encouraging you not to panic as you read all this. But to be honest panic and flight are smart responses when I come too close. There are too many pieces missing in me to be sure what the final picture will be.

As entertaining as those what-ifs are, it frightens me, Liv, to think of screwing up your life. I know that you are the only person in the world whose feelings and happiness mean more to me than my own. But I guess I don't trust me. Am I capable of happily ever after or am I forever doomed to self-destruction?

I haven't told you much about Wife #2. We were happy, Liv. I really did love her. Hell, I even loved her parents though they were the opposite side to my coin in almost every way. We were happy as clams as long as the future beckoned brightly to us. We even talked about having children someday. No, I'm hedging my words: we tried to have children. That was when the future began to cloud over with a chance of showers, just not baby showers. The early mutual encouragement we shared began to take on hints of blame. "Maybe we are just trying too hard." "Maybe if you drank less." "Maybe if you worked less and tried to relax some." "Maybe if you had a full time teaching or writing job instead of playing fireman. Maybe the toxic smoke has affected you." "Maybe you should get tested." "No one in my family ever had a problem producing babies! Maybe YOU should get tested."

Admittedly, it was a major disappointment. Probably we both should have seen specialists and therapists. But, each one fearing what we might find lurking in the results, we didn't. And the "ever after" part began to shrink in length. And the future became storm-laden. Even though I loved her dearly and I know she loved me the same, we couldn't make it work. Do you hear that, Walker? The Christian world's favorite wedding scripture is "Love bears all things, believes all things, hopes all things, endures all things. Love never ends." But it isn't true. No matter how hard you want it to be. Disappointment can kill love. Every period every month became death knells for our marriage. Every time I left for the firehouse, disappointment grew in her heart. Every time she won another award and agreed to new assignments, it grew in mine. Finally it obscured the love, like kudzu strangling roadside trees, until our love was dry, brittle, dead. And then it caused me to harbor feelings of enmity toward this one whom I deeply loved.

I fear that there is something in me that poisons those close to me. Though I can take that chance with my romantic "temps," it would kill me if that happened to us. You are the only person I have ever been able to love unfailingly. But what if that was only because we didn't see each other for 45 years? Or only because the brevity of "us" didn't give my aversion to stability time to kick in? Or didn't give the poison time to work on you? It scares me, Liv. I want to run to you and run away from you, both at the same time.

No, I won't hide from you at the reunion. Not physically anyway. But I am determined to protect you - from your self-critical tendencies, from faithless Rich, even from me. You know my biggest fear about the reunion? What we had back then was perfect, but can you recoup perfection? Will I somehow disappoint you?

Just so you know, my suite-sweet's name is Darryl Donoghue. She got stuck with a boy's name and frequently raises a toast to Darryl Hannah for paving a feminine road for her moniker. In adulthood she dropped the last three letters and is now known in the literary world as Dar Donoghue, pronounced "dare" and, boy, does that ever fit. You may have seen her name in your local bookstore. Barnes and Noble did a poster last year for her latest book, a biography, "Nancy Todd Lincoln: Ghosts to Bear." But you won't meet her, because she won't be coming to the reunion. She may not even be here by then. With us it is not "what-if," just "how long." Another example of why it is best to keep me

Your Best Bud,

Scotty
Thomas Alexander Scott

• • •

From: Olivia Walker MacLearn
To: Thomas Alexander Scott
Sent: Monday, May 13, 2013 11:57 AM
Subject: Written in the safety of the light of day…

Hey, BB, do you watch NCIS? Love that show! Anyway, the chief coroner is fond of telling stories — some of which have a relevance to the topic at hand and some that do not. You can decide for yourself about the following:

When I was in my early fifties I went solo (Ian was in Scotland) to a party at my parents in the Hamptons and an old high school boyfriend was there. He was "between wives" at the time, a not unusual state for him. Actually over the years, without the least bit of concern for my continuous status as a married woman, he would call or write me during his down time, routine behavior I simply ignored as I was quite content with the concept of marital fidelity. But this particular evening we took a walk on the beach and he offered me his jacket when the air proved a bit too chilly for my skimpy party dress. And perhaps it was a whiff of his cologne embedded in the fabric, or maybe it was the wine working on my won't-power, but when he suggested I come back to his place, I declined with less finality than usual.

I said: "Still no, but since you've proposed that idea so many times, I'll compromise. If you are still stuck on the idea when I'm eighty, I will meet you on the porch at the Hampton Senior Center and you can have your way with me."

We both laughed. And, I swear I did not mean it, yet I think I did. At fifty a fling with an old boyfriend felt possible as far as body image issues, but I was happily married and not interested in sampling from any other buffet. And eighty seemed possible too, because at that point my vision of me at eighty was more Katherine Hepburn than Sophia from "The Golden Girls." But not too many years after that evening I became acquainted with assisted living and nursing home populations thanks to Ian's illness, and now my own mirror keeps announcing the fact that I am not turning into Katherine Hepburn. (The fact that I never did look like KH should have made that obvious from day one but...)

What? Oh I have no "and therefore." Just sharing. Liv

• • •

From: Olivia Walker MacLearn
To: Thomas Alexander Scott
Sent: Monday, May 13, 2013 1:19 PM
Subject: Secondly... (No third happening.)

I am absorbing your email. All levels of it. I just wanted to say that in case my first email seemed flippant. Well, it was flippant.

Be assured though that my reactions are not flippant. Including sadness for your baby bump struggles. Ian and I had our own difficulties with that. Thankfully he viewed Holly as his own, so we were both helped by that.

I wish I could have comforted you during that time in your life. I never had a chance to be your place to come for comfort, as you continuously seemed to be for me. (Were you more evolved?) Liv

• • •

From: Rich Stapley
To: Olivia Walker MacLearn
Sent: Monday, May 13, 2013 6:30 PM
Subject: Legacy

Are you going to convince Mary to apply to Morrison? A family returns to the place where you pushed the boundaries. It's my belief that the school changed more in the four years we were there than in any four years before or since. There was dressing for dinner, formal teas with the housemothers in the girls dorms', no parietal hours (not just none, but unthinkable), freshman hazing, and a political consciousness that was MIA.

Maybe you don't deserve a statue in the quad, but at least a photograph in the gym between the 1967 tennis and basketball teams: "Gaze upon Olivia Walker, all you who pass by: when she arrived, Morrison was ante-bellum; when she left, the campus was anti-war and sex was out of the back seats of cars and into the dorms where it belongs. She did it without ruffling feathers." Rich

• • •

From: Olivia Walker MacLearn
To: Richard Stapley
Sent: Monday, May 13, 2013 9:12 PM
Subject: RE: Legacy

Rich, you must be thinking of Morrison at some later date than when you and I graduated. Did you stay around

Lexington until Susan graduated in 1970? If so you probably did see some drastic change, as I think those years, 1968
through the early '70's, were definitely a time of change —
much of it good: Expansion of woman's rights and opportunities; better access to birth control; a less sheep-like
acceptance of the value of war. Some of it not so good:
The explosion of drug use; an almost paranoid distrust of
government rather than a reasoned distrust of some who
govern; and perhaps for young people too much exposure
to sex – at least the fictional movie version – where there
once was too little.

As to the four years we were there, I don't remember any sex
in the dorms. There was in the frat rooms, sure, and definitely in cars, but not in the girls' dorms. We had housemothers who were some kind of supernatural creatures. I thought
they could see through walls and enter our rooms through
the crevice under the doors. (Although Scotty did occasionally sneak into my room for late night talks. I should ask him
how he managed that!)

Of course, I confess that I was clueless to the fact that one of
the Sigs had a telescope aimed from his room at the men's
dorm behind ours to the windows on the back wing of our
dorm. I only learned of that when I heard one of his frat
brothers commenting at graduation that he was going to miss
stopping by Lou's room for the nightly search for nudity. So,
maybe I was clueless to other stuff as well!

Anti-war? You were for sure. You were against the war from the
start, ahead of your time, not one of the pack. I loved hearing you debate the issue! But was Morrison actively antiwar in
1967? I don't believe it was, rather that it probably changed

after our class graduated. Most likely beginning in 1968, and possibly influenced by the My Lai massacre. But even then at least half of the adult population of the US believed Vietnam was a being fought for an important cause.

Do you remember that horrible dinner when my parents visited and mom was talking about how the US was protecting us all from the communists, and you fearlessly expressed your views about the war? I thought my dad was going to have you tossed out of the restaurant.

Oh and as to legacy, Mary, if she has her way, is so going to follow Holly (Yale '90), Great-Uncle Colt (Yale '66), Great-Granddad Walker (Yale '41), and various other Walker ghosts as a boola-boola bulldog. And if she gets in, I will be a forty minute drive from her. How delightful would that be?

I'm on Metro North, heading back from the city. Grabbed an early dinner with a friend. I do love Manhattan!

Excuse any typos. I'm getting too old to type long emails on the miniscule keyboard of my iPhone! Liv

• • •

From: Mary Alice Schneider
To: Olivia MacLearn
Sent: Monday, May 13, 2013 10:36 PM
Subject: RE: DNA

I don't know where to start. First, kudos for being such a good soul and going to the residences to cheer up the women who understand their plight. When my mother was in such a setting for the last few months of her life, I had a hard time with the whole concept. The worst thing was that her mind had left the building before she entered it and I couldn't get a grip on what she told me when I visited every afternoon. She loved watching TV with her new friends (new ones every day as Eddie defined the situation), but she started transposing the TV plots to people we know. I would go in and learn from her that her friend Kay's daughter had been brutally murdered only to find out from my aunt that it was part of a crime show and Kay's daughter had visited Mom recently.

For as long as I have what are left of my wits, I think I'll concentrate on meddling in your business and trying to referee various conflicts within my own family.

First, about Holly's view of Rich. She's a sensible girl to want to let her daughters decide if they want to meet their biological grandfather some day even though she does not have any desire to connect with Rich. In every way that matters Ian was Holly's dad. Rich simply served as a hapless sperm donor. Holly is probably the best mistake he ever made. Perhaps just knowing that he is a grandfather will give him some sort of boost. It seems that males in many species are proud of their progeny even if they don't contribute to their welfare. Think of that self focused stag, Bambi's father, feeling pride that he fathered the young prince of the forest even if the fawn couldn't have picked him out of a forest ranger's lineup or, better yet, a wall of heads in some hunter's lodge. One of my favorite old New Yorker cartoons is of a couple of animals saying "I'll never forget where I was when Bambi's mother died." The females in nearly every case of offspring rearing (OK, not sea horses) do the work and the males try to take the credit.

Your self-confessed "adolescent" yearning for a do-over of a long ago love affair probably won't fly. I am still hoping you work on a start over with Scotty. There's a guy you could walk and talk with forever. Or you could just be quiet together. With Rich there are always a couple of elephants in the room: your unknown pregnancy and his dumping you for what's her name. If I were a friend who endorsed romance novels, which I don't, maybe I could get the fog machines cranking, slap an eye patch on Rich and have you fall into his arms in front of a ruined castle. I almost forgot your ripped bodice, not of course from over eating, but from heaving lots of sighs. He could confess his undying adoration of you and beg your forgiveness etc. etc. and we could all gag. That fantasy aside, I think the guy needs to know what went down after you parted so that he at least knows who's who in your story – and his.

Eddie just gave me a turn. He bellowed from the family room and when I ran to see what was wrong, he was in a religious ecstasy over the Boston Bruins who had just vanquished the Toronto Maple Leafs (it should be leaves) against all odds. When I left him in his favorite chair about an hour ago, he had nothing good to say about his team, but now all is forgiven. He has a heart "how shall I say, too soon made glad," to borrow from Browning's "My Last Duchess," but I don't plan to ice him as the duke did his young duchess. The duke was a creep, no doubt about it.

You just listen to Malice. Get your wardrobe lined up, do all the glamorous stuff you need to get done and go to that reunion to drop some bombs on all the right people. Kick ass. Take names. Oh, and take pix because I'll be the missing party.

Malice

p.s. Eddie did not pamper me, but he did give me three big bags of potting soil for the window boxes along the front of the house and he fixed my "fright" mirror so that I can see all the things wrong with my face before we go out anywhere. He's a sentimental fool.

• • •

From: Olivia Walker MacLearn
To: Olivia Walker MacLearn
BCC: Mary Alice Evans Schneider; Thomas Alexander Scott
Sent: Tuesday, May 14, 2013 12:56 PM
Subject: Every defense attorney's dream juror...

Okay, M and Scotty, here is another joint email. (This does NOT count as a third email, Scotty, so stop grinning.)

Both of you have declared Rich unworthy of being told that Holly is his daughter. He is pretty much in your opinions merely a sperm donor, and an unfaithful one at that.

If we were on a jury, I would drive you both crazy. Here is how my argument would go:

We can only find Rich guilty of the lesser charge of being unfaithful, and even then we must consider whether there are mitigating circumstances (to be addressed later).

The main question is this: If the accuser had told him that she was pregnant, what would he have done? We cannot know, because she never told him, so we cannot convict him of the greater crimes of avoiding responsibility or rejecting fatherhood.

Instead of telling Rich, his accuser accepted her family's opinion that she made a stupid mistake, that her actions shamed said family, and that the only appropriate decision was to hide herself from public view until she could give the baby up for adoption by a proper family. She believed them so completely that she hid herself and her shame not just from "public view," but from her college friends as well.

In her defense, that behavior was rather typical of the 1960's. It was a time when girls heard the lovely saying: why would a man buy the cow, if he can get the milk for free? Think about what that said of the worth of a woman. We never heard: why would a woman buy the bull if she can get the beef for free?

In fact most of us did buy the bull. We bought into the false premise that honorable men can sow their wild oats, and then later can sow their real oats with the virginal women they marry, the ones whose milk was not to be had for free. The ones who stuck to the motto: You want it, you buy it.

She did not tell him, so we cannot convict him for not wanting a baby he did not know existed. And to the lesser charge of infidelity, the accuser herself has reconsidered her original testimony. She no longer asserts that she lost the love of her life. She admits that her infatuation with that brilliant young man, might partly have been because his opinions were delightfully opposite of her parents, or simply because they were young and sex was new and seemed like love. She wonders if just maybe it never was love. And, members of the jury, she acknowledges under cross examination that Rich might have strayed because he found someone who actually was in love with him – not infatuated with his political ideas, not swayed by the physical, but truly meaningfully in love.

We ask that you find him not guilty by reason of circumstance, and that you instruct her to clear the air, to put the truth where it belonged those many years ago, to give up the romantic tale of damsels in distress and men without virtue, and acknowledge that the bull we all accepted in those times might have had more to do with the decisions they each made than the innate guilt or innocence of either. Liv

• • •

From: Rich Stapley
To: Olivia Walker MacLearn
Sent: Tuesday, May 14, 2013 5:02 PM
Subject: Revisionist History

Could it be that I'm confusing Morrison 1963-67 with UCLA in 67-68? Maybe, because I do remember sitting poolside at UCLA in early September that year, having just arrived in town - two women (were they co-eds then?) were sunbathing topless, several couples - including two guys - were kissing, and some kid was eating an orange. Swear to God, the campus security guy ignored everyone except the kid who had to pick up the orange peel immediately and put it in the trash.

Chalk it up to bad memories and wishful thinking. As for dinner with your parents, what I remember was the bad form of picking a fight with people I liked and who were paying for dinner. That same conversation probably happened countless times on every college campus. We're slow learners though - I couldn't find anyone to be skeptical with me that Iraq had WMD's (it was probably my reflex inability to believe anything from the Bush administration), and when the war was in full tilt, I nearly got tossed from a cocktail party for complaining that the only sure result of it was going to be soldiers returning home screwed up and ready to boil over.

And the Sigs' telescope? If a Sig had to operate it, the one thing we know is that it was rarely in focus, was pointed the wrong direction, and the lens cap was glued on so they wouldn't lose it. Sigs did have active imaginations, though, so they didn't need to see anything to have unforgettable experiences to recount the next day.

You're right about the delights of having your granddaughter only 40 minutes away. Let's hope it works out. Do they still write essays as part of their application? (A friend of mine who wanted to get into an elite college was told by his high school guidance counselor to bicycle across Canada the summer after his junior year – "It will set you apart.")

Me, I'm going to the gym every day to get ready for this reunion. I'll be the one who can't stand up straight because of a strained back.

Rich

• • •

From: Rich Stapley
To: Olivia Walker MacLearn
Sent: Tuesday, May 14, 2013 5:31 PM
Subject: Your parents

Liv, I should have asked about your folks. If either is alive, I hope it's in relatively good health. If your mom is at hand, probably don't pass on my regards, only because I don't want to upset her. When you told her we were no longer a couple, she probably offered sincere and heartfelt congratulations.

My own folks each lived into their 90s, but died several years ago. My father didn't say anything from '67 until Susan and I split up, but after, he asked me once or twice if I knew how you were doing.

Rich

• • •

From: Olivia Walker MacLearn
To: Richard Stapley
Sent: Tuesday, May 14, 2013 5:36 PM
Subject: RE: Your parents

I remember your dad fondly. He was so kind and such a gentleman — as evidenced by his loyalty to Susan while you two were a couple.

My dad is chipper and active in an upscale (bar's open) assisted living residence in the Hamptons. My mom died several years ago. Her reaction to our breakup was complicated. I waver on explaining it.

Good luck at the gym. I once went religiously but have fallen off the wagon. Problem is getting back on the wagon can be challenge enough, forget remembering how to set all the machines once one has climbed back on.

I'm going to the theater with friends this evening here in Westport to see *The Dining Room*. I'm really looking forward to it. Such a wonderful community theater! Liv

• • •

From: Mary Alice Schneider
To: Olivia MacLearn
Sent: Tuesday, May 14, 2013 10:34 PM
Subject: RE: Every defense attorney's dream juror…

Liv, I like the clear and logical way you present your case, but I still think Rich is/was a creep and needs a jolt. He must know that he fathered a girl who has mothered two children who are his descendants. Beyond that, he doesn't need to connect or start sharing photos or going to graduations. He needs to think about his past and about having USED a nice girl who never got to have one of those "virginal" wedding experiences.

So you bought the bull and he didn't buy the cow. Nowadays girls are definitely not buying the bull. My friend Babs in England says it a bit more roughly, being an outspoken woman of means. "Why should anyone buy the whole pig when all she wants is a bit of sausage?" It sounds very refined in her accent.

Young people today idealize the 60's, having feasted on Forrest Gump and other glossy reminiscences. There were plenty more girls like us than like Jenny and the free love crowd. I lived in fear that I would give in to lust, or more accurately, convince Eddie to give in to my lust, and become pregnant. On the other hand I had a horror of being an old maid teacher, than which I still believe there is no worse punishment on earth. Of course I could have tried being a swinging single teacher like some of my more glamorous colleagues.

Given our place in history, I think you did the very best you could in view of your family's hang-ups. You made yourself scarce during pregnancy, clung to your beautiful daughter and married prince charming, maybe not in the order the fogeys would have selected, but with a very happy outcome. I wonder if in his entire life Rich has had the opportunity to demonstrate that type of courage. Back when I used to teach The Red Badge of Courage (note finger down my throat), the boys would get all smug about how a man must face the moment in war when he can't turn back. The girls would fidget and start to feel that they would never face a comparable test. Then I would tell them not to worry and write two words on the chalk board: DELIVERY ROOM. The boys would gasp and I would point out to them that some of the young men ran from the battle in fear. No woman gets that chance in the delivery room. There is no turning back. You faced it alone and won big. Rich must know the truth. He should have bought the cow, but now it's too late.

So OK, Rich is not guilty, but he still loses. He made the wrong choice for him, but in the long run the right choice for you. He remains a sperm donor and a cad (love that old word) who now may "raise a glass" with an early love interest and learn about himself. History can be unpredictable in some cases.

Keep listening to Scotty. He has a good soul.

Malice

• • •

From: Olivia Walker MacLearn
To: Mary Alice Schneider
Sent: Wednesday, May 15, 2013 10:04 AM
Subject: Branded…

Well, M, after reading your comment, "Rich must know the truth. He should have bought the cow, but now it's too late," I have this vision of me swaying into the room at the cocktail reception. I will be wearing a wispy beige outfit with amorphous reddish-brown globs, or perhaps the same dress in white covered with black amoeba like shapes. My altar of delight will be discretely covered with a sheer fabric. Not enough to hide the splendor from his view, rather just enough to declare that there will be no free samples today. I'll toss back my head before I turn to fasten the gaze of my big blue eyes on his, and moo, ever so defiantly. Liv

• • •

From: Mary Alice Schneider
To: Olivia MacLearn
Sent: Wednesday, May 15, 2013 4:43 PM
Subject: RE: Branded…

Don't change a hair for me, funny valentine. I like it. It sounds as if you may have read a romance novel or two. Malice

• • •

From: Olivia Walker MacLearn
To: Mary Alice Schneider
Sent: Wednesday, May 15, 2013 5:22 PM
Subject: Or even more disturbing…

Perchance my life has evolved into a frig'en romance novel – or two. Liv

• • •

From: Olivia MacLearn
To: Guendaline Field
Sent: Wednesday, May 16, 2013 5:30 PM
Subject: Time flies!

Thanks for your reassurance that no one is trying to figure out where I was those years, Guen. I still agonize a bit about seeing everyone but I am committed to attending.

I am nervous about seeing Rich. He has been very sweet in his emails so I should be relaxed but I keep debating with myself (and with my friend Mary Alice and with Scotty) about whether I should have — still should tell Rich about Holly. You must be thinking: really after more than four decades? Well, at least that is what I keep thinking.

Holly has always known about Rich but has never had any desire to meet or find out about him. Her daughters know also, although not his name. Holly will give each girl that information when she turns 21. She believes that is when each can make a reasoned decision about contacting or even about searching for more information about him.

At least I got over my initial adolescent fantasy about a relationship redo. Communicating with Rich has shown me that he's remained a good person and for some reason, I'm assuming he is still quite attractive, but there is just too much water under too many bridges.

Should be interesting! Liv

• • •

From: Guendaline Field
To: Olivia Walker MacLearn
Sent: Wednesday, May 15, 2013 6:45 PM
Subject: RE: Time flies…

Liv, just one more question. Should Rich hear the news from
you or from grandchildren that he doesn't know exist? None
of my business of course, but the question really does jump
out of your last email. Guen

• • •

From: Olivia MacLearn
To: Guendaline Field
Sent: Wednesday, May 15, 2013 8:45 PM
Subject: RE: RE: Time flies…

Guen, you always were the most practical of our group! Have
you ever considered becoming a life coach? Liv

• • •

From: Thomas Alexander Scott
To: Olivia Walker MacLearn
Sent: Wednesday, May 15, 2013 11:21 PM
Subject: RE: Every defense attorney's dream juror…

Walker,

In regard to your old boyfriend/beach/sex at eighty story–
what? My dear Ducky (who is by the way the Medical Examiner,
not the Coroner), I searched your story for some pearl of wisdom but found its oysters empty. Perhaps I did not dissect it

properly. But it is nice to know that you already have a hot date lined up for your eightieth birthday party. He gives you a real walker; you give him Viagra. Sorry I won't be able to attend, but I plan to be dead by then. But at such a party, who could tell the difference if one guest showed up dead? So maybe I'll attend after all.

Your following email, offering me assurance of non-flippancy, was very much appreciated since I had opened a vein or two and gushed forth my life essence in my last email to you, receiving in return a fable with no punch line. Then I began to weigh my email's heaviness and your email's obliqueness and I did find some meaning: I needed to get a hold of myself, to man up as us boys say. The student approached the Zen Master and asked him, "What is the meaning of life?" As his response, the Master hit the student in the face with a fish. I have always loved that story from Dr. March's World Religions class. To me it meant that life cannot be known except through our experiences. My recent email was a pointless search for self-knowledge and life-knowledge, leading me deep into the foul recesses of my cerebral cellar. Your "sex at eighty" story was the perfect fish. So I'm all better now. I bow before you, Liv Master.

Now, on to your email which was most assuredly not the third email but which I did receive after the other two and before I had a chance to reply to any. Call it what you will. (Big grin here.) The Trial. Juror No. 3 replies to Juror No. 1 and sends his sexiest regards and a wink to Juror No. 2. I have never blamed Rich for getting you pregnant, because, all these long, hate-Rich years, I never knew you had had a child. I only blame Rich for breaking up with you, which hurt you at the time something fierce. I remember too well all your tear-drenched agonizing and my inability to say anything remotely helpful. When you two broke up, you broke down, and I took the elevator ride with you to the basement. Having to watch you suffer like that was pure hell for me. And I rightly blamed it on Rich whether he was justified or not. Whether Susan's love for him was stronger, purer, righter than yours makes not one scintilla of difference to me. This juror doubles as a witness to the torture he put you through and I hold him accountable. Whether it was inevitable, even if it was unavoidable, Rich hurt someone that I care for deeply and so I know him to be guilty of that harm. That may be all for which he is guilty, but it is enough for me.

As for the bovine implications of your argument, I'm not sure what universe you lived in during the late 1960's, but I lived in one in which a sexual revolution was occurring. We were all trying to have as much sex as often as possible, so I'm not sure from whence all those virginal brides were to come. In those days the wild oats prohibition for women went right out the window as did many of the girls in the women's dorm on those nights. As your mother might say, "Why, it's been said that some women even began to enjoy sex! The very idea!" (Somehow my retro 1950's chauvinistic self keeps wanting me to write the old locker room boast, "Well, I never had to pay for it!" But I have been married three times, alimony-ed twice, and had my paychecks garnisheed, so there is little firm ground there on which to take a proud macho stance.) I know what you are trying to say, I think, and you are correct. But it is also true that, with guys, the beef is usually free for the asking. Since I am not sure of the intent of this meaty passage, this bull is leaving that pasture and closing the gate behind.

The simple truth is that you want me and/or Mary Alice to release you to inform Rich that he has a daughter. To which I respond, whatever you want to do, I will support you 100%. But let me ask you first to consider the possible consequences. You tell Rich and he wants to meet Holly, and be a part of her life, and come to family gatherings, and be a grandfather to her kids, and take family vacations together. In fact he says that you have no choice – that he is going to exercise his patria potestas (paternal rights). Does Holly want that for herself and her kids? (BTW, do your grand-teens even know your story?) Or, you tell Rich and he says, "Are you sure it's mine? You're not expecting me to pay child support or something (in this case maybe grandchild support), are you?" Are you ready for the emotions that rejection would ignite in you? Or, you tell Rich and he reads you the riot act for not telling him at the time, protesting that at this late date he has lost the chance of being a father to his daughter, leaving you feeling even guiltier than you do now with him not knowing. In fact, my dear supplicant on the way to the confessional, tell me one good way that this could turn out and I will cede my vote on the charges to Juror #1.

Non paterfamilias,

Scotty
Thomas Alexander Scott

• • •

From: Olivia Walker MacLearn
To: Thomas Alexander Scott
Sent: Wednesday, May 15, 2013 11:58 PM
Subject: Sorry

Oh, Scotty, it is hard to write through tears. But write I must. Everything you've said I already knew. That you opened your heart; that I wrote back meaningless drivel; that I should not tell Rich; that as M told me, I should "Keep listening to Scotty. He has a good soul."

I wanted to write back to say that you are capable of happily ever after, that you deserve happily ever after; that you are no more likely to screw up my life than I yours; that it might just be worth the thrill of trying, even if one of us does get hurt.

But you wrote all those "what if's" about why your feelings for me lasted, Scotty, and every "what if" rushed right in to shine lights on my own insecurities. I cannot imagine another chance at finding such love in my life as I so stupidly avoided seeing those years ago. Not now. Not this imperfect rendition of that young girl you once loved. I'm no hot gramma as you once asked. I am just an older neurotic Liv, who has weathered my storms without the comfort of your arms for the past 46 years.

So instead of risking what might happen if I wrote what I truly felt, if I agreed that you saw fantasies fluttering all around the edges of my words, I became flippant and focused on anything but the truth. That seemed less scary than my fear of opening the door completely and watching you turn away in disappointment. Only perhaps you have anyway.

Damn it Scotty. I wish Guen had never found me so I could at least be safe in that special place you tucked me away in your memory. Liv

• • •

From: Olivia Walker MacLearn
To: Thomas Alexander Scott
Sent: Thursday, May 16, 2013 9:14 AM
Subject: PS Post-coffee in the gentle light of morning...

It is also possible that I was a teensy bit – as in enormously –
intimidated by the photo I found online when Googling your
daring Dar. Holy crap, Scotty, intelligent, productive, interesting AND drop dead gorgeous? Just saying...

• • •

From: Olivia Walker MacLearn
To: Mary Alice Schneider
Sent: Thursday, May 16, 2013 11:45 AM
Subject: Off with their heads!

M, I am off to the mall for some warm weather outfits. Marcy
Blefton called me an hour ago to ask me to come down to
Orlando to talk with some of her benefit event planners at
a big meeting they are having. I'm a last minute fill-in for
someone who canceled, but who cares! I'll have a few meetings Monday and Tuesday, and then on Wednesday I'm
heading over to the Ritz Carlton (near Universal Studios)
for a morning to afternoon spa day. Meetings are at the
Grand Floridian, so I am staying there, but Holly, the girls
and I all loved the spa at the Ritz when we were there for
Christmas some five or six years ago. A nice combination
of interesting meetings and spa time, and I am thankful
for the opportunity to stuff my inner Princess/child back
where she belongs for a few days while I function as a competent adult.

Seriously, M, Princess Liv, is a pain in the royal butt. She avoided her college friends for 46 years, even though her handlers told her it was a tad unnecessary in these modern times; then whoosh, she decided to come out of hiding because her old friend Guen found her, and Scotty's sweet "come back to us" email tugged at her heartstrings.

Consequently she decided she might enjoy a redo (mostly sexual I fear) of the Liv-Rich failed romance; but when he seemed more bridge partner than sex partner in his emails she began to question her almost 50 years of silence on his contribution to Holly's DNA.

In the midst of all of that, the princess discovers that her loyal defender in the days of yore is actually one hot fellow — at least verbally as she has not had physical contact with him for what the royals call "a four-generation-peasant-turnover." She remembers their tantalizingly innocent yet intimate encounters and begins to fantasize about what it might be like to go to the royal ball with him. Sadly she is out of practice in the custom of verbal parleying, so she flip-flops between glib nonsense and gushy tear streaked confessions. (Hot Sir Scotty is probably signing up for the crusades just to find some peace from her machinations.)

So off with her head! I have quite had it with her. She is not any good at this reconnecting stuff. The queen is back! The corsets are on. Heads will roll. Sex is banished! Bring on the blue hair and hear me roar: BINGO! Elder Liv

• • •

From: Guendaline Field
To: Olivia Walker MacLearn
Sent: Thursday, May 16, 2013 12:00 PM
Subject: RE: Last Minute Prep

Liv, by Life Coach I assume you mean telling people what they should to do. Just ask my husband, son, and daughter. They will tell you that it is probably best, in most instances, that I keep my nose out of their business. They do have personal experience with me, so I think they are probably right. I know they are unanimous. Guen

• • •

From: Olivia MacLearn
To: Guendaline Field
Sent: Thursday, May 16, 2013 12:08 PM
Subject: I'd hire you...

I am certain they are wrong! Still if you are worrying about your advice, please don't. Scotty added a different perspective. He asked me to think about the consequences if Rich does not comply with Holly's "rule" that I would need to instruct him not to make any contact with her or the girls.

That is certainly worth considering, and I think the decision of when/if to tell Rich is best made at a later time, and probably with more reasoned consideration from Holly. (And I need to have a better idea of what kind of person Rich is all these years later; much better determined face-to-face at the reunion than through emails.) In fact other than you and Scotty, I intend to keep the details of my pregnancy private.

Nonetheless, I still think you would make a great life coach. Liv

• • •

From: Rich Stapley
To: Olivia Walker MacLearn
Sent: Thursday, May 16, 2013 1:19 PM
Subject: The Dining Room

Liv,

I'm glad about your dad – it's a rare sighting to see a man in assisted living centers. I'm guessing you stayed close to your mom until the end – and that you miss her. A toast to her memory and her stiff backbone. And thanks for the words about my dad. He lived a long time, saw and did a great deal.

Wikipedia fact: William H Macy was in the first production of The Dining Room, back in 1982. I had to look it up, and I had to look up the play as well. It gives me an idea for a non-credit extension course through UCLA Extension: "Plays We Haven't Seen or Read: In this no-credit course, you will read and talk about plays that no one in the class, including the instructor, has seen or read until now. Follows the courses 'Novels We Haven't Read' (fall, 2012) and 'Poets We Haven't Read (spring, 2013) - which are not prerequisites. Instructor, Mr. Richard Stapley, M.A."

This is my post-career career – talking about literature with the blue-rinse set, people for whom a book group of pals is not enough. I stayed in touch with people at UCLA, mostly through the professional association of teachers of English, and it's borne fruit now through the extension program – I help fill their diversity quota – "Old guy? Check."

So, let me know how the play is and if I should put it on the potential-syllabus list.

At the gym, it's easy. I use the smallest dumbbells and barbells, and set the machines on the lightest possible weight. I fancy that I hear people mutter, in a Liverpool accent, "He's a clean old man."

Rich

• • •

From: Guendaline Field
To: Olivia Walker MacLearn
Sent: Thursday, May 16, 2013 4:28 PM
Subject: My nose gets bigger...

Liv, now that we have opened the subject of Rich in a rather dramatic way I am compelled to be even more of a nosey parker. I never knew why you two ended things so suddenly. If I recall correctly I had even bought a new dress to wear to your wedding. I was looking forward to a trip to the northeast. Is the reason for the breakup something you can share? It is none of my business so I surely will understand if you don't want to share. I always thought you broke it off, but now I think I was wrong. Guen

• • •

From: Olivia MacLearn
To: Guendaline Field
Sent: Thursday, May 16, 2013 9:14 PM
Subject: Busy time for everyone...

No problem, Guen. So much was going on that last spring of our college life, and you missed a lot of my angst after the breakup because you were living off campus.

Rich and I were not engaged. Perhaps you remember one of our all-girl dinners when we all planned our weddings, whether there were actual grooms in sight or not.

Rich broke up with me. He became involved with Susan, a freshman at the time, and they eventually married. As I said: lots of water, lots of bridges. Liv

• • •

From: Rich Stapley
To: Olivia Walker MacLearn
Sent: Thursday, May 16, 2013 9:25 PM
Subject: I'll take your silence as an invitation to keep talking

A-liv, E-liv, I-live, Olive,

I was just outside watering plants (no green thumb, I've parched as many as I've drowned over the years), and managed to surprise a pair of ducks (mallard and what's a female duck besides Daisy?) in the creek that runs through the back yard. They flew off, but they will be back; maybe there's a nest nearby and I'll soon be in the midst of *Make Way for Ducklings*.

For whatever reason, startling the ducks got me thinking about you and the reunion. Sort of a petite Madeleine moment that had me looking back for a few moments, then jumping ahead. The National Writing Project asked me to present its model at an international conference of teachers of English this fall – in

Florence (Firenze to you). So, if our exploration in cyberspace
and at the reunion as ex-lovers goes well, I invite you to think
about being Beatrice during my first visit to Tuscany. Separate
rooms, and if the squalor of my pension leaves you horrified
(think Forster's *Room with a View,* which has a rather nice small
hotel), we could stay in separate hotels, but would share meals,
car, etc. If you need to slip away to Switzerland for a few days to
visit your money, I'll head for the coast and follow the footsteps
of Shelley, Byron, and Keats – Lawrence's Etruscan places.

I know there's nothing you've written to suggest even the
remotest interest in such an adventure. But, I see it as something more than fun. How many people know me as well as
you do - or as I do you? My mother's dead, my sisters don't
count, and Susan is the least likely travel companion I can
imagine. I suppose that you have girl friends who know you
better than I, but not in the same way. Maybe it's just that we
know each other's fears and limits and moments of despera-
tion that a girlfriend (or in my case, a colleague or former
roommate or drinking buddy) doesn't know. So, the rich-
ness of northern Italy just might be more accessible to us
traveling together. And if that's complete and total horseshit,
I'd still like seeing the Uffizi with the help of your eyes. No
comparisons to David allowed.

So, tell me about the play last night. (And you have studiously
ignored my requests that you describe a typical day of charitable fundraising – people who ignore seem to do it studiously,
don't they?)

Cheers,

Rich (in expectations)

• • •

From: Olivia Walker MacLearn
To: Richard Stapley
Sent: Thursday, May 16, 2013 9:28 PM
Subject: awkward…

I just finished answering an email from Guen when yours arrived. She wondered if I broke up with you or visa versa.

I had been thinking about whether The Dining Room would be a good play to read. I would say probably not. Hard enough to flow through the multiple vignettes when actors help by donning different clothing, changing posture and voice, etc.. Of course I am not a language arts major, so perhaps it would be okay.

A more complete answer to your email in a day or two. It is night here in the east, and the ducklings are fast asleep. Liv

• • •

From: Olivia Walker MacLearn
To: Thomas Alexander Scott
Sent: Friday, May 17, 2013 9:17 AM
Subject: Sometimes a third is really a third…

Could be third time's the charm. Could just as well be three strikes and you're out! But either way, one thing is obvious, I have a somewhat pathological need to fix anything I might have screwed up. So, here I go again with each email trying to explain the last. (And in advance, to avoid a 4th email, I apologize for my tendency to quote songs and non-literary sayings and proverbs. Remember I majored in math, so I have nothing Shakespearian upon which to draw.)

When I read your email, which ever so appropriately scolded me for my stupid NCIS story, it was late at night and all I could see was that I had hurt you. My tears were real and my response was true, but poorly worded, because it may create in you a feeling of expectation on my part. There is no expectation. Fantasies fluttering around? Most definitely, and somewhat of a surprise to me although perhaps not to you, but no expectation, because you are not unfettered. Because Dar seems like a girl I might even have liked, and the grass is not always greener, and you don't know what you've got 'til it's gone, and all that.

If I could numb the principled part of my brain, I would hang any concerns on the ever so handy but false "what she doesn't know, won't hurt her" hook and send you an invitation to take our wordy foreplay to another level, to see if what could have been might become what is, with the caveat that the RSVP is for one night only. What will be, will be. Que sera sera. Worry about ruining each other's lives is not allowed.

Perhaps we find heaven on earth. Perhaps we skip off into the sunset together. Or perhaps we have a Casablanca moment, or spend the next two days of the reunion looking at the ground whenever we come in contact. But at least we avoid the eternal "what if" question.

'Tis tempting, but not without danger. So, perhaps the safer course is to just file all this recent email exchange away as if it was one of those back in college mornings that required we say: "We drank way too much! Did I do or say anything I shouldn't have last night?"

I suppose the mature decision is simply to meet as two old friends grateful for the chance to be in each other's lives again. Because however angry I made you with my insecure backpedaling reaction to the sudden self-awareness that I had been verbally hitting on you, I still believe I am snug and safe in your heart, and that your arms will always be open for me, even if just in my memory.

Okay, Scotty, please don't make me write a forth email before you respond, because sure as God made little green apples, I will read this again after sending and feel a need to explain…
Liv

• • •

From: Mary Alice Schneider
To: Olivia MacLearn
Sent: Friday, May 17, 2013 11:01 AM
Subject: RE: Off with their heads!

Yikes. You lead an exciting life. New clothes. Exciting trips. However, I know that in the back of your mind, you are thinking about that reunion and about whether you are really a bridge player or a much more physical person.

That's a telling remark about adolescence. It's too short a period in our lives and now that we are nearing the other end, why shouldn't we go back? There's something thrilling about having a few do-overs, but with whom? You know where I've placed my vote.

One other point, harsh though it may seem. Don't expect a whole lot from men our age. I refer you to Mark Twain's recently released autobiography, which he insisted be withheld until long after his death. He pointed out that women can perform as well, if not better, as they age while men have a much shorter shelf life.

One might argue that today's medical advances give men an edge that they did not have in Twain's time, but all the meds have their limits. I've overheard Eddie and his two best friends heckling the Viagra commercials, when the smooth talking announcer warns men to contact their doctors if they have an "erection lasting more than four hours." They vie with each other for the nastiest options, shouting "call all your friends" or "rent a billboard" and more that I won't share. They save their best attacks for the dual bathtub ads. Maybe men don't mature, but simply age.

So about that plan for corsets and Bingo. I don't buy it. Remember the constricting garments we wore under prom dresses? Those days are gone. We would have been hard pressed to get into any trouble in those virtual chastity belts. We're free of all that. Give whatever you want a try. How often do you get a chance to be with people you haven't seen in more than four decades and might never see again? It's a free for all out there, so go have some fun. We used to think everyone was watching us, but it isn't true. They're all too worried that someone is watching them.

You know I won't let up on you. Stop over thinking this reunion. Just go and have a great time doing whatever you want. You are single and affluent and healthy. What more do you need? I'll write you a note. "Liv has my permission to do whatever she damn well pleases with the person(s) of her choice."

In unrelated news, Eddie and I went to a christening last week at which one of the young mothers wore lavender pants tighter than her skin, a red sequined top cut down to her navel and bejeweled spike heels in an animal print. She was easily forty five pounds overweight and felt great about herself as we could all see. It really is a "brave new world." Anything people of our age can think of to do will pass unnoticed.

Malice

• • •

From: Olivia Walker MacLearn
To: Mary Alice Schneider
Sent: Friday, May 17, 2013 12:31 PM
Subject: tick-tock, tick-tock

NOT READY! NOT READY! NOT READY! NOT READY! NOT READY! NOT READY!

There now, I feel better. And I was referring to the Orlando trip not the reunion issues. Well, mostly. More later. Liv

• • •

From: Olivia Walker MacLearn
To: Mary Alice Schneider
Sent: Friday, May 17, 2013 8:23 PM
Subject: The Dr. Ruth of Cape Cod

Okay, between the few items I bought (few because I think this is the year of outrageously ugly clothing) and what is

in my closet already, I think I have assembled enough outfits for all possible talks, social events, and plain old Disney
wandering.

Now back to chapter 12 in *All You Need to Know About Sex Before
Attending a 46th Reunion,* by M. A. E. Schneider.

I hear you about not expecting too much. But shelf life is
a funny thing. Is it really as bad as people say, or do we
need to redefine good sex? I think our expectations have
been tinkered with by ads for little blue or white pills. Two
bathtubs facing a lake? Really? How many people do you
know — outside of Hollywood — who can look good getting into a craw foot tub? I would be so freaked out after
climbing in while yelling: "Close your damn eyes," that I
would never emerge from the bubbles, let alone be ready
for sex.

And aren't there options other than popping pharmaceuticals?
Do you remember the scene toward the end of *The Best Exotic
Marigold Hotel* when Carol reveals that the sex pill Norman
thinks he took was actually aspirin? I know that sometimes
a real medication is needed; I just think we reply too much
on an outdated adolescent view of sex. Get'ter up and get'ter
done – no up, no done.

So much pleasure occurs on the way to what is undeniably
exquisite but relatively short-term bliss, especially, if one can
enjoy the journey without focusing on any particular part of
the trip. It also helps to avoid being too rigid (Ha – pun not
intended — made myself laugh!) about what we are willing to
do along the way. Oh well, memories of the joy of sex with a
scandalous Scotsman I suppose.

But assuming such activity can be found in this gathering of the Class of 1967, I am confused by the note you've given me: "Liv has my permission to do whatever she damn well pleases with the person(s) of her choice."

Person(s)? Now there's something I've not yet tried, nor am I all that tempted. It would seem to me to require just too much effort. For example, I would have to hold my stomach in and maintain appropriate control in the back at the same time, so as to look relatively toned from all angles. Way too much work!

Or did you mean with one person OR the other? Or one and then the other? Oh my, M, so many options, and I remember that you previously demanded photos. You wicked woman! Is this weekend to become a paperback novel, tucked discretely into the upper right hand drawer of your desk, edges bent back to recall the location of your favorite passages? If so, perhaps you better call your friend from the baptism to find out where she purchased her lavender pants and red sequined top. Sounds perfect for the group photo. (Don't shoot me. I've perchance had too much vino.) Liv

• • •

From: Rich Stapley
To: Olivia Walker MacLearn
Sent: Saturday, May 18, 2013 9:15 AM
Subject: The Play's the Thing

I didn't read your note until now — yesterday I saw the heading "Awkward" and thought I'd wait a day or two. But, not so bad. Tell Guen that "he was a bastard, but not all men are, thank goodness."

As for *The Dining Room,* let me know if you have seen contemporary plays you recommend. It should be easy to find lots of plays that a classroom full of adults haven't seen or read. We have the Ashland Shakespeare Festival on the West Coast and an L.A. Shakespeare festival, but it's easy to miss out on everything except revivals of Les Misérables and Andrew Lloyd Weber.

I did see the ducks yesterday afternoon, but they were down the street, not in the creek behind the house. I'm hoping they'll be a cache of eggs somewhere. Two years ago, I did see a line of five or six ducklings trailing behind mom. It's a lovely sight in urban America. We have wild turkeys, too, sometimes alone, and sometimes in a raffle of a dozen or so — on a slow meander down the street. For some unknown reason, the dogs let them alone.

One more thing: if we are going to present our case for why there should be a photograph of you in the student union near the various male athletic teams of the 1960s, can we tell the provost or the college president that you wore Morrison's first pair of granny glasses (those red-lens sun glasses) and the first batik shirt. "Fought for gender equality and did it in fashion."

Call me a bastard, just don't call me Dick,

Rich

• • •

From: Olivia Walker MacLearn
To: Richard Stapley
Sent: Saturday, May 18, 2013 10:12 AM
Subject: RE: The play's the thing

Loved your end paragraph, and I think I actually may have owned a pair of those glasses at some later time, but perhaps we should stick with the realization that it was UCLA, not Morrison, that you were remembering. No photograph in the Student Union of me.

But on to more pressing matters — your invitation. First of all, let me offer congrats on the presentation. That is quite an honor. And Florence no less! Not a shabby location! I've never traveled there. Most of our early trips to Europe included Holly, and the grounds at Ian's home were indescribably beautiful and child friendly. So every time we went, we would consider all sorts of stops and in the end remove most of them. (Later we did often fit London and Paris in coming or going.) And then when Ian's illness began to surface, we stopped traveling outside of the US.

But your offer of traveling together, even with separate rooms, is not something I can do. I know I had a "let's try this romance thing again" reaction when I first heard from you, but I eventually realized from your emails that you were not thinking that way, and that led to an understanding that my own thoughts were fueled by nostalgia with a twist of "I want to be young again." (In truth, the second part is still alive in me. I don't want a platonic travel mate. I want the whole package. Same room and all that entails. And we both know that certainly was, but just as certainly is no longer us.)

I hope this is not too upsetting. I have no other answer. Our time together was something I will always hold dear. I would not lose any of what we had — well, maybe the part when you were with both Susan and me. But oddly not even that. If I were offered a *Back to the Future* opportunity to end our relationship earlier than when it did, even knowing that it would lessen the pain, I would not. I would keep it all, because much more wonderful than bad came of what we were.

And please also know that this has nothing to do with where we would stay. In the end it really is more about with whom and why, than it is about the where.

Anyway, Rich, you painted a lovely picture of a trip together, but I think if we are lucky we will leave the reunion able to say that we have begun a journey toward friendship, and for now that is all I can offer. Liv

• • •

From: Guendaline Field
To: Olivia Walker MacLearn
Sent: Saturday, May 18, 2013 12:43 PM
Subject: Red faced…

Liv, Could I really have assumed so much! You two seemed like the perfect match. Clearly I should not be the class historian. I feel like a fool. You on the other hand have incredible grit. You must have known about Holly before graduation. I can't even image the decision making trauma you went through. How on earth did you pass your final exams? Red Faced Guen

• • •

From: Olivia MacLearn
To: Guendaline Field
Sent: Saturday, May 18, 2013 1:30 PM
Subject: Orlando bound!

Well, Guen, if it makes you feel any less foolish, I also thought Rich and I were a perfect match. But you know, we were so young, and I think sometimes it takes a lot of years of growing up before one can look back and say, maybe I was wrong about this or that. Not just love but choices we make, things we thought we were or were not good at, chances we took, chances we shut our eyes to. I think we are pretty lucky if we make it through those times in one piece!

As to graduation and final exams, remember there were no little plastic wands to pee on in those days to instantly find out if one is pregnant. We might suspect, but we had to wait, sometimes for a month or two and then a trip to a doctor to find out for certain. For me it was the end of June, after I was already home and packing for my post-college-glad-the-freaking-liberal-broke-up-with-you-now-stop-moping gift from my parents. When you and I get a bit of alone time at the reunion I will tell you about the months between graduation and Holly's birth in a wonderful little Cape Cod hospital.

I leave for Orlando tomorrow afternoon. I'm filling in for a speaker who canceled at the last minute for an annual meeting of charitable groups. I'm just there until Thursday morning, but it will be a nice break.

Maybe the Florida sun will add a bit of color to my complexion, although if you remember how I looked after those ridiculous tanning sessions of the roof of the dorm, sadly that means red and freckled. Liv

• • •

From: Guendaline Field
To: Olivia Walker MacLearn
Sent: Saturday, May 18, 2013 7:24 PM
Subject: Counting on your presence!

Liv, so glad you are getting away. Revisiting old memories that had probably completely left your mind must be taxing. I hope this is just a quick fill-the-gap working get away and that you are not changing your mind about coming to the reunion. Please don't change your mind! No excuses accepted. Guen

• • •

From: Rich Stapley
To: Olivia Walker MacLearn
Sent: Saturday, May 18, 2013 9:04 PM
Subject: Icarus

It's not too bad to be back on terra firma. Thanks for being gentle. I guess there isn't providence in the sighting of ducks.

I'm glad about the reunion and the path back to friendship — my ignorance about gardening leads to some spring delights when most everything has started to grow again and I'm convinced that a plant is dead and gone, but I water it anyway, then after way too much time, green shoots and leaves appear.

I've been receiving announcements of a high school reunion (#50) in the fall — it was a big class, with nearly 600 graduates, so each announcement I get reminding me to register includes a couple more names of classmates who've died — "on Saturday afternoon there are golf and tennis tournaments, and we're sorry to report that Fred York, Patty Hansen, and Jim Stoddard have passed away."

Is the message, "Show up to ward off the reaper," or is it "Come to show respect for the dead"? The working class kids from my high school aren't living as long as those of us who went to college.

I haven't studied the Morrison reunion calendar (don't actually care much, just glad to be there) — but will you compete in a tennis or golf if there's a tournament? My golf game, which in 1963 looked like I could flirt with a 28 handicap if I applied myself, is completely gone. Fifteen years ago I went to a driving range and did not hit a single ball straight. A Japanese woman was at the tee to my right having a lesson, and I swear I almost hit her two or three times. I feared I was W.C. Fields perfecting a perpendicular shot. But if you're in a golf tourney, I'll caddy, or cheer from courtside if it's tennis – Lithe Liv

I've attached a photo I enjoy titled "Life."

To life,

Rich

• • •

From: Thomas Alexander Scott
To: Olivia Walker MacLearn
Sent: Sunday, May 19, 2013 1:58 AM
Subject: RE: Sometimes a third is really a third...

Just a few more hours, my Liv, and you will have my response. No fear, it's good; it's all good. Got to catch some sleep. Exhausted, mind not working. Know this doesn't make sense, but it will, I promise. Sleep peacefully tonight, my lovely Liv.

Scotty

• • •

From: Mary Alice Schneider
To: Olivia MacLearn
Sent: Sunday, May 19, 2013 7:13 AM
Subject: RE: The Dr. Ruth of Cape Cod

Liv, I've been insane these past two days with all the hoopla surrounding the birthday weekend (Josie turned four yesterday), with Amy's in-laws staying at our house, so will write a long note tonight after the third birthday fete in three days. She had a "do" at her school on Friday, a big adult/family thing at our house last night and today a huge kid party just over the bridge on the mainland at one of those kids' club gathering places where they have huge bouncy houses and a racetrack for foot propelled cars. It will be just their group, not the usual crush, but still enough to give any grandparent the vapors. The kids will have at least a one to one ratio of attentive parents, not what one sees there on an "open play" session. Shudder.

More later.

Malice

PS I meant OR, not AND when I said persons and tonight I'll explain my thoughts on twosies, threesies and more.

• • •

From: Olivia Walker MacLearn
To: Mary Alice Schneider
Sent: Sunday, May 19, 2013, 11:57 AM
Subject: Boarded the plane but…

Weather delays possible both here and in Orlando, and there
is no Wi-Fi on this plane, so I am cut off from when they close
the forward door until I get to the hotel. Good thing I brought
a book! Liv

• • •

From: Mary Alice Schneider
To: Olivia MacLearn
Sent: Sunday, May 19, 2013 4:15 PM
Subject: RE: The Dr. Ruth of Cape Cod

In vino veritas as they say. I get the best truth out of you when
you've had a few. Now to explain. I never meant for you to have
more than one partner at a time, this being the country of
serial marriages and relationships. To refer to Cabaret again
"Twosies beats onesies, but nothing beats threes" was more of
a decadent Weimar Republic view and not one that works for
us now, certainly not for folks of our age. So do them one at a
time, ideally with a nice break between sessions.

Your Marigold reference reinforces my belief that the writers
of that film have yet to reach the age when nothing, not even
Dumbo's magic feather, can help, let alone naproxen sodium
substituted for a Viagra. Romance is still fun. Living life and
loving slowly and savoring each minute can be wonderful still,
but given that women become more orgasmic with age and

men, still caught up in hydraulics, can't keep pace as they age, offers us one of life's wryest ironies. So we soldier on with the more infantile men blaming their partners, something they ate, the pharmaceutical companies or maybe fate. Nobody wants to face up to age.

Funny that you thought I support group carnality. I don't even like group dancing, the horrible moment when the orchestra leader or DJ at a function thinks it is time for "HOT, HOT, HOT" or the electric slide to get everyone on the floor. I much prefer dancing that showcases one man and one woman moving almost as one. Nearly every time Eddie and I dance, we get mean glares from husbands and wistful ones from their wives. The place we frequent in Bermuda is full of couples who don't dance together and who, after a few drinks, ask us how we do it. Eddie says "It's simple: we've been dancing together since we were thirteen at Sunday night church gatherings. All you have to do is the same moves at exactly the same moment, and do it to the music. Also, somebody has to lead and the other has to follow." After this I often hand him over to the young woman of a couple and he dances with her to show the husband how easy it is. If the woman knows how to follow, the husband is usually so demoralized that he wants to kill Eddie and turns up at the pool next morning to discover Eddie out on the water doing slick windsurfing moves while his wife says "You should try that. I'll bet Eddie can teach you." Eddie is such an ordinary looking dude, but sly.

Speaking of the dear man, he is out mowing the lawn while I'm hiding in the house from the pollen. What a year!

We survived Josie's party at Kidz Party Center. When there's just one party happening it is a lot saner than during a rainy summer free play day when the place fills up with kids in every bounce house, on every pedal car and on every flat or vertical surface and nobody can figure out which adult goes with which kid. I think adults have to sign a waiver to take away at least as many kids as they brought in. Today we beheld a mass of yuppie parents, kids dressed in costume, younger sibs and the requisite four grandparents, an aunt and various other relatives. Nobody got injured or had too serious a meltdown. They gobbled masses of pizza and cake and carried off their loot bags. The new trend is not to open the gifts in situ but to take them home and open them to prevent the "I've already got this" or "I hate this game." I wonder what kind of a world awaits these kids. Let's hope it's a safe one, but I have serious doubts.

Shudder. Enough of the downer thoughts. Congratulations on finding the right duds for you upcoming trip. The thing about this year's fashions is that they scream "THIS YEAR ONLY" and nobody is calling them classic, so whatever you buy you will be hard pressed to integrate into the years to come. Remember the big shoulder pads of yore!? Gross. Who knows what lies ahead?

Have a good time and wear whatever you please — to BOTH events. I repeat: take pictures.

Malice

• • •

From: Thomas Alexander Scott
To: Olivia Walker MacLearn
Sent: Sunday, May 19, 2013 7:37 PM
Subject: Explanations

Liv, I have been writing and rewriting this damn thing since 2:00 PM today. Probably it still doesn't say what I want to say but, hell, somewhere along the way one has to speak and move the conversation along. So first let me explain the delay in responding.

I last wrote to you on Wednesday. On Friday morning Dar and I woke to a pounding on the door of our apartment. It was Dar's editor who is based in New York City, but there he was in real life, looking none too well for the wear. He had come to claim her. Pouring a cup of coffee with copious amounts of cream and sugar, I sat back as a keen observer to watch the drama unfold in the familiar confines of my living room. He declared his love; she declared him an idiot. After all, she said, didn't he see me sitting there on the couch? What was he doing?? He laid out a line of completely clear logic that proved that she would be better off with him in the city than stuck out here in the semi-urban sticks with an unpublished hack writer (the hack part didn't bother me but I have been published in a number of journals). It turns out that every time she has gone to NYC for a consultation on her new book, she has been staying with him, telling me that she was at her beloved Grant Hotel, a 2-star pretending to be a 3-star. That's the problem with this cell phone age, Walker; you never phone your partner's hotel, just her cell, so you never actually know where the little cheat is at the time. She could tell you she was in San Francisco and instead be at the Green Acres flop-house on the next block. Well, this pleading and outrage was a lot better than daytime TV, but as the morning wore on, the outcome was obvious. Logic plays a strong hand. Just after noon the obvious was stated and she began to pack her things. And she had lots of things. By late afternoon the freight office had been contacted to pick up her stuff and she and her illustrious editor were off to his company jet waiting on the tarmac at a private terminal at DFW airport. As she packed, I noticed for the first time how many of her clothes seemed to be missing and I had a good idea where they might be, serving as a spare set in his Central Park condo in NYC. They left just before seven so I went out for supper, deciding on a liquid diet for the night. I drank myself to sleep by 3:00 AM in the wee hours of Saturday.

She phoned me at 6:00 AM, regretful, apologetic, remorseful, stating that this was not what she wanted, saying she was coming home on the 10 AM flight and would I pick her up at DFW. So I brushed away the metallic aftertaste of alcohol and drove to DFW and waited in the baggage carousel. But she wasn't on the 10 AM flight. She texted that she was catching a later flight and would land at 1:40 PM. She wasn't on that one either. I was still there in their connected uncomfortable chairs at 3 PM waiting for what the attendant said was the next flight from NYC. She phoned me. He was in the background begging her to stay, but she said that she had had that Katharine Ross moment. You know the one from "The Graduate" where Dustin Hoffman (Benjamin) has interrupted Ross' (Elaine's) wedding and they have run off together, jumping on a city bus, she still in her wedding gown. After they quit laughing, there is this blank empty silence between them as they gaze out opposite windows of the bus. Dar had hit that moment after running off with her lover/employer. She wanted to come home and asked if I would wait for her. She would arrive at DFW on the 7:50 PM flight. So I grabbed some supper and a few drinks at an overpriced, under-qualified airport restaurant, somehow knowing that she wasn't going to be on that flight either.

We had had a big fight earlier in the week that had nothing to do with anything of importance. You say that you think she is pretty? Well, maybe she is when she isn't hurling a wine glass or a verbal barb at you. When her anger swells, she is a tsunami of rage. I had a feeling then that we had fought our last round. The 7:50 PM flight was delayed due to the ever-present Texas afternoon thunderstorms but finally landed safely near 9:00 PM with only one empty seat on board – hers.

By then I had been at the airport for twelve hours, operating on only three hours of sleep the night before. I was in my car headed for the south gate when she called. I calmly said hello and there was a long uneasy pause on the other end. I could hear her lips trying to form words. Finally I spoke up and said, "I'll pack any books and manuscripts you missed and send them this weekend. Any clothes will have to wait till next weekend." All she said was "Thanks, Scotty." I hung up and then I hung one on. I called a cab sometime after midnight. Now if I can just remember the name of the bar or its location, I can reclaim my car.

I had read your emails of Thursday and Friday on my iPhone while I was wasting my life waiting amid the sea of ebbing and flowing humanity at DFW. The love pouring out of your emails contrasted so powerfully and crazily with my mounting frustration with Dar and with my life. Add in the exhaustion and nothing seemed to make sense; the whole world was coming apart and the pieces were bouncing off the inside of my skull. I didn't dare write back while sitting in that pool of fury at the airport. And when I finally got back to my apartment, I was mentally incapacitated to say the least.

Now that you know why I haven't written, here is my more rested and hopefully more coherent response.

As for taking the "wordy foreplay to another level...with the caveat that the RSVP is for one night only." No strings, no regrets, no lingering expectations. No thanks.

As for the "mature behavior simply to meet as two old friends grateful for the chance to be in each others' lives again." I think I will pass on that also.

I don't want a one-nighter with you, as great as that sounds. I do not want a nice weekend rekindling old friendships and telling old stories. What I really want is to see Cape Cod. Monday I am going to tell the Dean that I am not available for summer term. That should probably do it for my job, but I've got some proposals circulating for long-term assignments and a series of articles that should support me for a while. And though I have never been to the Cape, I feel this incredible draw to it somehow. Any chance you might meet me there?

I have realized something in our correspondence and this latest fiasco with Dar just makes it clearer than ever. I have been looking for you since you vanished in 1967. In bars and classrooms, in traditional and disreputable relationships, in bottles of booze and thousands of words, I have been looking for you. But nothing worked because none of them were you.

I'll go to the reunion if that's what you want to do, but what my soul craves is time with you on Cape Cod. So, Liv, my friend, my love, how does that fit into the scheme of your life?

No matter your answer you will always be snug in the arms of my memory, but I had rather you be there in person.

Looking for you somewhere,

Scotty
Thomas Alexander Scott

• • •

From: Olivia Walker MacLearn
To: Thomas Alexander Scott
Sent: Monday, May 20, 2013 12:53 AM
Subject: Re: Sometimes a third is really a third...

I just finished a long day of travel from New York to Orlando. (A good friend asked me to cover for a last minute cancelation by a speaker at a meeting for charitable foundations.) What should have been an easy trip was not. Runway delays. Weather delays. Luggage delays. I finally arrived in my room at The Grand Floridian, opened the curtains, and looked across to Cinderella's castle just as the 10 PM fireworks began. And then I powered up my iPad, and there you were.

I've read your words, and reread, and reread again. Almost three hours have passed and still here I sit.

I'm scared. No doubt about it. Scared for every "what if" either of us could conjure up. But I told Malice a while ago that you feel like home. I miss your arms. I miss talking with you into the night. And there is that image you created of you sitting on the floor in front of your couch...

So yes, Scotty, I would very much like to be with you on the Cape.

I finish here Wednesday. The reunion is Friday. Guen has poured her heart into planning this for all of us, and she will be crushed if we do not go. You know how poorly I deal with guilt, so how would you feel about a short stop in Kentucky? We could meet there Friday and stay one day — two at the most — and then on to the Cape for as long as it takes for our souls to be satisfied. Liv

• • •

From: Olivia Walker MacLearn
To: Mary Alice Schneider
Sent: Monday, May 20, 2013 8:53 AM
Subject: Scotty

Thank goodness I am not scheduled to speak before 11! I was awake until 2, and when I actually slept my dreams were crazy!

Scotty wrote last night. Long email. Long story. Too long to sum up while I am gulping coffee, but he declared his love and said his soul craves time with me on Cape Cod.

I could have used another week to agonize and reply! But I said yes, M. Please tell me I was not foolish to reply so quickly! Liv

• • •

From: Olivia Walker MacLearn
To: Mary Alice Schneider
Sent: Monday, May 20, 2013 12:56 PM
Subject: PS

I am so thankful I had already declined Rich's invitation to Florence — with separate rooms — before Scotty's recent emails! (I may have neglected to share Rich's invitation with you in the craziness of the last few days.)

Rich replied sweetly to my decline. I think he was more relieved than disappointed. I perhaps presented as a bit unhinged in some of our previous correspondence — in truth, I was perhaps a bit unhinged in some of them.

More later. Am between sessions. Liv

• • •

From: Mary Alice Schneider
To: Olivia MacLearn
Sent: Monday, May 20, 2013 2:12 PM
Subject: RE: PS

Liv,

Thanks for the quick note between sessions. Florence!? Separate bedrooms? It sounds as if he wants to revisit the past, but remember Faulkner: "The past isn't dead. It isn't even past." So watch out.

Faulkner also mentioned that the dead have more power over us than when they were living, which I am coming to understand the longer I remain above ground. I can still hear my mother demonstrating the basics of grammar, telling me the party to vote for and enforcing what colors to wear and when. Just yesterday I wore white summer jeans before Memorial Day and lightning did not strike me. I got the jeans dirty, though, so Mom may have had a hand in that. Her two younger sisters, widows in their early 90's, still drive and live independently and tell me they often speak to my mother, not directly of course. It's kind of like communicating with God. If you speak to God, it's praying. If you hear God speaking to you, people think you're crazy. My aunts claim that their sister taught them everything they ever needed to know, especially the things the nuns left out at school. No doubt.

It's too bad that after we get all our life lessons completely organized and filed appropriately, nobody much cares to hear them. Maybe we should publish. Seriously. My grandma knew the answer to any moral dilemma. She should have had a hot line.

You must be too tired with all the activities to read for long. I'll preach at you later.

Malice

• • •

From: Olivia Walker MacLearn
To: Mary Alice Schneider
Sent: Monday, May 20, 2013 5:12 PM
Subject: What could go wrong?

Well I think my talks have gone well so far. Everyone is engaged in their projects and eager to brainstorm.

Of course, between sessions I think about all that's happened and I keep wondering how Scotty reacted to my email.

And at one point I had this momentary trip to "let's imagine everything bad that could possibly happen" town such as Scotty will email me to say the Dar (ex-live-in girlfriend) returned and that she is pregnant and says it's his and what should he do. And of course I tell him he would regret walking away from his child and we agree to care about each other in our hearts and exit stage right... What, me worried?

Okay, I have to shower and dress for dinner. In a great restaurant, but lots of speakers so could go late. Liv

• • •

From: Mary Alice Schneider
To: Olivia MacLearn
Sent: Monday, May 20, 2013 6:37 PM
Subject: RE: What could go wrong?

Good. You are thinking about Scotty. If he has a pregnant girlfriend at this age and she is anywhere north of forty five, good luck to both of them. They should rent a billboard and phone all their friends. And don't forget the lovely adage my city kids taught me back when I thought I was teaching them: "Mama's baby, Papa's maybe."

Malice

• • •

From: Holly MacLearn
To: Olivia Walker MacLearn
Sent: Monday, May 20, 2013 7:17 PM
Subject: Sending triple doses of love your way!

Mom, I got your voice mail. Sorry I was not here when you called. I was picking the girls up from band practice. I know you are struggling with some heavy stuff, so in case you are not back from your dinner meeting before I go to bed, (No later than 11 – I have parent conferences before school tomorrow.) I decided to reply by email so you would have my thoughts. (Bet you were shocked to find an email from me waiting in your inbox!)

First of all, this Scotty guy sounds pretty cool. Yes, I know you are scared, but seriously, mom, isn't it time to be brave and not play it safe? Sure I get it. You have been out of the "dating scene" for decades, but from what you've told me, you and Scotty were best buddies. So it's not like he's someone you found on match.com. Although they do have sites especially for "people your age" just in case this Scotty thing doesn't work out. (Relax, mom. That was a joke!)

And about Rich, it seems to me, and to your very sweet and brilliant granddaughters that you believe the right thing to do is to tell him. All three of us are okay with that. But we all think that telling him the first time you see him in 46 years might be a bit difficult on both of you. Maybe plan to go see him sometime this summer. We can decide before hand what the best way is to tell him. I might even be able to go with you. (Well, maybe not. That sounded like a better idea before I saw it in print.)

But seriously, mom, I have no worry that Rich will disrupt our lives. We've always known about him. I think his life will be the one impacted by the information. And should he ever demand more contact than we want, well, I can be a pretty good mama grisly if I need to be.

So, mom, to sum up: fly off to the Cape with Scotty. He sounds perfect for you. And wait to tell Rich but relax knowing that you have a plan to do what you feel is right.

We love you. Be safe! Enjoy the rest of your meetings and the reunion. Call if you need me. I would say text, but I've finally given up on that!

Holly

• • •

From: Thomas Alexander Scott
To: Olivia Walker MacLearn
Sent: Monday, May 20, 2013 8:27 PM
Subject: Re: Sometimes a third is really a third...

Liv,

After pacing the hallway outside the dean's office and rehearsing my spiel, I strode in and told him that I would not be available for summer term, know it's late notice, so sorry to put this extra work on you, blah, blah, blah, and he surprised me. I expected a suppressed inner mirth and a detached, "Oh, well, Thomas, that's how it goes. By the way we are downsizing for the fall, probably have to cut most or even all of your classes, and certainly won't have full time work for you. If I can be of assistance in your relocation, blah, blah, blah." But instead he got genuinely tearful, as if losing me affected his own life in some deep arcane way. He followed that by heaping tons of undeserved and heretofore withheld praise upon me. But then he segued into anger, profanity even. "Dammit, Scott, I have stuck up for you when department heads wanted your head! Now you walk out on me this close to summer session, you son-of-a-bitch!" I was proud of his sputtering tweedy soul, though his swearing brought to mind what Mark Twain said of his wife's attempt to curse, "You've got the words right, Livy, but you ain't got the tune." Of course long before his swearing commenced I had stepped away emotionally and had taken my usual seat in the bleachers of the observation deck. I was so entertained by his tirade that I wished for a bag of popcorn and a coke. So, no matter how it arrived at the point, the eventual result was what I had expected. Jobless again.

I retreated to my favorite nearby watering hole and ordered two beers so that I could toast to me on my wide-open future. I drank one and my inner observer quaffed the other. Then I checked email and a day of much thunder and lightning turned to cool breezes and blue skies. I swear I felt sand between my toes. In celebration of your reply, I ordered me and myself two more beers and lifted our glasses to you, singing (in harmony no less) "The Drinking Song" from "The Student Prince."

We may have put on a few decades, Liv, but our heart's are young, aren't they? And the long time of separation is soon to end. May young hearts never part. I loved the setting for your email: fireworks, Cinderella's castle, and me. Who says fantasies can't be real? Or that Fantasyland can't evolve into Tomorrowland?

Do you want to know how happy your response made me? I was so euphoric that I actually *stopped* drinking! I wanted a perfectly clear head as I re-read "Yes, Scotty," until the phrase burned like a brand inside my eyelids and I could hear your voice saying it, a voice I haven't heard for 46 years. God, that sounds goofy!! See what you do to me, Walker, I feel shaky sixteen and virginal again. And we both know that neither of those is correct. Scared? Damn the what-ifs, Walker, full speed ahead! To the Cape!

But yes, loyal Liv, yes. We can't disappoint dear Guen. And I won't, unless she asks me to wear a freshman beanie at the reunion. Let's do the whole two days. Otherwise I would feel as if I am cheating the others by hoarding our long lost treasure for myself. Plus it will tantalize my senses to watch you interact with everyone (maybe not so much with Rich) knowing the whole time that very soon you will be by my side on the shore.

I am packing tomorrow and tossing the perishables out of the fridge. Who knows when/if I'll be back again. Early Wednesday morning I'll hop in my banged-up convertible and stop in Memphis to reconnect with some friends and family there. Then I'll be Kentucky-bound on Thursday. On Friday the rest of my life begins.

Holding you — in thoughts tonight, in my arms on Friday,

Scotty

• • •

From: Olivia Walker MacLearn
To: Thomas Alexander Scott
Sent: Monday, May 20, 2013 11:18 PM
Subject: Four days!

I'm reserved at the Griffin Gate. Checking in about 2 or so on Friday.

Holly says you sound cool. She is a bright, accomplished woman, who occasionally talks like a teenage Valley Girl.

Waiting for your arms. Liv

• • •

From: Olivia Walker MacLearn
To: Mary Alice Schneider
Sent: Monday, May 20, 2013 11:27 PM
Subject: Onward and Upward

Well, M, I heard from Scotty. Guess my answer was okay, because four days from today we will say hello for the first time in 46 years, and proceed from there "to infinity and beyond!" (Lots of little boys running around the hotel in Buzz Lightyear gear.).

I guess it's too late to join weight watchers and go back to the gym?

Now, please put on your Lucy hat, because as usual I need advice. Rich has been very sweet in his emails. He writes about looking forward to seeing me, and he accepted my answer that I would not go to Florence with him in a very gracious manner. So, do I give him a heads up on the Scotty development? It seems the kind thing to do, but also seems weird. Liv

• • •

From: Mary Alice Schneider
To: Olivia MacLearn
Sent: Tuesday, May 21, 2013 8:02 AM
Subject: Lucy Speaks

Lucky you! The doctor is IN and ready to advise. First, forget the weight watcher and gym BS. You are who you are and you are wonderful. Anyone who disagrees can screw off or speak to me and get a more severe suggestion.

It's good to hear that Rich is being sweet, but please remember that we aren't in college, or high school or the dreaded middle school years, so you don't have to share with him the fact that you have a crush on another "boy." You didn't share with him the fact that he impregnated you and you disappeared to Europe to incubate his child, did you? Nor did you share your nearly solo delivery on Cape Cod in the coldest December I can recall. He deserves no heads up on your love interests. This is your chance to explore old relationships and begin some new ones and he can just take a number if he wants to be included.

Never a fly more eager to be on a wall,

Malice

• • •

From: Rich Stapley
To: Olivia Walker MacLearn
Sent: Tuesday, May 21, 2013 10:22 AM
Subject: No Tennis, but No Cold Feet

Hey Liv,

I finally read the itinerary. No golf or tennis tourney. But I hope you're packing anyway. It's supposed to be in the low 70s this weekend — perfect weather for Merlot on the porch.

I suppose that state law requires a ceremonial mint julep as well.

Your memory for when and what is far better than mine, but I did look up a few things: *Sgt. Pepper* was released the month we graduated. *Bonnie and Clyde*, *Belle de jour*, and *The Graduate* the same year. There's a wonderful moment in *Belle de jour* when Catherine Deneuve, wearing nothing, walks away from the camera. This is arguably the most beautiful actress in the world at that moment, and we don't see a single muscle. It's all soft curves. Within 25 years, muscles matter – imagine Angela Bassett in "What's Love Got to Do With It?" Those are ropes in her arms.

No ropes in mine, but after two months at the gym, there are nascent triceps — the radish of muscles, the easiest to grow. Now, if I can only figure out what triceps do, I can show off.

See you soon.

Rich

• • •

From: Rich Stapley
To: Olivia Walker MacLearn
Sent: Tuesday, May 21, 2013 10:41 AM
Subject: PS

Liv,

Even though the reunion is in the 21st Century, I hope you'll bring real photos to share — not those stored in cell phones:

pictures of Ian, Holly, and Mary as well as of you across the decades (but none of your cat please). Most people, I find, hate pictures of themselves, but still, the weekend a little bit about what's happened this past umpteen years as well as what's going on now and what's in coming.

Wait, have you discovered the school of Buddhism that teaches that there is only the present? (I saw a t-shirt last week that said, "Meditation: don't even think about it.")

I hope you'll bring a few photos to show both the slow inexorable march of time and moments of significance — let's not pass around phone screens to ohh and ahh over people and places in images too tiny to decipher.

Do you think the TSA screener will notice I've been working out?

Cheers,

Rich

• • •

From: Olivia Walker MacLearn
To: Richard Stapley
Sent: Tuesday, May 21, 2013 5:36 PM
Subject: RE: PS

You will probably have to settle for iPad photos. (Still digital, but easier to see than on an iPhone.) I am at a conference in Orlando (leaving for another speaker-type dinner shortly) here through Wednesday night, arriving back in CT Thursday early afternoon, and I have a morning flight to Lexington the next day, so no time to dig out hard copies, but I have a plethora of photos, on my iPad. (Although current ones only.)

As to the TSA screener, I hoped to say something witty, but it is almost the end of a busy day and I am all out of witty. It could be an interesting story for your "tell us something about yourself" introduction. See you Friday. Liv

• • •

From: Olivia MacLearn
To: Guendaline Field
Sent: Tuesday, May 21, 2013 5:40 PM
Subject: RE: RE: Orlando bound

The meetings have been interesting and rewarding, Guen. People are so devoted to their charities and anxious to learn anything they can about successful fund raising, so I am delighted to help where I can.

I finish here on Wednesday and will fly back to CT in plenty of time to repack and get to the reunion. I promise I will be there. Would not miss it! Liv

• • •

From: Olivia Walker MacLearn
To: Mary Alice Schneider
Sent: Tuesday, May 21, 2013 8:20 PM
Subject: Last speaker dinner is over!

Oh, M, you keep me sane, or laughing, which is close enough. I agree with your advice, and am leaning toward telling no one about Scotty and me, and definitely not Rich.

I have to confess that as I sit here in my room at the hotel, looking across the lake to Cinderella's castle, it feels a bit ironic that I am, at this age, acting somewhat like a character in a fairy tale. It has me reflecting. (I know, what else is new.)

A few weeks ago I was flying somewhere, and as I sat at the gate, waiting for my plane to arrive, I thought about how I soon would be going to an event full of people I've not seen in decades. How would we look to each other? I glanced around and tried to find someone my age I found attractive or to be more honestly precise, whose bones I would be willing to jump. No one passed muster. In fact I would be willing to bet that a good number of the men I visually rejected were younger than I. Yet, here I am sight unseen anticipating nights of delight with Scotty.

Why? And why does Eddie still light up your life, and fill your world with song and other good stuff? Is it because we all knew each other when we were young? Does the before image superimpose on the present? Why do couples who have been married for decades, half a century, or more, still call each other sweetheart or beautiful girl or my guy?

Is it for real or for show? Remember, M, I have known young love that was hot, but not true enough to last. I've also known married love that was sweet and warm, but that began to fall apart in almost imperceptible ways in the spring of my 49th year. I was still so young then, and even though our marriage lasted long after I could be called young, it was never again what it had been, so I do not truly know what it is like to love or be loved in this stage of life. I suppose I should just lift my chin and set sail, but I just might need you to give the boat a push. Liv

• • •

From: Mary Alice Schneider
To: Olivia MacLearn
Sent: Tuesday, May 21, 2013 10:04 PM
Subject: RE: Last speaker dinner is over!

You couldn't find a more experienced boat pusher, Liv. You should just set sail and with Scotty. How right you are about superimposing yesterday over today. To Scotty you will still be the petite girl who reclined against his legs and shared all her secrets. He will see the "now" you but in a haze of the "then" you and remember, please, that he has now regained a friend whose earlier loss he couldn't comprehend. I have nothing but good vibes about your reunion with Scotty.

And why does Eddie still light up my life when I have loved him forever? I can see past the thinning hair and the extra weight to a boy who made me wonder at my good fortune the first time he said he loved me (I was fifteen). Just to be his partner transformed my life. At the end of sophomore year I went from being a goof off in an experimental class for high IQ kids to being the straight A student my parents had always wanted. If they had known my motivation, they might have been shocked. It was love. I wanted to be worthy of Eddie. He tells me I am still magic when I am perfectly able to see the white hair I don't bother to color and the inevitable lines of time. To pick up on our previously discussed Sonnet 116 by Shakespeare, "Love's not time's fool, though rosy lips and cheeks within his bended sickle's compass come." Real love, it appears, is supposed to go the distance. I also can't rule out great sex, a good brain and a super sense of humor. Also there's nothing on earth or in a house that Eddie can't fix.

The great experiment is that you and Scotty, after all these years, may begin again and have a bond that never was fully realized but might just become something that can last. OK, if it doesn't last, a splendid one or two nighter might be fun too.

About checking out guys and wondering who would be a good match, I think everyone does that at some level. I can honestly say that I have rarely seen anyone I'd like to try. Loving Eddie is just too comfortable a lifestyle to risk losing. However, you are an absolutely free agent at a time in life when almost anything you want to try is permissible.

About being loved at our age I turn again to Will S., who said "to love that well which thou must leave ere long" is precious indeed. We don't know how much time we have left, so if there's anyone we want to love or to give love to us, we must take the chance while we can.

One last English teacher reminder (thanks, Andrew Marvell): "For every at my back I hear time's winged chariot hurrying near." That's from To His Coy Mistress, which got a southern mother all worked up a couple of decades ago when her daughter brought the poem home from college and Mama saw the line in which A.M. suggests that a maiden put out before dying: "where worms shall try thy long preserved virginity…" I believe the state college system banned this poem until people objected. Virginity? Remember that?! It used to be such a big deal. We've seen a lot of changes in sexuality, but like every generation, we think we invented sex and we definitely did not.

So..."Gather ye rosebuds while ye may." Now I'm off the rails. Just go to the reunion and have a blast and don't forget to dish up everything when you get home. I expect essay answers.

Malice

• • •

From: Thomas Alexander Scott
To: Olivia Walker MacLearn
Sent: Tuesday, May 21, 2013 11:18 PM
Subject: Packing

Liv,

Tell Holly that not only am I cool, but also rad, fly, boss, and gucci. That ought to cover the generational jargon spectrum. I hope to meet that young woman on some not-too-distant day.

Found my Morrison yearbook for our senior year. Damn, we were cool. It's amazing what you can find when opening boxes that have been snoozing for ten or fifteen years, when trying to whittle your life down to traveling size, when tossing out leftovers from several live-ins and lovers. How did their stuff get in THERE? I think old girlfriend litter intentionally migrates into the deepest crevices of one's habitat just so it can jump out into the middle of the blissfully long-forgotten and startle one into remembering. Toothbrushes that I didn't recognize (maybe I'm a somnambulant ortho-klepto), black lipstick (I never dated anyone who wore black lipstick, I swear to Goth!), a tax return that I forgot to mail five years ago — with the check attached (maybe I should balance my checkbook once in a while?), flotsam and jetsam of a life lived mostly in whitewater. I taped up two boxes of Dar paraphernalia and a long tube filled with Barnes and Noble posters of her bemused face and forwarded them to NYC. Since the United States Postal Service is now in charge of my mementos and memories of Dar Donohue, and since I am certain they will lose them, we need never worry about reappearing recollections disturbing our peace in the dunes.

Since the detritus and debris of my debauched decades will not fit into the pint-sized trunk of my '94 Mustang convertible, I have rented a storage unit at Wee Keep — an inspired name since, if you forget to pay, they get to keep. One day I may see my stuff on Storage Wars! Boxes of already-yellowed paperbacks, the hand-typed original pages of my first Master's thesis, a gaggle of unmatched Christmas ornaments dating back to my childhood, bits and pieces of outdated electronic band equipment, a painting that I started but naturally never finished (thus making it the defining opus of my life), a wooden sled (Really? In Texas?), various and sundry tools, and paper files, oh my God, think of the trees that died (my storage unit has become a veritable Forest Lawn), plus this and that, more that than this — my material world crammed into a 5'X8' shell of tin. One good Texas tornado and they'll be picking up pieces of my life in Texarkana.

The linens and furniture (what wasn't rented) were given away or returned to their original owners (if said owners were still alive and willing to take back their loaners). Unwanted items were curbed. The rest is packed carefully in the trunk of my car without benefit of suitcases in order to maximize the space. My laptop and external hard drives will ride shotgun with me since they are by far the most important "things" I own, containing my thoughts, contacts, writings, and photos. Odd to think that a compact jumble of electronic circuits is the most intimate object that I will bring with me into our "nextness."

Empty now, the apartment waves at me by means of the dust wafting in the sunbeams streaking through the open windows. I take a deep breath, let out a long sigh, and cry out despairingly, "God, this place is a mess!" So it appears I will spend the evening with my good friend Mr. Clean and his faithful sidekick Lysol. Even with that, there is little hope of getting back my security deposit. Funny that a place that once held such fun and fury is reduced now to just walls and doors. I guess the rest finds its home in us.

I should be working instead of writing, but something keeps dragging me back to this email. It feels as if, when I write, I am already holding you. And I don't want to let go — ever.

On the road tomorrow,

Scotty

• • •

From: Rich Stapley
To: Olivia Walker MacLearn
Sent: Wednesday, May 22, 2013 10:36 AM
Subject: Be sure and wear some flowers in your hair

Probably not the summer experience of any of our classmates, but still, a whiff of nostalgia: http://www.sfgate.com/news/article/Summer-of-Love-40-Years-Later-1967-The-stuff-2593252.php

See you soon, Liv,

Rich

• • •

From: Olivia Walker MacLearn
To: Richard Stapley
Sent: Wednesday, May 22, 2013 5:02 PM
Subject: RE: Be sure and wear some flowers in your hair

Rich, that site was fascinating. Not sure about everyone else, but I fear I missed it all. Sometimes I think I was living in an alternate universe, one grounded firmly in the 50's. I do, however, believe I finally am ready at last for the '60's.

Travel safely. Good luck with the TSA and your new physique. Liv

• • •

From: Thomas Alexander Scott
To: Olivia Walker MacLearn
Sent: Wednesday, May 21, 2013 6:15 PM
Subject: Bridges...

Been burning up the road and burning bridges behind me. First the long causeway over the Ray Hubbard Reservoir east of Dallas burst into flames after I passed. Then the Arkansas

River Bridge in Little Rock fell to the water in ashes. And the granddaddy of them all, the Mississippi River Bridge at Memphis, melted like molten lead as I sped across leaving me no avenue of return to my old life. Each flaming structure lent its own particular exhilaration to my new venture — and extracted its own particular toll on my nerves and self-confidence.

Speaking of nerves, are you anxious about the umpteen times you will have to repeat your abridged life story to your many admirers and more than a few curiosity clingers? If it gets tiresome, just start making up stuff. Tell them you developed amnesia and had been living in a Buddhist monastery in the Tibetan Alps until a Zen Master hit you in the head with a fish, restoring your memory. Tell them you have been staffing the space station and were unable to hitch a ride home until now. Fiction is usually more interesting anyway (your case being the exception of course).

Sitting in a Beale Street bar right now, sipping a Glenmorangie 18-year-old scotch, killing time (and a few random brain cells) until I meet some of my grad school buds at the Rendezvous, the best rib joint in the Southeast. They will have to swallow more Liv stories than ribs, I fear. If I bore them into desertion, I shall have my dessert alone and entrap the server into listening to more of my Liv-ly tales. My mind is voraciously out of control; I can't get enough of you.

I just had a horrible thought: you're not rooming with Guen, are you?? If so, I hope she can deal with it when you tell her that, most likely, you will be out late — as in "all night." I broke my piggy bank and reserved a suite at the Griffin Gate just so we could have a couch to lean back against.

Soon, my Liv, soon now,

Scotty

• • •

From: Olivia Walker MacLearn
To: Thomas Alexander Scott
Sent: Wednesday, May 22, 2013 6:41 PM
Subject: RE: Bridges

I will tell them that I was "getting over my breakup with Rich and learning to embrace life as an independent woman," and that afterwards I married a man in a kilt.

It is 6:41 PM now. I just returned to my room from the "do it all" treatment day at the Spa here at the resort. I will leave Orlando as scrubbed and polished up as I can be.

By the way, I noted the current time because you once remarked that my writing is hotter late at night. So in this cooler light of almost evening, I thought I would write that I am sitting here thinking about how I do not want to tell anyone at Morrison about thee and me.

I want us to be our secret, a secret that feels delightfully sensuous. I don't wish to let anyone else into our beginning. Conversing about it feels too commonplace. I prefer total magic. I want to feel sweet electricity as my fingers brush yours when you hand me a glass of wine. I want to sit across from you at a table and move my foot closer to yours as I exchange pleasantries with whoever is seated next to me. Perhaps I will steal a quick glance when you respond with a slight bump of your shoe against mine.

And I want to dance. I want to drown in a ballet of emotions as we draw close, then apart to converse, then close again, the sensations greater each time. And when the housemothers are busy complimenting the organizers, I want to sneak past them, as I have never done before.

Two more days, dear Scotty. Liv

• • •

From: Thomas Alexander Scott
To: Olivia Walker MacLearn
Sent: Thursday, May 23, 2013 12:49 AM
Subject: Secrets

I love your plan, Liv. An undercurrent of passion felt only by those two in the know. Furtive glances, double entendres, secrets — perfect! Normalcy as abnormal as it can get. The momentary denial followed by the explosive moment of YES. My God, girl, you ought to be a playwright!

I'm for it, my love. Of course at this moment in time I am easily agreeable, having just returned from the blues, booze, and barbecue of Memphis to a hotel room that was empty until I entered it and now, because you are so present in me, it is so full of you that your name bounces off the walls. I feel like I'm in a scene from West Side Story. It's such a beautiful world that I feel drunk all the time! Wait, I am drunk. But that takes not an iota away from the loveliness of a life that includes you. OMG, I am talking like a 2 PM soap opera! Yet, amazingly, it isn't sappy theater, it's reality. Holy shit, Walker, I think I hear the Righteous Brothers singing *Ebb Tide* on my balcony.

Shhh, don't startle them; they might leave. Let's make their song come true, Liv, as I rush to your side. It is Thursday already by a few minutes. Later today I will burn a few more bridges on my way to you, the miles and hours between us melting away. I will fall asleep tonight without undressing, listening to my illusory serenade, content to imagine that I hear the rippling waves of the Cape and that, miraculously, I am holding you in my arms.

Shhh, sleep well, my Liv.

Scotty

• • •

From: Olivia Walker MacLearn
To: Thomas Alexander Scott
Sent: Thursday, May 23, 2013 1:02 PM
Subject: One day...

I am in flight to LaGuardia. Thank goodness there is Wi-Fi on this plane. I do love emailing from the air. Feels like magic!

I've been thinking about one of your suggestions for an answer to my disappearance. You wrote: "Tell them you developed amnesia and had been living in a Buddhist monastery in the Tibetan Alps until a Zen Master hit you in the head with a fish, restoring your memory."

I may just go with that one. It will be more effective than my heal-grow-kilt story, and is actually quite close to reality.

Just one more day, Zen Master. Liv

• • •

From: Thomas Alexander Scott
To: Olivia Walker MacLearn
Sent: Thursday, May 23, 2013 11:12 PM
Subject: In Lexington

Okay, I apologize for being gassed, gushy, and giddy in my email last night (or the wee hours of today, take your pick). I sounded like one of my Air Force pals who was the biggest, rawest, roughest brute — until he floated far enough down Liquor River to go over the falls. From that moment on you couldn't get near without his big paw bear-hugging your neck and his wet breath blowing spittle in your face as he proclaimed, "I love ya, buddy. D'ya know 'at? I love yuh, man." Then he would drop his grip, step back, extend his arm shoulder-high, point his finger at me, and just nod like a bobble-head doll. Every time our eyes crossed paths up would come the arm, the finger, the bobbing head, and that knowing, locked-in, squint-eyed gaze. But, you know what, Walker? That was his true self staggering out. Tipsy but truthful. It was his sober self that wore masks and put up defenses. So, if I sounded sloppily sentimental last night, influenced by alcohol, I plead the fifth (in fact, I drank the fifth). But I meant what I said. It was the raw, unsophisticated, inebriated truth. However, I doubt that the Righteous Brothers were really on my balcony. Though they sure were in my head.

I was awakened today by the phone ringing much too loudly. I fumbled the receiver to my ear and the desk clerk said, "Pardon me, Mr. Scott, but do you wish to extend your checkout time?" "No," I told him, "I plan to leave before 11:00 AM." "Which day?" he asked. That was my first clue that maybe I should pry open my other eye and look at the clock. It was already past noon. So I unfurled myself from the tangled sheets, showered off the effects of last night's celebration, poured myself some wake-up java with lots of cream and sugar, and revved up the 'Stang on my mission to burn the remaining bridges.

The arched bridge spanning the vast Tennessee River exploded into fireballs like mortar rounds on the Fourth of July. In Nashville my afterburners annihilated the Cumberland River Bridge. The bridge over the narrow Green River in western Kentucky went up in a puff of smoke. Finally, the last one. The Kentucky River Bridge on the Bluegrass Parkway seemed to disintegrate under my rear tires, debris cascading into the deep gorge of the riverbed. I have arrived, my long lost love, and now there is no turning back.

So, Madam Director, how do we play this? You are checking in at the Griffin Gate about 2 PM tomorrow. Do I pick you up at the airport? Do we meet at the hotel? Or did you really intend for us to see each other for the first time at the cocktail party? If so, what if I break and just scoop you up into a lingering kiss right in front of the canapés? I may have aged but I am still dangerous!

Waiting for you,

Scotty

• • •

From: Olivia Walker MacLearn
To: Thomas Alexander Scott
Sent: Thursday, May 23, 2013 11:41 PM
Subject: RE: In Lexington

I've rewritten my Madam Director plan numerous times. Too funny; too hot; too OMG I just wrote things I would blush to have you read.

I think if you picked me up at the airport that we might never get to the Griffin Gate. So Zen Master, what would you say to this plan, I taxi there, check in, unpack, and freshen up (quickly) and then we have a little pre-canapé time. Your place or mine? Your Shameless Liv

• • •

From: Thomas Alexander Scott
To: Olivia Walker MacLearn
Sent: Thursday, May 23, 2013 11:58 PM
Subject: RE: RE: In Lexington

I would say yes – oh yes. My suite, because I have the couch, a balcony large enough for a couple of old ballad crooners, and Ebb Tide on my iPod.

I'll have my hand on the door handle so it may open before your second knock. When it does, well, who knows? But I can hardly wait to find out.

Scotty

• • •

From: Olivia Walker MacLearn
To: Mary Alice Schneider
Sent: Friday, May 24, 2013 12:05 AM
Subject: Yikes…

Well, M, I am packed and ready for bed. The driver comes in the morning and I leave for Lexington about 10.

I'm meeting Scotty at the hotel before the cocktail party. That is incredibly exciting and horribly terrifying at the same time. I'll keep you informed and if I get in trouble I'll send up a flare. Liv

• • •

From: Olivia Walker MacLearn
To: Thomas Alexander Scott
Sent: Friday, May 24, 2013 9:45 AM
Subject: Hours...

I'm on the plane. It's drizzling but our crew says we are good to go and should arrive fairly close to on time. No Wi-Fi so no magic emails from the sky. :(

Soon! Liv

• • •

From: Thomas Alexander Scott
To: Olivia Walker MacLearn
Sent: Friday, May 25, 2013 2:48 PM
Subject: RE: Hours...

Liv,

I can't believe that in a few minutes you will be standing here beside me.

After all these years,

Scotty

• • •

From: Olivia Walker MacLearn
To: Thomas Alexander Scott
Sent: Friday, May 25, 2013 3:15 PM
Subject: minutes…

On my way in minutes. Changing clothes. Still blushing from opening the envelope containing a key to your room that you left at the front desk for me.

I'll knock this time, though. Liv

• • •

From: Mary Alice Schneider
To: Olivia MacLearn
Sent: Friday, May 24, 2013 5:10 PM
Subject: Thinking about you

Have a wonderful reunion. If Karma works, you will feel me with you.

Malice

• • •

From: Olivia Walker MacLearn
To: Mary Alice Schneider
Sent: Friday, May 24, 2013 6:35 PM
Subject: Cocktails

M, I'm back in my room to quickly shower and dress for the "official" welcome cocktail party. However, I am fairly certain the party has already started for Scotty as I know it has for me. I've already had a cocktail, and I have never felt so welcome.

In fact, if the rest of the weekend is half as wonderful as the first few hours, well, let's just say, "Hooray for long shelf life!"

I'll email you in a glorious day or two. Oh, and if Karma IS working, I hope you will know when it is appropriate to look away. Love you, dear friend! Liv

• • •

From: Mary Alice Schneider
To: Olivia MacLearn
Sent: Friday, May 24, 2013 7:53 PM
Subject: RE: Cocktails

OK, I'll look away if I must, but please remember that I have a great imagination. Go for it!

Malice

• • •

From: Olivia Walker MacLearn
To: Mary Alice Schneider
Sent: Friday, May 24, 2013 10:55 PM
Subject: Dessert

We're back at the hotel and I've stopped in my room for a minute. I wanted to let you know that all went well this evening. Guen's planning resulted in party perfection, old friends were pleasant, and no one even mentioned my disappearance, so that was a lot of unnecessary angst.

Scotty was charmingly attentive without drawing anyone's attention. (Well, I am fairly certain Rich noticed, but that is a problem for another day.)

Tonight my love is in his suite, gallantly awaiting my arrival, and I'm like a kid at Disney with a key to the castle. How amazing to be in this moment after all these years. Liv

A sequel to MIND OVER MIRROR, book one in the

series *LIFE, LOVE, AND BIFOCALS*, is scheduled

for publication in the summer of 2014

AUTHORS

Jan Allinder Anestis provided four creative friends with a skeleton plot and basic character facts. She and her four co-authors dug into their artistic centers, gave birth to unique characters, and MIND OVER MIRROR evolved.

Jan created the character Olivia Walker MacLearn (Liv). Jan's weekly Op-Ed column "I Wonder…" was featured on the editorial page of *The Weston Forum*, Weston, CT, from 1995 to 1998. (Those articles are available on her website www.jananestis.com.) She also authored "Laughter Therapy" in 2004 for *Bountiful Health*, a magazine briefly available in health food stores in Tennessee, and she has written a forty-something romantic beach read, BLUE LIGHT SPECIAL. Jan's brain is always imagining stories and she treasured the challenge of weaving the characters' stories together for MIND OVER MIRROR.

Wandaleen Cole penned Guendaline (Guen) Field. Wanda is a retired corporate lawyer who practiced for over thirty years. Her creative talents were spent writing pleadings, briefs, contracts, software licenses, opinions and instruction manuals. Stepping into Guen's shoes was a pleasant and relaxing experience for her, a relief from years of convincing, protecting, securing, opining and instructing. Wanda also hosted a local television program for several years that invited the audience to ask questions related to the law.

Richard (Rich) Stapley's writer was Jack Hailey. Jack is a policy analyst in health and human services in California. He wrote "Teaching Writing, K-8," for U.C. Berkeley, distributed by the National Council of Teachers of English, and he was for many years a teacher-consultant for the Bay Area Writing Project. Jack spends weekends at his sweetie's gallery, talking to people about how art feeds the soul.

Bill McDonald authored the character Thomas Alexander Scott (Scotty). Bill has published one book and numerous articles of historical research plus several devotional works. He lectures on the topics of racism, religion, and other simmering realities. McDonald spoke at the Kentucky Governor's Inauguration in 2007 and 2011. From 1983-2008 Bill penned a weekly faith and humor column, *Out of My Mind*, often stolen by or quoted in other newsletters and columns. For 18 years McDonald has managed and played bass for a classic rock band.

Jo Ann Walther authored the character Mary Alice Evans Schneider (Malice or M). Jo Ann spent thirty-five years teaching secondary English in Cambridge, Massachusetts, writing recommendations for many of her more than three thousand students and three dozen student teachers. She is currently working on a memoir, "November in My Soul," a cautionary tale for her grandchildren.

Made in the USA
Lexington, KY
24 November 2013